"Feel sorry for yourself and you're dead, you might as well give up, desexualize yourself, fall apart," Aunt Eleanora had told her. "Don't do it, I'm telling you, don't do it. You've got good genes, you come from strong stock, and, by God, you can do anything."

And Mary Catherine discovers that she can do just about anything—from running her own real estate office to sleeping with a series of married lovers.

Nobody Makes Me Cry is the gutsy, un-inhibited portrait of a restless ex-wife in the uncharted world of the newly divorced.

A selection of the
Women Today Book Club

NOBODY MAKES ME CRY
was originally published by
Saturday Review Press/E. P. Dutton and Co., Inc.

NOBODY
MAKES ME CRY

Shelley List

PUBLISHED BY POCKET BOOKS NEW YORK

NOBODY MAKES ME CRY

Saturday Review Press/E. P. Dutton edition published 1975

POCKET BOOK edition published September, 1976

This POCKET BOOK edition includes every word contained in
the original, higher-priced edition. It is printed from brand-
new plates made from completely reset, clear, easy-to-read type.
POCKET BOOK editions are published by
POCKET BOOKS,
a division of Simon & Schuster, Inc.,
A GULF+WESTERN COMPANY
630 Fifth Avenue,
New York, N.Y. 10020.
Trademarks registered in the United States
and other countries.

ISBN: 0-671-80702-1.
Library of Congress Catalog Card Number: 75-6514.

Printed in the U.S.A.

To Jerry

Acknowledgments

The author would like to thank Paul Pollaro and Conrad Sponholtz of the MacDowell Colony in Peterborough, New Hampshire, for time and space, and Gail Collins for her invaluable help. And to my daughters, Julie and Abigail List, a special thanks, since they somehow always seem to understand.

NOBODY
MAKES ME CRY

Chapter One

"Mary Catherine, do you have trouble walking in the cold weather?"

The doctor kept feeling for a pulse in her feet.

"Why are you poking me like that?"

"I'm trying to find a pulse in your feet and it's not easy."

"I have a pulse in my feet?"

"Yes, everybody has. Be still so I can feel it, ah, there it is."

The doctor had sores on his hands. In between the giant freckles, the large snowflakes of freckles on his hands were red and purple scabs.

But she liked him. Forthright, not mysterious, matter-of-fact. He had known her since she came east. She had wanted a New York doctor.

"Sex life? Good, no hang-ups?"

First time a doctor had ever asked her that in getting the family history.

"What can I do to stop the pain during my period?"

"For a woman of your age—"

"I wish you'd stop saying that."

"For a woman of your age, whenever there is a case like this we advise taking out the ovaries and the uterus and giving hormones by mouth."

"I want to secrete my own estrogen in my own way. I'll bleed."

"Suit yourself, when it gets as big as a basketball,

then we'll worry. The size of a small grapefruit or a large orange. That's how big they are."

"What?"

"Your fibroids."

"I don't like the idea of them floating around in there."

"They do not float."

"Well, I'm not going to have all my insides out, I'm very attached to them."

"Nobody said you have to, it's your decision if you can stand the pain of your period and the heavy flow."

"I'll stand anything."

"And at your age you have much less likelihood of ovarian cysts if you have no ovaries."

"I don't intend to get ovarian cysts."

"Don't be so smart. Anyway, your grapefruit or orange, actually two-month-fetus-size fibroids are not ready to be taken out anyway, so stop worrying."

"I just don't like the idea of those foreign bodies floating around in there. I'm too fat."

"You're no such thing. Don't lose a pound. As a matter of fact, you could gain a little. This is February. Come back in June."

So far, her New York day had been only fair. She would give it a C+. She had been to the gynecologist, had lunch, went to the museum on Fifty-third Street. She had an hour and a half to kill before she met Deborah, so she walked down to Forty-second Street.

She walked between the two massive lions at the Forty-second Street library, looked up at the stairs, went to the ladies' room. She turned around and walked out of the library. God, I'm restless, she thought. New York did that to her: overexcited her. She went around the corner and walked to Bryant Park in the back of the library. There were only a few derelicts there now, thanks to someone running for office who had decided to clean it up. She sat down on a bench where a woman was huddled into a corner. There were a few pigeons, a man reading Thorstein Veblen on the next bench. It was quiet. Cold.

Suddenly there were outbursts from the corner of the bench. The woman sitting there wrapped in a red wool shawl and plaid slacks shouted to the world at large, "Sure all the girls that got the jobs were Jews. They were all Jews." They followed her, lay in wait for her, the talking-to-themselves brigade.

The voice was unreal, pushed out of the diaphragm, like the diabolical tones coming out of that little girl in *The Exorcist*.

A moment later, out of the same larynx, out of that voice box, came soft, genteel, ladylike tones. "Pardon me, miss, do you have a nickel or five pennies?" Mary Catherine gave it to her.

Silence. And then the other self of her, the red-shawl-lady other voice would crash forth. "Thirty-seven years and she's still building in the Bronx," she said. "The statue of Columbus is still there. Boarding houses, all your life you lived in boarding houses. Oh, shaddup." The "shaddup" made Mary Catherine jump. It was loud, harsh. "Oh, shaddup. I didn't wanna build here too. The Knights of Columbus, they did it."

And then with a guttural growl she let forth, "Ver . . . ra . . . zan . . . o." It was scary. She was so lonesome. She was like a toy that someone had wound the back of too tight. "Who cares about your bar mitzvah," she said, followed by "Mm . . . mm . . . mmm . . ." like a motorboat warming up. "What are you? What are you?" she shouted to the pigeons.

Mary Catherine never looked at her. She would allow her the dignity of talking to herself in peace. But a man of about sixty-five sat down next to her. Between red shawl and her. Mary Catherine was writing a shopping list for tomorrow.

"I see you're left-handed, I am too, but I don't write with it. But it didn't harm me in other ways, I'm still a perfectionist in life. You know, they should do something about people like that," he said, looking knowingly in the direction of red shawl. "Put them away or something."

What is it about me, Mary Catherine thought. They follow me. They know I care.

"You know," he said, settling in for a long conversation, "this is one of the most sorrowful days in my life."

"Why?" She wanted to know.

"My girl friend and I broke up. After seven months. I furnished an apartment for her, used to take her to lunch at the Commodore, ten dollars it used to cost me. Listen, it's not the money, believe me."

"How old is she?"

"Twenty-one. You know, she just got in with the wrong company. I think"—he leaned over conspiratorially (there were blue veins in his bulbous nose, and folds where the frown lines had deepened so)—"I think she turned out to be a lesbian. I called up this afternoon . . ." Mary Catherine was afraid he was going to cry.

Sniffing: "I called up this afternoon, we were supposed to have lunch and she was still home. Well, she told me she couldn't come and she had been partying till five in the morning. Now, she didn't mention anything about men, only the girls, so I don't think there were men there. Anyway, she has hurt me in three ways. First, she broke my heart; second, the money, but really the money's not the thing; and third, she turned out to be a lesbian. I met her on a train, you know, the commuter train, and then put her up in the city. That was my mistake. And then she turned around and is having a ball. You get what I mean."

"Well, I've got to get my train. You see, I work at the New York *Post* at night and I don't get out of work till after midnight. It's hard for me to meet people. I'm going to call a dating service. I wish I didn't have to go. I need someone to talk to."

"Well . . ."

"Are you Catholic?" he said, getting up, adjusting his raincoat.

"Not really."

"Well, say a prayer for me."

The lady at the edge of the bench was snoring softly. And all the pigeons had flown away.

Mary Catherine, sitting an hour later in the Oak Room bar, sipping her scotch, was happy in that anonymous room, comforted by the fact that she didn't know a soul, hoping it would swallow her up. The warm dark brown of the bar's walls was turning almost black as the sun was fading outside over the park, across from the Plaza. Anyway, she thought, I've got to do something, I've got to get out of that town, that Long Island lethargy, away from other people's husbands and PTA meetings and leafless winters, the lifeless trees this time of year. They were bleak and blank and she wanted out. No more leaflessness no more lovelessness, I will find sun and solace.

For Deborah, however, Bloomingdale's had been a collage of blue-uniformed girls with pink smocks and thin slits of heels behind makeup counters. They were wearing the newest thing in makeup: no liner, heavy mascara, each separate lash a world unto itself, it was a wide-eyed look and it was indeed in. Deborah felt faint at the activity; bustling, moving with ladies trying on wigs, curly-headed young men with small bottoms smoothing on lipstick with the third finger, pinkie extended out, matrons in from Rye and Westport. Their wrinkles stood out in the cruel light of the multi-bulbed makeup mirrors; mirrors everywhere, and paint pots, pencils, isotoners. "Beautiful, we can make you beautiful," the first floor of Bloomingdale's was shouting. "Trust us, just trust us, put yourself in our hands."

The lady at the earring counter where Deborah felt herself propelled (one didn't walk on the first floor of Bloomingdale's, one was wound up in the middle of one's back, spun around three times and headed for whatever direction one was facing) was at least seventy, her face had so many folds and crevices. She probably never left that counter all day, Deborah thought. That is her life. Life among the gold loops and the pearl drops. Deborah bought some loops. She wanted to buy something and the crowd was not so oppressive here.

Deborah found herself on the escalator and almost tripped off as it got to the second floor. She moved up to the fourth, fifth, and sixth floor. Raffia chairs, Siamese statues and pluperfect luncheon settings, fake flowers, luxurious green hangings and thick luscious towels, delicacies and curtains and fixtures. Deborah, finding the cacophony and color too heady, turned a corner, found the down escalator, and, heart beating, walked out of the store. The black nun at the subway entrance sitting on a bridge chair was nodding. Someone could have taken her can with a cross on it and run away.

Deborah leaned against the window, as the mannequin wearing a pink fluff of something for cruise wear stared imperiously down at her. Unsympathetic. She needed a drink. Bloomingdale's was not a good place if you need a drink.

"I'm sorry I'm late." Deborah came in, her nose red and running, hair struggling out of the careful bun she had pinned on when she took the train into the city that morning. But the rest of her looked fine. She had stopped in the Plaza ladies' room to freshen up, determined to make some sort of reasonably assured entrance into the bar; so her makeup was new, a little bit of blue liner made her eyes stand out, and the creamy rosy-fingered rouge gave her cheeks a glow through which the freckles showed.

She carried a shopping bag from Bloomingdale's, *House Beautiful* and *Vogue,* looking somehow very much the country cousin visiting the city. A bit of the Long Island Rail Road sticks to one's clothes, a bit of the station wagon and the beach stays with one on Fifth Avenue. In the summer months the coiffed suede slick too-tan twosomes on Main Street in the country are unquestionably New Yorkers summering. One knows that after one glance at the car, the shiny spotless one without baseball bats and gloves and broken flashlights and leftover de-icer from last winter in the back seat.

Deborah was glad to see Mary Catherine.

"I must look a mess, haven't looked at myself since seven when I caught the train." She smiled, crossing her legs under the table.

"You look fine," Mary Catherine said. "I've ordered a martini for you."

"Thank God. I've just fought the battle of Bloomingdale's. Don't you look smart. What's new. What are you reading?"

"Things are starting to happen."

"What kinds of things?"

"Well, internal things."

"Like what, for God's sake."

Deborah squinted into Mary Catherine's eyes.

"Like my period is all of a sudden very erratic."

"So?"

"And it hurts a lot."

"More than usual?"

"Yes, I went to the doctor this morning."

"And . . . ?"

"And he said I had little tumors inside."

Mary Catherine twirled the swizzle stick into her scotch.

"A lot of people do. And . . . ?"

"And they're always benign."

"Well, that's good."

"But it makes my period hurt."

"All right, that's not so terrible. What else?"

"Fibroids they're called."

"I know."

"So he took out his big book."

"And?"

"And he's talking about my insides, right?"

"Right."

"And he shows me pictures of how they're attaching themselves to the lining of the uterus. And he said he'll keep checking them every four months and . . ."

"And what?"

Deborah was impatient.

"And if they get too big they take out the works."

"He said that?"

"A hysterectomy."

"You're kidding."

"It just so happens that I am much too young for a hysterectomy so I'm not going to have it. I told him that. He said they give estrogen easily now, and it's no big deal. Sure it's no big deal for him since he doesn't have a uterus, but I do and I'm not going to walk around uterusless. He couldn't get over how outraged I was at him. How would he like if I told him, "Well, castration is nothing, snip snap, off it comes. It's no big deal." Well, he's not going near my insides. I'm very attached to them. I will ignore the pain, live with it, not pay any attention to it, but all that business is staying in there. Deborah, I'm very attached to my insides."

"If it were me, I'd have it all out. Who needs it."

"I'd rather secrete my own hormones, thank you. Of course I don't want any more children, he asked me that, but I am secretly very comforted by all those organs inside me."

"I think you're crazy."

"Why?"

"Because I can't stand my period. It's a bore, a bloody bore, and it's inconvenient and I cry before during and after. Abe used to say that I never had a normal moment, being afflicted by premenstrual, menstrual, and postmenstrual tension. Maybe so, but if it were I and it came to that, and it probably will, I'd have the whole thing out, done away with."

"Not me. I just can't believe that I've gotten old enough to be menopausal. The pausal that refreshes. Deb, I'm getting loaded."

"Pissed. Pissed, my dear."

"That's a loathesome expression."

"Honestly, what a hypocrite. So ladylike on the outside you make me sick, and only I and God and a few men know you're not a lady at all at all. All of us, we're all old enough to start menopause. I started this year."

"How do you know?"

"Your period starts getting lighter, sporadic."

"And do you really flush?"

"Well, sort of, but the weird thing is you feel so sensitive all the time. Like being premenstrual, teary all the time. I burst into tears at the oddest times."

"Well, not me. I refuse. It's not necessary, irrelevant, and I'm not going to let it affect me one way or another. But, Deborah, how can it happen, we're young, we feel young, we're still attractive and sexual and we're there already, at that time of life. I can't believe it, it came so fast. It's like yesterday my mother had her hysterectomy. God, of course that's why I feel the way I do. My mother was suicidal. She'd had this mammoth fibroid that looked like a baby inside her stomach and she went to the hospital to have it removed and they took out everything and she cried and cried, it had hurt so much. I was thirteen and my aunt Eleanora had come back from New York and took care of us. My father was a mess, positively useless with my mother away, and I remember feeling so sorry for her. All the pain. And she was so sad all the time. The Catholic thing helped her, but after that her skin dried up and she developed these black circles under her eyes that she would never try to hide. They gave her hormones too, but it didn't matter, she dried up as though her whole body had been submerged in water too long. I don't know. It seems to me she never felt like a woman again. From then on she went to church more often, read the Bible a lot, took care of my father, but her heart wasn't in any of it. It was as though something had died in her. And neither Dennis nor I could tap her mothering again. We tried. And we loved her, I suppose, in our way. She made me feel so sad."

There was a silence between them as Mary Catherine's gaze stayed fixed on the window boxes lining the wall. This is the time, lady, she thought, this is the time for all good women to come to the aid of their bodies, this is meaning time maudlin time this is the time of your lives time.

Mary Catherine's positive feeling about her period was comforting. Aunt Eleanora had seen to that. The nuns had never never talked about it, and she had learned from Janet Hugo, a German girl, whose mother never mentioned it either. Mary Catherine's mother had always been terribly embarrassed by the whole thing, so she didn't want to disturb her. Janet Hugo and she had discovered a dog-eared book in the library with lots of illustrations about where things like the vulva were, and they taught themselves everything they wanted to know about everything. Without realizing it, even though they dreamed about big careers in New York, the thought of having babies enchanted them. As she looked back, she couldn't figure it out, with all the negative emphasis on the body and its functions and her mother's martyred involvement with them, but Mary Catherine's romantic nature transcended it all. She and Janet pored over books with photographs of benign mothers gazing down on sleeping infants suckling, or books on childbirth without fear, the ultimate fulfillment. She was looking forward to it.

After she got her period she would struggle to find the right hole to put the Tampax in, confused, utterly frustrated at all those unknown orifices. She had no idea what they were. Janet would stand outside the bathroom door reading the instructions out of the Tampax box next to the handy little container you could carry to school. They had giggled and laughed so loud, and finally one day, eureka, Mary Catherine found the hole.

The day after her wedding night, she had written Janet, was a Sunday and she had woken up at noon and realized she had missed mass for the first time. "Deep down," she wrote her friend, "I was really amazed I was the same person, no lightning, no feeling of total corruption, in fact no guilt. I felt totally released as though I'd been followed around all my life by some sort of oppressive guardian who kept track of everything I did, and suddenly he disappeared. At that point I now had a temptation to try it out all over the place and test my new freedom."

But of course she didn't and lived with the exigencies of Carlos's penis for all those years.

So despite the nuns, despite her mother, but because Aunt Eleanora had pushed the affirmation-of-woman-hood theory from the beginning, her period was something she almost enjoyed. In an odd way the discomfort, the teariness, the forlorn feeling gave her pleasure. She would read poetry at these times, or a novel guaranteed to make her cry, and lie, wrapped in her own comfortable sadness, her proof that she was, after all, indeed a woman.

Her daughter, Francie, of course, was another story. When Francie got her period after months of careful preparation, Mary Catherine was delighted, bought her a Joni Mitchell record she knew she loved, wrote her a note, and when she gave it to her, kissed her, welcoming her into the world of women. She asked her, "What do you think, Francie, what do you think about it?" "You know what, Mother, you know what I think," she had answered, "I think it's disgusting."

Well, you can't win them all, Mary Catherine had thought. She was certain, however, that somehow some of her feelings had to rub off.

"My doctor wanted to fix me up with someone, can you imagine, Deborah?" Mary Catherine was doodling on a napkin.

"You're kidding."

"No, a friend of his is getting a divorce. This, of course, is while he's got me up in the stirrups investigating my vulva."

"You love that word."

"I know. Do I use it often? I love the sound."

"So what did you tell him?"

"I wanted to be sure he was single. I happen to

adore my doctor, and I trust him. But then the truth came out. The man had just left his bed and board, like last night, and is excruciatingly lonely, which means he is what you call a married man, and I've got enough of those."

"You know it's true, where are the single men for us. All I've got is Sam, who I don't even like, who on February twenty-eight I may marry. Mary Catherine, there must be unmarried men around somewhere, someplace."

"There is no such thing as an unmarried man in our age bracket. Forget about it. My wise aunt who knows everything told me once a long time ago that if a man is worth anything he's worth taking away from his wife. And that's how she got all three of her husbands. It's true. She used to tell me that there was no such thing as morality involved. It was just the rule of the game. And you just have to be as smart and as beautiful and as shrewd as the next one or you won't get anyplace."

"O.K. So that's the way you function. Right?"

"Of course not. I try, but I'm not good enough, or is it bad enough? But somehow I know that that's probably the way to do it. I just bumble around, and it is true that all you meet are married men, and sometimes I have succumbed and sometimes I don't. Actually, it's not a very nice thing to do and I am just goddamned determined to remain intact."

"What on earth does that mean?"

"It means that nobody's going to make me do or be anything I don't want to."

"I'm smarter than you are but you've got more sense," Deborah said.

"How do you know you're smarter?"

"I read more. I'm more sophisticated. I know more about opera."

"Big deal."

"I'm not being insulting. It's the truth. What do you know about Baccarat?"

"What?"

"See?"

"See what?"

"You don't know about Baccarat."

"So what, Deborah. What is it?"

"It's crystal. It's the finest crystal in the world. My ex loved it."

"What on earth does that have to do with anything?"

"And also I know about Lorca. What do you know about Lorca?"

"His name was García Lorca and he was a Spanish poet."

"And playwright."

"So what, Deborah. This is dumb."

The waiter brought another round. The fine veins pushed through the corners of Deborah's nose. Her cheeks were flushed. She was happy.

"Mary Catherine, why do you make a fuss? I'm really complimenting you, for heaven's sake. I'm just saying we are an unlikely pair."

"Is that what you used to tell Abe?"

"Well, yes, as a matter of fact. We were unlikely. But it worked for a while. And I loved him."

Tears.

"But why do you think we're friends? You and I."

Mary Catherine wished seamed stockings were back in. She ached to smooth the back of her leg to straighten something. Something to do with her hands. She did it anyway, feeling the bulge of her right calf.

More tears.

"Because I love you, Mary Catherine. You're the only one I can be honest with. I went to that rap consciousness thing and all they kept telling me was to fulfill myself and go to work. So I'm working, but it doesn't do anything about the loneliness. It doesn't do anything about the silence. Anaïs Nin said that the only reason for madness is loneliness. It's true. Not to have anybody. Especially on Sundays. I will die on a Sunday."

They were bad enough at college, Deborah thought, when the dormitories would empty and people would go to the movies on dates or into Boston for Sunday dinner at sympathetic families' houses, for leg of lamb and mint jelly and a fire in the fireplace and white tablecloths and crystal glassware. The Commons would be half-empty on those nights and the bare linoleum tabletops and rabbit stew and raspberry Jell-O made it all seem lonelier than usual. There would be a quiet sound on the campus those Sundays, the light coming on in the dorms, one by one, and then night would finally and gratefully come.

"Divorced Sundays are the worst," Deborah said. "How they could be is beyond me, because nothing could be lonelier than college Sundays, but divorced Sundays are. Much worse. Always a fitful sleep on Saturday. And, you know, a country Sunday is different from a city Sunday. For a divorced woman especially. For one thing, people don't do anything during the week. No one just says come drop over for a drink or come for dinner, or let's go here or there. The week is tired time for husbands who stumble off the train and the bar car, or even if they haven't had one drink they are walleyed from the rush to the station, the dash for the train past cops and whores and news vendors and doormen and mink ladies and hustlers and just people rushing, rushing to get home.

"So they get off the train. And they see the kids. And the wife, martini in hand, maybe meets him at the train, and the mention of going somewhere upsets him and so no one goes anywhere on weeknights.

"But when you're alone. And it's just you and your children and then nobody and the night sounds and the oil burner clicking on and off, it's pretty grim.

"And then the rap ladies kept talking about putting whipped cream on the vagina, to stimulate their husbands, and why do husbands hold money over their wives' heads and things like that, and is it so terrible to covet the neighborhood liquor man. I couldn't relate to any of those ladies and none of them gave me comfort. You give me comfort."

Deborah didn't want the waiter to see she was crying. She was going to be fifty next month and she would be damned if a waiter that she had flirted with surreptitiously would see her crying with Helena Rubinstein's non-smear, non-running mascara streaking her face. So she hid her face in her bag, searching for something, and gingerly patted her eyes and cheeks with the back of her hand.

This Mary Catherine, this little beautiful woman with the disarming direct look and such little hands and feet and such a girlish body, seemed to care. And she seemed so strong. That little self of her had so much buoyance; she would not use her, she would try very hard not to depend too much on her. But she wanted to be blood brothers—sisters, even though the word *sisters* unless you were related seemed rather sophomoric to her, she wanted to take a scout knife and slit wrists together as they did when they were kids, as she had done with Sarah Cohen when they swore allegiance forever and ever to each other. They had put their wrists together and let the bloods blend. Sarah's had seemed redder than hers that time, but no matter, they became sisters, they became one. How nice to slit wrists with Mary Catherine, Deborah mused, bloodletting bloodbath bloodless Captain Blood bloody bore blood brothers sisters be my friend.

She took her tiny rouge compact out of her makeup kit and with trepidation looked at her eyes, puffy now, narrow. Grateful she was a woman, grateful for artifice and paint and repairability—a woman's face is always repairable. So she dabbed a bit here and there with the shiny new pinkening stuff, smoothing it up under her eyes onto the cheekbones. Was it her imagination or did it seem, with the softening light creeping through the window, could it be that her eyes were moving lower on her face? Could it be that the cheekbones had fallen ever so slightly since morning?

"I give you comfort," Mary Catherine said, "because I sit here and listen to you and don't coddle you. You're spoiled and don't have any sense of humor and feel so self-pitying."

"My husband, Abe, used to say that, Abe used to say that all the time, but what's good about me is that I care. I may be weak and I may be frivolous or whatever, but by God I care. My kids are in good shape, nobody's on drugs and nobody got anybody pregnant, and I suppose I should be grateful for that. And the reason is that I really do care about people." Deborah threw out her arm, and in emphasizing the point spilled her drink on Mary Catherine, on the table, into the peanuts, and just missing the shiny-haired young girl at the next table's brown fur-trimmed coat resting on the seat.

"I'm so sorry," Deborah said, her face getting very red. "I'm so sorry. Oh, God, look what I did."

"It's all right, don't pay any attention to it, I'll get you another drink."

"I want to get married," Deborah said. "I want to do for someone. Go to the gourmet cheese store and bring home the Brie and goat cheese for someone. I want to chill the wine and have champagne on ice for him, and cook his favorite Hungarian goulash with sour cream, and wear a long hostess gown when he comes home." Mary Catherine was wiping up the mess, the napkins were soggy. "I don't care how corny it is, goddamn it, it's what I want." Deborah was beginning to get a little noisy. "And I want him to be there to take me to the theater and send me roses on our anniversary and help me, be there when someone is sick so I don't have to do it by myself. I don't like to do those things, Mary Catherine, by myself. Can you understand that? I want to be married"—she was whispering now—"I don't want to be modern and live with someone, I want someone no matter how boring we get to each other, I want a husband. If it means we are actually using each other, then that's what it is. But in the meantime I know what I want, I want to get married."

"So get married."

"Well, what do you think of that, tell me what you think."

"I think it's fine for you, I do."

Deborah was crying and all the mascara and thin liner were smudges. Her face glistened with tears. The waiter didn't pay any attention.

"Deborah, get married, go on, it has nothing to do with anything. Why do you feel guilty if it's what you want?"

"I don't know what to do with all this freedom in the air. It has nothing to do with me, everything to do with me. All this alternative-life-style business and group this and group that, and the other day someone stuck a thing in my hand that was pushing a commune for divorced people. He had a white mustache and a greasy look and looked at least sixty, and I certainly couldn't think of sharing a bathroom or kitchen chores with him, that's for sure. The point is, I like it, the freedom. I like coming and going and not being beholden and all that, and I like being appreciated for my brain and talent instead of my rear end, but goddamn it, I like it the old way. I'm free enough sexually, I suppose, but I'm not interested in exploring some woman's tits or putting my mouth on her or carrying on like some of the Women's Lib ladies are yelling for me to do. I feel like every time I pick up an article or turn on the television my whole life has to be reorganized. I start questioning every goddamn thing. Why can't it be the way it was? Why can't people love each other and grow old with each other and care about each other? Just this week I saw three TV panels on alternative life-styles, that term makes me sick, and this one girl said seriously, and she made a lot of sense, that we must do something about the boredom. Marriages don't last because people get bored with each other. I saw *Blood and Sand* on television the other day and they're all dead. Tyrone Power is dead, all that black eyebrow and sweet face, and Linda Darnell. Dead too. Nothing lasts. Whoever said anything lasts. Nothing lasts. So leaves and flowers and things die too, but they always come back, something always replaces them. Why can't people replace, replenish their love? Why, Mary Catherine, why doesn't anything last? Why does it go away? Six years, seven years, and the people are tired of each other. I don't get tired of my kids. I always love them, it changes as they change, as I change, but it grows, why can't it be like that with a man and woman, why does someone always look better once the sex loses the bloom? Why does sex have to complicate everything? I don't want to be bisexual like *The Village Voice* tells me to all the time, I don't want the alternate route or the detour or whatever, I want it to be the way it was. Do you have to go through a depression together like my parents to stay together?

"Why can't one woman love one man for a long time and the other way around? I'm so terrified I'm thinking of marrying Sam because he's the first man that looks halfway decent to me who likes my cooking. Is it crazy, does it make me terribly insecure? Does it mean I'm hopelessly neurotic because I can't stand to be alone, because I know that I'm a fairly interesting person and I read a lot and am moderately well versed on what's going on in the world, but I don't care, I'm only half there when there is no man with me. I want to share, I don't want so much variety, I'm tired of all those magazines telling me I should expand my horizons."

"Deborah, why do you buy those magazines, for heaven's sake? *Cosmopolitan* and *Playgirl,* for God's sake, you're not twenty, you're too old for singles bars and all that shit. If you want to get married, go to Parents Without Partners, for heaven's sake, and meet some nice widower with three kids."

"Do I sound dumb, do I sound ridiculous to you?"

"Yes, you do, you're a pain, but I understand. But where are you in all this?"

"Doesn't it bother you in the same way, don't you tire of lack of security, the not knowing, the getting old? We are getting old. You said it yourself, the affront of our getting menopausal. David Susskind is telling me how to run my life. The other night a bunch of divorcées were sitting around commiserating, and one said you might as well masturbate instead of the one-night stand, so debilitating it was, and another one said sex and love are separate of course, the one-night stand is all right if it is gratifying, as long as it doesn't debilitate you. And, Mary Catherine, the one who wouldn't masturbate, 'I'll be damned if I'll do it,' she said, 'it's just too undignified.' Goddamn it, I don't want to either, I want to get married."

"Good God, you're beginning to sound like a broken record."

"Mary Catherine, all I can get is a two-hundred-pound monster. Is that what I have to look forward to? Oh, Sam, he takes me to dinner, then up to his apartment high in the sky and you know what? I hate it I hate it. I hate him and he's all I've got. How do you like that?"

"I don't like it. So find someone else."

"I can't. They don't want me. I'm too old. My thighs wobble and my eyes aren't my eyes anymore. So I said to the plastic surgeon, there's this stranger in the mirror and I don't know who she is. It takes longer and longer and longer every day to put myself together. It isn't till eleven o'clock that my face gets to be normal again. It takes all morning till it falls into place."

"Deborah, you're making me sick. You're forty-nine years old."

"Too bad. Just too bad. You're younger. You're not as vulnerable as I am."

"Oh, God, we're all made of glass, for heaven's sake. But I've got Francie and my work and for God's sake I've got myself. And you, you've got so much you can't see yourself. You can't see who you are. If you didn't drink so much you might be able to see yourself clearer."

"I don't know why you keep telling me how much I drink. You're the one who drinks. I am not a drinker. Are you intimating that I'm an alcoholic? Jews don't get to be alcoholics, you know. Don't you know your sociology?"

"In the first place, that hasn't been true for years, and in the second place, who are you kidding. I can take it or leave it."

"Now. Now. Be honest. Now you can take it or leave it. You told me you and Carlo used to drink deep into the night. And I only started sipping the way I do when Abe left. Why did he leave, Mary Catherine? Why did he leave me? I wanted him to stay. I begged him to stay. He went off with a twenty-two-year-old girl who looks just the way I did when I was young, his student his student. I didn't think people did that anymore. How gauche, how typical, how unoriginal, to go off with your student. She's a poet, you know. Writes for the *American Poetry Review* or something. He promised we would be together forever. He is the only man who gave me an orgasm, you know. Unlikely, we were an unlikely pair, but he was the only one who gave me an orgasm, who I wasn't afraid of dying with. The only one who stood up to Daddy and the only one who held me all night long. I wasn't lonely when Abe was around. And now I find out that he's had women all these years, he told me, he told me. I am bleeding, I am bleeding, Mary Catherine. He was my rock and he left me, we left each other. She saw him on the street, Lolly told me the other day, with a 'gaudy lady' with long gold earrings.

"Why care, why not be big and wise and wonderful with no jealousy and no possessiveness, I said to myself, but somehow I always thought that someday we could get back with each other, that someday everything would be all right again and we would love each other again and make love with abandon, and now his gaudy lady has a pin in the back of her hair and pulls it out and pricks my balloon and it is over. He has his gaudy lady and I my fleshy fan who makes his tepid love and has no idea who I am. He did and he is gone, gone to gaudy-lady land."

Deborah took a long sip of her drink. "What about you, Mary Catherine? You never tell me anything about yourself, you keep it all in like beans in a bean-bag but I know something is happening because your eyes shine and you have a wild look under all the quiet."

"Oh, Deborah, why do I trust you. I don't know why. I guess because we're both in the same kind of scene in a way. There are two now."

"Two men?"

"Yes."

"And they are both married."

"Yes."

"Do they know about each other?"

"No."

"Mary Catherine, how can you do it?"

"I don't know. I just can, and not only can I do it, I enjoy it. Deborah, I love the differences. And I love to stay home alone on Saturday night and not see anyone and read and fill the house with music or talk to my child. Is that heresy? Is that blasphemy? All I know is that once I decided to let go of all that believing, it set me free."

"I could never do it. I am a one-man woman."

"I used to say that."

"How can you, how can you enjoy it with different men? You don't belong to either."

"No."

"Will you ever belong to anyone?"

"You sound like a little girl. Nobody belongs to anyone, ever."

"I am a little, I am a little bit like a little girl."

"I don't know. God, I don't know. All I know is that I discovered this thing in me and it was a body and it was alive and could function in a million different ways with lots of people. Now I sleep with two. And whoever else comes along. What's such a big deal about that? My guilt is at a minimum, it almost doesn't exist, I have to force it, if you want the truth.

"If I could have it this way forever I would be preferably happy; it's playacting and it's romantic and it's full of no responsibility and I can be loving and wise and sexy and I don't have to sneak putting olive oil in my hair all night long or I can run naked through the house if I want, not make the beds for three days if I don't want to.

"Anyway, I have gotten out of the habit of being faithful. All right, blanch, it's an old-fashioned word. But I have. I seem always ready for the next encounter, always open to whatever is going to happen."

"Something will change it."

"Maybe. Maybe you're right. Security doesn't mean a damn to me. Sometimes when things get physically rough and a bore like the toilets overflowing or getting stuck in a snowdrift, but other than that security is a strange and confining word."

"You, my dear, are missing something."

"I guess so, Deborah, I guess so. But I found out something. I found out a sad truth and I hate to admit it to you. I don't know why and I probably shouldn't, but I will because for a strange reason I want you to be happy, I want you to be the incurable romantic, if that's what you want, or I want you to have affairs that titillate you and make you feel beautiful."

"So?"

"So it's that I can get the same amount of pleasure in bed, or even give the same, to anyone. Anyone. One lover I have says to me every time we have finished making love and being together for a long time, 'I can't ever imagine your being this way, this responsive, with anyone other than me.' And I never give him a direct answer because, Deborah, the answer is, he is fooling himself. I can come and be aroused and sexually excited

by any man. I've proved it. I've lived it. And you know
what? So what? No one moves me, no one makes me
feel different from anyone else. No one, Deborah, no
one no one no one ever makes me cry. With Carlo at
the beginning I cried. I cried and I thought every time
I was having an orgasm I would die. That it was like
going into a world that was close to the beyond.
Romantic drivel, maybe, young-idealistic, who the hell
knows.

"All I know is that I've proved it. I didn't set out
to, I didn't set out to make a test case for heaven's
sake, but there it is. I can function like a man. I can
take it or leave it if I am horny enough. And if it
sounds harsh from a nice Catholic girl who already is
condemned to purgatory anyway, I don't care. The
point is that I proved it and I'm left with two men who
what, who what, who suit me, shall we say, at least
for now."

"Oh, Mary Catherine."

There were tears in Deborah's eyes.

"Don't you cry, don't you dare cry for me. I'm fine.
If you feel sorry for me, I'll scream. How dare you.
You're wrong. I'm better off than you are, that's for
sure."

"Oh, Mary Catherine. What above love?"

"I don't know what it is. I can care and take someone to the doctor if they're sick maybe and darn their
socks, is that it? I don't know. And I can give them the
warmth of my body just like I do to Francie. But nobody yet touched me, for God's sake. Nobody makes
me cry."

Deborah looked at Mary Catherine, whose hands
were clenched, whose eyes were defiant. She put her
arms around her.

"Deborah, why is it that anyone can make me come?
Anyone can rub and hold and carry on with me and

I can come. Did you ever read *The Golden Notebook?* Where Doris Lessing's liberated ladies can only have orgasms with men they love? Not true. No truth to it. Our bodies are limitless. Sure, some men make me feel better than others, the rhythm is right somehow. It has nothing to do with anything else. My sexuality is total. Of course, it's better if I could love, but love sifts through me like flour; I don't love, I just don't love. And really, I don't know if anyone loves me either. It's all a game we play; we play at love, we play at all the romantic stuff we were brought up with. I'm not saying it wouldn't be nice, and I'm not saying that men I've been involved with in my head were lovers. I'm saying they were infatuations, silly no eating and sitting like a fool by the telephone and no more. By God, no more, I just don't want to be disappointed anymore. I don't want a man floating away to booze or other women.

"Deborah, I've discovered such a force inside me, a force that astounds me. Yes, I can do anything, I proved it. No, I do not want this to be the way forever. Yes, I want to love someone but, Jesus, I want to be free, I want to trust first. I found this other Mary Catherine and I can't let her go, eenie meenie miney moe I've caught myself by the toe if I holler let me go. I'm not, I'm not letting go. Life's too short. So I'll be lonely. I don't like it either. I've been lonely all my life but it's not devastating anymore. It's just not devastating. I can be useful; yes, I can.

"But by God, I'm not going to be a whiner like you. You whine and cower and drink up a storm and don't do anything about your insides. So give Sam the gate. Find someone, take up Tab. Get off your ass. Advertise in the *New York Times* classified for a husband, do anything, but stop waiting for something marvelous to fall into your lap. You told them all off in your group therapy, yoga doesn't do a thing for you, you meditated and that didn't give you any peace of mind. Do you honestly believe that if you had someone to bring cheese home for, that everything would change? Did it ever occur to you that Deborah, good old boozing, sunning Deborah would still be there?"

Deborah started to cry. Her shoulders went up and down with the even tempo of pumps drilling for oil. She put her hands over her face. The sobbing made her lose her breath, and her face, under her fingers, as much as Mary Catherine could see, was red.

Mary Catherine helped her up. In the lobby it seemed all pink and pocketbooks, tea sandwiches and string strains in the Palm Court with its maître d' in a tuxedo and bags piled high, its Caron window, silks and furs, a lobby collage. She held her in her arms, ignoring the few stares, and felt her friend's thickening waist. Mutt and Jeff they must look like, she thought as she led her into the ladies' room. Which one had the Toni. She had not meant to make her cry.

Chapter Two

In 1973, the year of the divorce, Mary Catherine Romano took herself to a psychiatrist.

Everyone in Eastville, or everyone who could afford it, or somehow get it covered on the Blue Cross or Medicare or Major Medical, was taking himself to psychiatrists or transcendental meditation (TM), mind control or encounter or transactional analysis (TA), or yoga or Catholic family service. Eastville was going crazy just like the rest of the world, and Mary Catherine needed help too. She was getting rid of Carlo.

Sara Jane Laverette around the corner, whom she knew from Girl Scouts years ago when the girls were young (trim in their little green dresses, bony ribs feeling vulnerable, sweet through the cloth, little cap folded through the loop on the shoulder) was in real trouble. Her husband had come home one night, sat her down along with the five kids on the blue-print couch in the living room, and told them he was leaving. Just like that. He had had women here and there, Mary Catherine knew that and Sara Jane certainly did, but she had loved him and waited up for him every night no matter how late he had come home from New York. Once she had called his office every hour on the hour till three in the morning, till he finally came tiptoeing in through the door. He had admitted that he had impregnated a girl with whom he had been having an affair, that she was having the baby the next week, and he had agreed to give her three hundred dollars a week. Just like that.

And now he had taken off. Like the welfare fathers, like the construction workers and bus drivers who became so frustrated because they couldn't support their families. But Sara Jane's husband had been an advertising man, a king of the bar car, the hail-fellow, hi-there cocktail-party backslapper, the champion of the subliminal image, defender of people's life, liberty, and pursuit of cigarette sales. Manny Laverette just took off, telling his fifteen-year-old he could have the suits in the closet. The new baby needed him more, he said to the six of them seated wide-eyed on the blue-chintz couch, the picture window coated with steam. All he took when he left was his guitar and his copy of *On the Road*. A beat late perhaps, but he took off.

She finally traced him to Montana, where he was working on a ranch with the girl and the baby.

That, according to Mary Catherine and everyone in the upper-middle-class suburb of New York, was trouble, real trouble. Sara Jane hadn't worked since she was twenty, there was no insurance on the car, and no promise whatsoever of how Manny was going to support them all.

That was real trouble.

So that whenever Mary Catherine heard a story like that over morning coffee at the Cupacoffee on Main Street at 8:30 A.M. before all the tradesmen opened their stores and before she unlocked the door to her real estate agency, she, as her mother would say, counted her blessings.

At least she had gotten her divorce, Carlo had promised to support Francie, who although sixteen would be going to college soon, and she herself had worked on and off since she was sixteen, so was not catapulted into a job market swollen with nubile long-haired blondes with pink cheeks and long torsos. She wasn't complaining. She was better off than most, she thought, and somewhere, somehow had a built-in cope machine that got her through things. Even now; but she needed help. She had to get her thoughts clear, see where she was going, learn what to do with the loneliness.

"Feel sorry for yourself and you're dead, you might as well give up, desexualize yourself, fall apart," Aunt Eleanora had told her, "don't do it, I'm telling you don't do it. You've got good genes, you come from strong stock, and by God you can do anything. All you've got is you in this world. Just you. Depend on yourself; if you find someone else to support you and believe in you, by God, Mary Catherine, that's gravy. Life isn't like that. Life's hard and full of cruel ironies, but by

God you've got it inside you to do anything, be anything."

Aunt Eleanora used to tell her that when she was ten, maybe twelve, because the doubts had already begun to set in. She felt skinny and ugly. Oh, to be beautiful, she would think, walking home from school with Janet, her best friend, oh, to be beautiful, she would think, walking into the house, putting her books down on the kitchen table, glancing at herself in the mirror with philodendron on either side next to the telephone. Janet's skin had no pores, how could anyone live in a poreless state she would think, and her cheeks had a high rose color, always.

Mary Catherine was sallow, pale yellow, especially in winter, and on the very cold days she would notice a gray tint. Green eyes were different and lovely, but hers looked like pea soup, she thought, murky. And why didn't she have the traditional silky Irish complexion like every other girl of her lineage? Why did she break out? Sometimes she couldn't look at her face in the mirror, there was never a place that wasn't covered with some raw blemish. She thought of herself as scarred. You gave me brains, Lord, but are pimples the price I have to pay for them? Take them back, make me dumb, but give me a decent skin.

Once her mother, in a burst of untypical generosity, had saved some money and had just taken Mary Catherine to a fancy dermatologist in Boston after Aunt Eleanora had berated her sister for not doing anything about her daughter's skin.

The waiting room was enough to send her back home swearing to every saint in the book that she would never touch a shrimp, a piece of chocolate, or fried food again, ever, ever till hell froze over, till the millennium came. Pits and purple, miniature breasts, protuberances with white nipples needing to be squeezed all that poison spread over all those faces. It had seemed to her that some of the boys looked worse than the girls, getting the scourge of acne as torturous, as disfiguring as the bubonic plague, leprosy, and smallpox all rolled into one great pimple.

She felt cursed by her skin, and the doctor, all smooth baby face of him, not a blemish in the world, spent two minutes with her for his thirty-five dollars and told her not to eat shrimp, fried foods, or chocolate, which of course she knew already, to please go down the hall where one of his starched sirens would steam her, boil her, squeeze her, draw and quarter her, tar and feather her, or whatever, and she would be as smooth as new, and would she please make another appointment with the peaches-and-cream girl (just to rub it in) at the desk.

Miss Hill, as she cheerily told Mary Catherine her name was, wrapped her and steamed her as promised, and squeezed all the evil out of her, all the white little heads and black little heads, all the oily sebaaaacious, as she called them, glands would dry up and she would be Lana Turner, Betty Grable, June Haver—poreless queens all.

An hour later, exhausted, feeling cleansed, as though her face had undergone the highest of high colonics, she had walked out into the bright sun, squinting into the street. She rushed to the first window she could find. At the corner a florist had a wall of window on the outside of his shop, next to some hanging wandering Jew.

She looked worse. What had been fairly benign blemishes had turned into a rubbed-raw red-brick surface. Spots. Spots were all over her face like the Mark of Zorro, like the stripes of a zebra, the trunk on an elephant. She felt betrayed. Thirty-five dollars' worth. She would never go back, couldn't afford to go

back certainly, wouldn't do any good to go back anyway. "You'll outgrow it," Miss Hill had said consoling-
ly, and of course that's what did happen, finally, in
college, all those oily sections of what the girl at Filene's
Revlon counter had haughtily called "a combination
skin" finally caught up with the rest of her face. And
by the time she was twenty-one she felt a little more
in control of the situation. Salves and ointments, steaming, and oatmeal and honey packs, almond paste, egg
white, cucumbers, strawberries, mayonnaise, and lemons, she used them all, smelling like a salad gone rancid
in the sun. But sooner or later her skin caught up with
the rest of her and she was glad God hadn't taken
her up on her Faustian bargain. Her brain became her
saving grace when all else failed.

Today at forty-three the murky green of her eyes had
cleared, and if she wore blue, they turned aqua. She
had learned to like her eyes. Slowly, as the years had
gone by, she had learned to like the whole thing. She
was small, just five feet, with very black hair sprinkled
with a snowy streak in front. The white streak had
started to grow in when she was twenty-five and she
would stand, fascinated, at the mirror watching this
premature sign of age attack her head as the years
rushed past overnight.

But she had decided not to dye it, since black dye
always looked as though someone had taken Griffin's
number two shoe polish and with short swift strokes
painted on youth with a capital Y. Mary Catherine
had been determined not to fall into that trap, even
though Aunt Eleanora, who seemed to know everything
about how to combat the ways of the world, had insisted she do something about it. She had refrained.
Somehow she felt comfortable with it.

Her skin was fair, prone to freckle easily, and her
body designed, except for her bosom, which was full,

for the teen-age department of women's stores. She was a size five, with size-five shoes, narrow ankles. She dressed simply because at her age she couldn't get away with teenybopper bell-bottoms or swinging short skirts, and since those were the only clothes she could fit (she always had to let them out in the bosom), she chose carefully, picking a medium-length skirt with a matching sweater and colorful scarf attached with a smart pin, leather boots, or tight-fitting slacks with matching longer jackets to give her more length. She looked neat, ladylike. There was always a secret, though, in her eyes, a promise.

She had seen the psychiatrist on her lunch hour, or whenever it was she could get out of the office when clients from New York weren't coming out to the country to look for summer houses or winter rentals or to buy the cherished house in the promised land.

Eastville, Eastville, Long Island, one hour from the big city, close to the Atlantic Ocean, where you could take your kids in the summer and they could dig in the white sand, where boating and boozing bedding and bundling were suburban pastimes, where forty black families sprinkled the school system with their children, where the turnover was heavy, as oil companies and giant industries transferred their men every few years, sprinkling the schools with their midwestern-, Saudi Arabian-, or German-schooled children, where teachers came and left like summer storms since they couldn't afford to buck the affluence, pay their rent, cope with a system that had all the earmarks of progressivism but which relied heavily on grades, achievement, conformity. The town had the reputation of liberalism, progressivism, enlightenment. But it was not the prevailing motif. A recurring theme perhaps, but only that. Real estate moguls gobbled up precious land, cut down two-hundred-year-old trees, built one shopping center more prosaic, more California-crass than the other, rainbow flags fluttered at used-car lots, drugstores had begun to plaster their windows with garish signs promising drastic slashes on vitamin prices, and no ordinance, no law could prevent it.

It was a town like anywhere else, Mary Catherine supposed, except that because of the proximity to New York and because of the enlightened reputation, and because one after another Hollywood star saturated with the sun and surf, lobotomized by the logy southern California rhythm, had settled there. It was some kind of status symbol. Actors doing Broadway plays would commute for the hour, affording their children the fresh air and sense of normalcy. In the five years that Mary Catherine had lived there at least ten movie idols had moved into the town.

She saw them in the sport store, at the movies. And the town left them alone. The stars were good neighbors; but, when Mary Catherine made her pitch to sell a house, she always let it slip, who lived where, and how long, and what schools their kids went to. One brown-eyed granite-jawed sun god still dazzled them on Main Street. They were always reporting accidents, torn ligaments as women smashed into the car in front of them, catching a peripheral glimpse of Mr. Brown Eyes nonchalantly walking his towheaded daughter downtown for a chocolate ice cream cone.

During the twenties it had been an endless flat expanse of potato farms, and soon after, the artists, painters, the majority of whom were illustrators, heard about the loveliness of it and moved out, and remained.

They began dying off, but the reputation of the artists' colony remained. Artists or reasonable facsimiles flocked to the town even though it was more beautiful and cheaper farther out on the Island. They wanted to live in Eastville.

More than one of the writers in the past twenty years had satirized the place, made it the locale for their books or plays. The combination of the original residents, the old-timers, the potato farmers and their descendants, and the newcomers (sometimes it took twenty years to overcome that appellation) was like the proverbial oil and water. But no matter, it was the place everyone had heard of back there, wherever it was they came from in Minneapolis or Des Moines, Ames or Canton. Eastville was where they wanted to end up.

Those who made up the majority now were those people for whom Eastville, Long Island, was the last stop on the gravy train, the status-quo land, the American dream come true. As a result they wanted to keep it that way.

There were other groups, of course, who gave substance to the liberal reputation. One proud and dedicated group for seven years had withstood the stony gaze of firemen with American flags sewn on their shirts, and the taunts of young and old passersby, through stinging winter winds as they stood in front of the courthouse all through the war conducting a peace vigil. It was a moving sight. Every Saturday morning from 10 A.M. to 11, ten stalwarts had stood with signs, Peace Now, holding pictures of mutilated children. They would hand out pamphlets, engage in friendly exchange, and return the next Saturday.

There were also groups of innovative energetic young teachers and administrators who wanted to confront the malaise of the young, victims of the torpor growing out of the money and the drive of the fathers, the shattered goals of the mothers.

It was like any other town, Mary Catherine supposed, but certainly preferably to the Midwest, where she and Carlo had come from in 1968. It was slow back in Wisconsin, the pace was quieter, the people more open and accepting, but it was duller, less intense. She couldn't get used to the mothers in Eastville when she first moved there, always in the car, always driving their kids to this lesson and that one, filling up every minute of their lives. She had felt intimidated by the town, but soon decided that with or without Carlo she would extract the good out of it. She would protect Francie somehow from the temptations, the accessibility and peer pressure of drugs, the anti-intellectualism that hit when the kids were about twelve, the lack of emphasis on doing for themselves, finding their way. Everybody had too much or at least lived as though they had too much, and she didn't want Francie to be a victim of that.

When Mary Catherine was young she used to cry a lot. She took refuge in, sought after, films. She went to the movies often. It was a good place to cry. Lots of reasons. Ronald Colman going blind in *The Light That Failed,* Shirley Temple dying in *The Little Princess,* and when Emil Jannings pressed his nose against the window on a snow-studded night watching his family eating a dinner with turkey and candlelight, tears streaming down his face, in *The Way of All Flesh,* she had sobbed so loud the usher came to shush her. But it felt so good, she used to think, that marvelous kind of giving in letting the tears flow. How refreshed, how renewed.

When she got her period, those were the best kind of tears. Tears all day long. Teary in the morning, at lunch, in Latin class or at field hockey, at dinner, and then if she were in the middle of something like a nineteenth-century romantic novel, that together with the moody, morbid tears was glorious.

She was a romantic. Very emotional, and used to cry a lot. She didn't cry much at all anymore.

And now, in 1975, two years after the divorce, a

year after her short stay with the psychiatrist, Mary Catherine had become tough. Hard as nails. Liberated.

That is, if you call being liberated making her own living, supporting her child, cleaning out the gutters herself in the spring and fall, pumping out the Atlantic Ocean that seeped into her basement after the most recent rain or when the snow finally melted at the first green sign of spring. She could do anything, Mary Catherine could, anything a man could do. That she had learned. As a matter of fact, sometimes she felt quite superior to her married suburban sisters, if she was being honest about it, especially those who were saddled with boring husbands, for whom they had to cook and entertain deadly business colleagues. Some of those ladies envied her, she knew that: her freedom, her job, the traveling she got to do occasionally; and most of all, she imagined, the sexual experimentation that they surmised she had, that they would like to have. They didn't think about the loneliness.

Once, a while ago, Mary Catherine picked Francie up at school at 5:30 in the afternoon. The sour stench of scotch was on her breath after a long business lunch, and Francie noticed the telltale bumping over curbs and stones, the short stops at streetlights, the peering closely through the windshield to see what the street signs said. Francie had calmly asked her, "Would you ever commit suicide?"

Mary Catherine had looked at her. Her daughter's long, blond hair was streaked with past summer suns, her eyes were blacker this year. "No," she said slowly. "No, I wouldn't. The closest to a deep, deep depression I've ever gotten is when I gorged myself on thirteen Mounds bars. Never fear, Francie. Never, never fear."

They had laughed, but Francie had been serious.

Mary Catherine was married when she was eighteen,

six months after Carlo Romano had seen her at a
sorority dance. It was her freshman year at the University of Michigan (where she went because she heard
that Arthur Miller had gone there and in her eighteen-
year-old virgin mind thought that if that giant could go
to that school she would too and would become a great
playwright. It turned out that poetry suited her better,
but it didn't matter).

Carlo told her he liked small women. Her diminutive
proportions excited him for some reason; perhaps because he had been in the South Pacific during the war
and had fallen in love with a Japanese girl on Okin-
awa, maybe because his mother, who had long since
died, had been short, smart, strong. Whatever it was,
the look of Mary Catherine had delighted him. And
the fact that she was from Massachusetts and Irish
and he was from Wisconsin and Italian had nothing
to do with anything. He pursued her. He cajoled her.
He painted a glorious picture to her about their future.

"Mary Catherine," he had said, fondling her breast
in some deserted meadow off campus, one half hour
before the night watchman would lock up the dorms,
"Mary Catherine, we will have three kids and I will
go into my father's insurance business and we will live
happily ever after." And he would touch her nipples
and kiss her softly on her mouth and rub her till she
thought she would float away.

She wouldn't go to bed with him. She was scared.
The sisters at school had already told her what would
happen if she committed that sin. Just as they had told
her little brother that if he touched himself one more
time his penis would fall off. Just as they had crushed
the ruler down on Dennis's knuckles in school, so had
they never touched her but put such fear of the holy
fires and eternal damnation into her that even then,
as Carlo fondled her so deliciously, was she sure some-

how Sister Mary Alice was lurking behind a tree somewhere, the flames mirrored in her blue eyes. But that
new thing, that mysterious loveliness of friction, took
her off guard. Carlo was so gentle, so tender as he
smoothed her hair strand by strand, held his hand on
her cheek and looked long at her. It was all so new and
so fine, she had thought, on top of which she felt so
many new things in her breast and groin that would
never be settled unless she could spend long, lazy
nights in bed with this loving man.

The wedding had been simple. Mary Catherine's
parents didn't have much money. Her father was a
stationery supply salesman, happy to be on the road.
He had been in AA twenty years. Her mother weighed
two hundred pounds, had diabetes, and once was very
beautiful. They were relieved their only daughter had
married a Catholic, and that her virginity was intact
(the doctor told them so), and that Carlo had come
from a family that had prospects.

She was married the June of her freshman year with
all the sorority sisters there to throw rice in their aqua
satin gowns and gabardine hair bows to match and
$7.98 shoes dyed the same color. And Carlo's fingers
trembled when he put the ring on her finger, and when
he kissed her, after lifting up the veil with the priest
looking on, the gold on his robes catching the soft ray
of the stained glass from above, catching also Mary
Catherine's eye, blinding her for a moment, as Carlo
put his lips on hers, those familiar lips, he trembled
again; what was he worried about, Mary Catherine
thought.

She found out soon.

And ten months later she was pregnant. Those 3
A.M. fumblings, only consummated after Carlo had had
about twelve beers, and those unloving brawling bouts

of lovemaking resulted in Francie, that blond sweet thing.

And the fondling was never the same as it was on the meadow with the white moon smiling down on them with the moans of other couples reverberating in the hills, because he turned out to be a good man, Mary Catherine supposed, who loved Francie, who took them to church every Sunday, that he did, but he turned out to be a fraud.

When they earned ten thousand dollars a year, they lived as though they had twenty-five thousand. And when, thanks to Mary Catherine, who finally finished college at night and had gotten a job teaching school, they were pulling in, the two of them, about thirty thousand, they lived as though they had fifty. Boats, and lavish entertaining in the Madison suburb in which they finally settled, and booze. Booze came to a lot, Mary Catherine figured as the years went by. If only she had the money now that they had spent on liquor.

The only time Carlo could make love to her was when he was drunk. Once they had been fooling around in the back seat of a neighbor's car on the way to the movies and Mary Catherine touched her husband's penis, smoothed it, cupped it, and he carried on so, he recriminated and made her feel so guilty for her forwardness, that she never did it again. And Carlo the virile, like Eric the Red, faded, faded. He became a money-maker, a neighbor-impresser, a phony. And the weaker he got, the stronger Mary Catherine became. By necessity she was liberated before her time. She began to belittle him in public, and she also started to drink as much as he did, since it was the only time she knew he would make love to her.

They moved east, after Carlo lost his job when his father had died and the insurance company changed hands. And they settled in Eastville. There was just as much liquor there, and a dock for the boat Carlo would buy, job opportunities for Mary Catherine, cultural activities in New York, and good schools for Francie to attend. Mary Catherine took a course, passed a test, and got a job in a real estate firm. She was very good at it, and when the owner's husband was transferred and they had to move, she sold the whole firm to Mary Catherine.

It all fell apart. So fast. Carlo drank too much. Made a fool out of himself too often. There were flirtations for the two of them, and lots of heavy drinking parties, and she necked with their accountant by somebody's tennis court, fooled around. Eighteen years went by. Just like that.

Till one day, when Francie had had her fourth note from school in a month saying that she was failing, that such a bright lovely child was falling apart and what were you parents doing about it, the great blowup of all time came and went.

So Mary Catherine moved out. She left him. Took Francie and left.

And Mary Catherine, who had long ago (consciously anyway) stopped worrying about those inflammable adulterous guilts that Sister Mary Alice had pricked like tiny acupuncture pins into her head, Mary Catherine, whose Catholicism had long since gone by the wayside, Mary Catherine took herself to a lawyer, and decided to grow up and see what life was all about.

She had slept with one man.

She loved her child.

She could always work and make a living.

She felt strong.

And she had been so lonely she thought she would die.

But no more worrying whether the curtains were

frayed, no more wondering whether the liver was rare enough or the freezer stocked with pistachio ice cream. She would grab at the opportunity. She wasn't Elizabeth Taylor and she didn't have violet eyes and she wasn't Madame de Staël with a brilliance and a wit, but she was Mary Catherine with all this churning potential and by God she better do something about it before it got too late.

So she did what she had been threatening to do after every drunken lovemaking empty sweaty grunting empty empty evening. She left.

She didn't hate him. She didn't even hate herself for being so dumb as to marry for sex and then have the tables turned on her. So, after so many years of acting by the rule, by the catechism of her life, she was loose, breaking loose. Getting too loose maybe, she thought, getting to be a loose woman perhaps.

It was all changing so fast. It used to be that you don't go to bed ever before marriage, you stay faithful no matter what. You plan, you do the American thing and start out in an apartment and move to the country and get one, two cars, and your husband comes home every night with the rumpled suit in the summer with the paper tucked underneath his arm, and you have the martini in the car under the dashboard so the policeman won't see it. And tennis and sailing and keeping the status quo, the two weeks in Maine in the summer, putting the money away for college for the kids, for a rainy day.

It's not our fault, it's the way we were brought up, as the professor they had in college said, who identified their time as the "postponement of gratification time."

She had done it so long, the postponement, she decided she wanted her rainy day to be now. She wanted to be gratified. Unpostponed. She would be like the kids. She would live for today.

Carlo, of course, didn't know what hit him.

He promised to stop drinking. She stopped easily when he wasn't around. He promised he would mend his ways. It was too late. It didn't matter anymore. She didn't need him. She didn't need anybody.

That's what she had thought.

That's what she told the psychiatrist.

Chapter Three

Dr. Harold Stander was a handsome man. He wore a beige sports jacket with white threads staring through like ticking in a mattress, with a brown turtleneck sweater underneath. His brown shoes were shiny and had gold buckles on them. He was forty-five but looked collegiate, the gray tufts of sideburns only adding to the total effect calculated to be casual. He smoked a pipe, puffing and pulling on it, pressing the tobacco down into it with the eraser on the end of one of the many yellow number 2 pencils he had sitting in a pewter vase on his desk.

Mary Catherine had seen Dr. Stander through the years on the tennis court, his thighs spreading out of his shorts like oranges in a Christmas stocking. Her friend Lolly had been in therapy with him for a year and felt that he was helping her enormously. Lolly had undergone a crisis a year ago when she turned forty, and had gone into therapy.

"Mary Catherine, I don't know myself anymore," she had said to her friend at lunch one day, her fingers smudged with ink. She kept rubbing her eyes absentmindedly. It looked like Ash Wednesday in the corners of her face. "Eighteen years of marriage, a good marriage, and I feel free to tell him everything there is. And, Mary Catherine, ours has always been a good marriage sexually, tempestuous."

"Lolly, what a word," she had said.

"Well, it's true, but, God, I feel so vulnerable these days. I am this much away from other men. I sense in myself a whole nondiscriminating thing, I think I could go to bed with anybody. Listen, aside from the money, I could never understand Jackie Kennedy's attraction to Onassis.

Lolly was running her fingers through her thick hair, toying with her earrings. A successful writer, she had a master's degree, had taught English in college before she started submitting pieces to the magazines. She had had cover stories in many of the women's magazines and had earned a fine reputation. Her husband, Dave, was immensely proud of her; quiet where she was ebullient, soft-spoken where she would rush her words together, her voice high-pitched and excitable.

"I discussed it with Dave and we've decided that maybe I should go to one of those encounter weekend things. I've got to sort things out. I'm not thinking it will be some great panacea or anything, it's just that I've got to unburden myself and somehow a group of strangers is appealing to me."

Mary Catherine put her hand on her friend's arm.

"Drink your wine, Lolly. Come on, calm down."

"Mary Catherine, whether it means getting laid or not I don't know. Listen, maybe, just maybe, that's what I'm looking for. Maybe, and yet sexually Dave and I are fine, perfect, and yet maybe not, maybe I'm not being entirely honest. There are some things that aren't quite right. And sometimes, sometimes, Mary

Catherine, like last night, I could have walked off and left my children and not thought a thing, not one thing about it. Have you ever felt like that?"

"Of course, Lolly."

"I've got so many feelings in me now, I can hardly write and concentrate on whatever I'm working on. I don't eat or sleep, it's like being sixteen. Remember, Mary Catherine, when we were sixteen and those feelings, when you were sexually aware all the time at every minute, well, that's the way I am now, vulnerable to anybody. And you know, I love it, I love living at this emotional peak. It's important, it's important that I settle it now that I've turned forty."

"Why, Lolly, why, what on earth changes when you're forty?"

"Listen, I've only had two other affairs in my whole life. Can you understand that I've only gone to bed with three men in my life. Dave's the best, of course, he is the best and I love him in bed and I love him out of bed. I adore him, but someday I'm going to wake up and it's all going to be over and nobody will want me anyway, all masses of cellulite crinkling up like cottage cheese wobbling away on my thighs and crepy throat."

"Good Lord, you're crazy."

"I'm going to have it all fixed."

"Lolly, listen to yourself."

"Listen, if I'm going to go crazy I may as well go the whole way. Listen, I've got to decide. I could be one of three old ladies when I get to be eighty, I could sit by the fire with my husband thinking back on our closeness and family, an old lady who looks back on a marvelous past, or an old lady who only thinks of chances not taken advantage of."

Lolly had found Dr. Stander after a volcanic experience at the encounter weekend. She had gone to one run by the alumni group of the college she had gone to and was unlivable for two weeks after she came back. She was high and Mary Catherine couldn't stand it. Lolly's usual enthusiasms had multiplied so that she was manic, as though she were continually inhaling some kind of high-priced speed. Mary Catherine couldn't wait for her to come down, which, she had read, usually takes a few weeks, when the person realizes that the world outside that cocoon of good feeling and catharsis was still the same old world after all. The withdrawal from the euphoria of self-discovery took a long time for Lolly. She never told Mary Catherine exactly what it was that had changed her, what she had revealed at the encounter weekend in a rush of extravagant relief, but she had assured her that her malaise disappeared. So she followed it up with Dr. Stander.

"He is really fine, Mary Catherine. He's so bright and he of course is totally nonjudgmental and is helping me to understand what to do with this fortyitis that I'm suffering from. I'm putting a lot of the pieces together and Dave and I are really so much happier. Go see him."

So Mary Catherine found for the first time in her life, after priding herself that she would never need it, that she was certainly strong enough to cope with her own life, take responsibility for her own actions, she found herself sitting opposite a good-looking psychiatrist in his diploma-lined office, with bad paintings given him by patients lining the walls.

"I'm scared," she said.

"I thought you said you've been on your own so long, worked, earned your own money, etcetera, why are you scared," he said. His eyes were blue, she noticed. She decided to fall in love with him.

"I know, but even though it's an incredible relief to

get him out of the house and it is, it really is, it's like not preparing for your old age. Here I am alone. Me and Francie, a few friends I love, a good job, a lot of bills, with no plan. I want you to help me make a plan."

He laughed. What even white teeth, she thought; the better to eat you with, my dear. She was getting as bad as Lolly. Menopausal madness or whatever was attacking all these horny middle-aged ladies.

"Mary Catherine, what kind of plan do you want to make? What do you want to do with your life now?"

"I've only gone to bed with one man in my life."

"So?" He didn't blink an eyelash.

"I feel silly saying it. I don't admit it to anyone, these days. I know seventeen-year-olds who've already lived a lifetime, and I've had Carlo. That's it. Good old Carlo. I feel like a virgin practically."

"So what are you saying?"

Dr. Stander you are beautiful. When I was a little girl I used to have the same dream every night. A tall thin man stood at the edge of my bed and like some Giacometti sculpture stretched, loomed up at me out of the darkness, and around his middle finger he had tied a long rubber band and at the end of the rubber band was a little red round ball and he would bounce the ball, throw it attached to the long rubber band against the wall over the headboard on my bed, Dr. Stander, I can see the man now as though I had the dream last night but it was maybe over thirty-five years ago and in my dream my eyes were open, and I would watch him do it. Bouncing, bouncing.

"I'm saying that I'm an organized person. I want to organize my life so that I won't fall apart. I have to admit it: as independent as I am, one of the reasons I stayed married as long as I did was that I didn't know, I wasn't sure what was on the other side of that coin, I wasn't sure. And it got so finally that it didn't matter being alone, God, so what, I'd rather be alone for the rest of my life than live with a man where there is no love anymore, where he has to get drunk to make love to you, where he doesn't even put his arm around you, where maybe he will josh you like one of the boys or pat you on the behind like you just made a home run or something and that's all, that's all the affection you are doled out."

"That's quite a sentence."

"It was quite a marriage. I guess if I hadn't always had good jobs and was always so busy and took so much responsibility on myself I would have noticed how miserable I was. I took all my sexual drive and just barreled it into my work and my child. And like Lolly and everybody else, I know I'm forty too, and I think it's about time I found out how to live. Dr. Stander, I don't know how to start. You know, I can be daring in my work and take chances but I never have with men. I've never let myself. I'm not even Catholic anymore, it can't be that. Part of it is I've been ridiculously loyal. Does that sound silly?"

"Of course not. It's just that you denied yourself so much all these years."

"I know. . . ."

Mary Catherine decided that she couldn't afford to fall in love with Dr. Stander, since business wasn't too good this year, and figured that Lolly and a lot of other people could. She saw him for about six months and learned a good deal about herself. But, she realized, much of what she was going to learn, embracing, confronting that Mary Catherine self for the first time in her life, was going to have to come about by just living. "Put yourself in risk, Mary Catherine," he had said several times, and it was the last thing he said again to her as she shook his hand good-bye at the door.

Such an ordinary phrase. She heard it ten times a

day. "Put yourself in risk." "You don't necessarily have to put yourself in danger," he had gone on, "but open yourself up to possibilities. Think in that way and see what turn your life takes." He liked her. She could tell. "I wish you so much luck, Mary Catherine."

She reached up and kissed him, a little teary at the thought of leaving him. Impulsively she put her hand on his cheek. He smelled like her father, the tobacco sweet in his hair. She wished he were hers.

Chapter Four

It was not going to be one of Deborah's better days.

For the fourth day in a row Deborah Shapiro had a hangover. Ten brandies last night made today a squint squint day, a headache day, a day like all other days. Why is this day different from all other days, she said to the gray eminence in the mirror through squints and screwed-up forehead lines and eyes. She would not look. Feeling for the cold water, she turned it on and put her palms under the faucet. She drank from her hands. She patted the water over her eyes, onto her cheeks, down the front of her nightgown. "God, I feel awful," she said aloud. Crinkling her eyes, she looked at the calendar resting in the corner of the mirror. Six days in February had been crossed off. The twenty-second was circled in blue, the twenty-eighth in red.

She bent down again, cupping her hands into the ice-cold liquid, and rested there for a minute, wet hands over her eyes. "Another day another dollar," she said to the empty bed in the corner, the pillows on the floor alongside, the quilt knocked off in restless sleep during the night.

Picking up her head slowly, so she wouldn't get a wave of vertigo, she decided to take the plunge and look into the mirror. Pretty awful, she thought. When the red red robin comes bob, bob, bobbin' along, she thought, maybe spring will come sometime, somewhere, someplace, this year, certainly not here. Spring tempts us, taunts us here, the crocuses come out and then it damn well snows on top of it and the buds peek out during the day and close up at night. She viewed the damage, took stock of the necessary repair.

Every year putting makeup on in the morning took longer. Usually, Deborah thought, at about eleven in the morning there was a face there coming out of her skin, before that everything was spread out like cream cheese and jelly. No definition.

She stared back at herself. Upright now, she put her fingers around her neck. It felt soft but looked rumpled, with hundreds of little white dots where the jugular vein was supposed to be. Do women have jugular veins? Of course; it's Adam's apples women don't have. Those little white dots, a mottled polka-dotted panorama, had attacked her neck and chest when she was in her twenties, and now that she was forty-nine it really was ghastly. Usually she covered it with Revlon's Moon Drops, then Esté Lauder's Sunburst number 2, and that helped some.

Protruding brown eyes were half their size this morning. Above the lashes a spider-web-thin film of extra flesh seemed suspended. Although it was winter, she still had yellowing vestiges of deep summer tan. Her eyes were beginning to crack at the corners where the lines were very deep, and the frost tipping in her hair made her look as though she was going gray, which she was, but that was not the intent. The intent, she told Paul the hairdresser, was to make her look young and chic and irresistible. He said he would see what he could do.

"I've got to keep out of the sun this year," Deborah said out loud. She was beginning to get like an old lady, muttering to herself. I'm like an old crotchety lady with cats and saucers of milk and feeding the pigeons in the park, little bags of bread crumbs tucked neatly into the pocket. I've got to stop talking to myself, she thought.

Deborah had the kind of skin that, although swarthy, still wrinkled easily, especially since she had lain in so many summer suns, so much sleeping in so many scorching places had leathered and weathered her. As had so many diets, so much putting the weight back on. She had once been very beautiful, she knew that, and here she was a pocketful of vestiges, of what was and had been. She knew that she looked older than her years, and she knew that ten brandies a night was certainly the best way to lose her looks. Already little blue lines were nestling in the corners of her nose and she had a stomach that bulged out with all the audacity of a seven-month fetus.

Since Abe left last year, since her second son had gone to college in the fall, it had been just her and that house. Essie Holt, her cleaning woman, slept in sometimes, just so Deborah wouldn't be alone. Essie knew how Deborah hated being alone.

"I'm just one of those people," she used to tell Abe when they were married and he would go off on business trips, "I can't stand it, the house just shouts its silence to me. I hear it in the pores of the walls. Take me with you." That, of course, as she found out later, was about the last thing in the world Abraham Shapiro wanted to do, take Deborah to New Orleans to address a business seminar at the graduate school of business at Tulane, or to San Francisco to attend the Paper Owners of America convention. She stayed home. Minded the store. Got jealous. Started to drink. Climbed the walls. And last year he had married some Gentile girl almost as young as Roger, their older son, some student of his in the Graduate School of Business at NYU where he taught two nights a week. "It's my chance, Deborah, and I'm leaving," he told her. He had come back from a business trip to Cleveland, where he stayed three days longer than he had planned. She was lying in bed reading, the bottle of scotch on the night table. Louis Jourdan was trying to kill Doris Day on the color TV, Harvey was asleep down the hall, Roger was away at school.

She heard him downstairs, heard him come in the closet door, take out a hangar, hang up his coat. She heard the hat hit the shelf. He tripped over his own suitcase, bumped into the wall as he made his way into the kitchen. She sat upright in bed, making sense out of all the sounds downstairs, hoping against hope she could keep her temper in check. Hoping against hope she wasn't so drunk that she wouldn't be able to be brilliant and articulate, sweetly caustic. She decided to pretend she was asleep to avoid the worst. She couldn't quite tell what stage of drunkenness she was in, and that was a bad sign. Every night the week that Abe had been away she had finished almost a whole bottle. She had squinted at the red and yellow label resting by the telephone and seen that there was still quite a bit left, so she probably really hadn't had that much after all.

"You still up?" Abe had said, an apple and some tollhouse cookies in his hand. He had put his suitcase down in the hall.

"Yes."

"Sorry I was delayed, they held over the whole

meeting, everyone got screwed up. The Plotnicks say hello."

"Did you see them?"

"I had dinner there one night. You look like you've been having a fine old time."

Control. Beautiful control.

"What on earth do you mean?"

"The booze, Deborah, the booze."

"Oh," she said grandly, "I had a few, just to get me off to sleep. I didn't know exactly when you were coming home and I was worried. I think at least you could have . . ."

She stopped. The liquid in her glass was spilling on her frilly white nightgown, the ruffles fluted over the top. It suddenly felt cold on her breast as the scotch seeped through the fabric.

"Deb, I'm awfully tired," he said, taking his clock and two copies of the *Wall Street Journal* off the night table on his side of the bed. "I think I'll sleep in the guest room tonight. And you look like you could use a good night's rest."

She wasn't too good at these cold war tactics. The Maginot line was falling, Guadalcanal was being lost, Quang Tri was burning, and all the king's horses and all the king's men couldn't put Abe and Debbie . . .

"Abe, you've got a fucking nerve."

Here it comes, she never was good at strategy, she was a rotten student of logic and would probably be thrown out of the diplomatic corps.

"You've just got such a fucking nevre leaving me here alone all this time, not a call not a telegram nothing and you know, you know, goddamn it, how I hate to be alone."

"I thought you had registered for a course."

"What the fuck does that have to do with anything? That's all you ever talk about is registering for a course, fill up my time. I've got a damn job for God's sake, I work every day down at that shop, every damn day like clockwork in at nine out at five. I'm busy, I'm furtively, fruitfully occu . . . occu . . ."

"Occupied."

"Listen, Abe, I can finish my own damn sentences."

"Deborah, how many days did you go to work this week?"

"What business is it of yours? If you really cared you would have been here to check up on the whole damn thing. As a matter of fact I had a cold Monday and Tuesday and stayed home. It just so happens."

"Harvey wrote me that you slept three whole days. Just went to bed and slept."

"I'm going to kill him."

"Deborah, you can't go on like this, it's crazy."

She had started to cry. Another bad move, she knew it, but at that point the finger came out of the dike, lava was spilling all over the bedroom. Yosemite steamed out of her mouth.

At any rate, Abe had finally said that terrible night, "It's my chance, Deborah, and I'm leaving. I can't stay anymore, I've got to have a life for myself. You've got to do something about your drinking. You won't go to AA or talk to someone, you won't do a thing. And I feel for you, I really do. I'm leaving."

And that, of course, had been that.

A year ago. She had used all kinds of wiles and manipulations to get him to stay. But he didn't love her anymore, he had said. He told her about all that potential that she had had, all that beauty inside and she had let it erode, disappear from her repertoire. Sure, she had said, after I stayed home and brought up two terrific boys for you, after I entertained all your goddamn boring clients and business people who I couldn't stand when I'd rather be upstairs with a good book, after

Daddy had given you the money to start the business
with in the first place, sure now you disappear, now
you run away and leave me holding the bag. What bag,
he had said, and she couldn't think of what to answer.
But she had never done anything, for heaven's sake,
and she couldn't now at forty-nine go get a job, what
could she do, all she had was a college degree, she and
a million other women twenty years younger than she
was. Go to school, he had said till it was coming out
of her ears. She couldn't, she had answered, I can't
concentrate and do papers and be with kids, I'd go
crazy just crazy. You read a book a week, he had
reminded her. That's different, and lately she had had
a hard time concentrating anyway, so school was out.

So she had gotten that job in the bookshop where
they were lovely to her and where they seemed to like
her, where she had a place to go, a structure around
which to build her life. Abe was all right about the
money, but business wasn't good now and he had two
in college, so he was sending her less and less. Life
was pretty grim, that was for sure.

It was 8:30 A.M., February 7, 1975, and she had
to be at work at nine. March 7 was her birthday.
Deborah had been staring her face in the mirror for
almost twenty minutes. The cat came into the bathroom
and rubbed her ankle. She kicked it. She hated the
cat. It was as needful as she was, more. It never really
related to anyone, just demanded attention, never really
gave of itself, just took, ate slept rubbed against you
and cried to be held and rubbed. Deborah hated it. The
cat reminded her of herself.

"Except for this damn pot my figure's not so bad,"
she thought, looking down at herself. It was true; her
legs were slim, almost too slim, her bosom still high.
But she had lost her waist somewhere in the last year.
It met her rib cage and her hip, it was all one straight

line, and her belly ballooned. She had taken to wearing
full, modified tent dresses to hide it. She ate almost
nothing, was dieting all the time. Munching on celery
and drinking water at the shop.

She didn't know how she did it but somehow, for
the most part, she always managed to get to work. She
rinsed her mouth with glassfuls of Listerine after taking
a sip of brandy that was left in the glass from the night
before. The house was very quiet, so she put on television and the radio. Barbara Walters was interviewing
Nancy Kissinger and "Dance of the Hours" was playing.

Slowly she began the ritual. When she was young,
and going to Music and Art high school in New York,
she and her friends would meet at a drugstore. She
could sip a malted, dip into her bag, and take out her
Rosy Future lipstick and put it on without a mirror.
The girls were pretty impressed by that, especially since
most of them didn't wear lipstick anyway. Her best
friend, Beatrice, played the clarinet, so there would
have been no point. Today Deborah was back to wearing lipstick, having eschewed it several times during the
years. She thought it made her look younger.

She rubbed on her Moon Drops, smoothing the
cream into her skin the way they had told her at a
beauty course her mother had sent her to once when
she was in high school. She was grateful to her mother
for that, since it was the beginning of a lifelong involvement with taking care of herself. She spent a
fortune on creams and makeup, the minute something
new was tantalizingly advertised in *Vogue* she went
out and bought it. Her bathroom shelves were lined
with products she had used once or twice, the prices
still pasted on the bottoms. Throat creams, eye
creams, tightening masks, wrinkle cream, crow's-feet
cream, corn cream, crease cream. Lately she hadn't

been using them too much, but it was comforting to
see them there every morning, staring out at her from
the shelves.

She smoothed up her forehead, erasing the frown
lines, with the third finger of each hand, thumbs on
her cheeks. Around and around, I'll fox you, wrinkled
lady, they will disappear like those pads we wrote on
when we were kids with a special pencil with no lead,
doodling on something like a heavy cellophane, then
magic of magic, pick up the bottom and no writing!
That's the way my wrinkles will go.

The puffs under her eyes were fuller today. She
must do something about that, she thought, leaning her
face against the mirror. It was cold on her cheek.

The moment she put her base on was the beginning
of the formation of a face, she thought. It was as
though she had on a stocking mask, the kind robbers
used to hit banks, blank, expressionless, dead. Planes
and protuberances, shape and color then would emerge
quickly under her fingers.

The eyes took the longest. They were her best fea-
ture, she knew that even though they weren't too clear
this morning. Her hand slipped as she drew the thin
black line over the lid. As her left index finger pulled
back the loosening skin at the corner, the right tried
to line the lid evenly. It was a losing battle today, but
she did her best. Without liner her eyes disappeared
into her face, so deepset were they. She never went
anywhere without doing her eyes. Next the mascara,
over and over, curling up, over and over. She really
was getting too old for rouge, she thought, but put on
the three dots they had taught her in Makeup II, a
triangle under the eye and on the cheek, and smoothed
it in.

There. There was a face on top of that after all, it

wasn't the face she wanted or the face she used to have, but it was the face she had.

The phone rang.

Turning down the television and the radio off, she picked it up. She was late.

"Deborah, are you all right?"

"Mary Catherine, of course I'm all right, why shouldn't I be all right?"

"I called you last night up till about 1 A.M. and I knew you said you were going to be home. Where were you?"

"I was here. Mary Catherine, I'm late as anything and haven't had any coffee yet. What . . ."

"Can I show your house for summer rental this afternoon? I've got a client I think may be interested."

"Oh, God, it's a mess and I don't think Essie is coming in today. Can't they come tomorrow?"

"Deborah, that's the third time you've done that. You'll never rent it at this rate. Don't you want to rent it?"

"Mary, do me a favor, don't start in on me so early. I've got a headache."

"Did you turn your phone off last night?"

"I think it slipped off the hook or something. I caught it this morning.

Mary Catherine and Deborah were an unlikely pair.

They had met over a year ago one Saturday morning when Deborah's gray Cadillac was pulling out in back of the library and backed smack into the orange front of Mary Catherine's car. Mary Catherine's Datsun pumpkin had turned into an accordion.

Mary Catherine had smelled the alcohol on Deborah's breath, and Deborah was near tears but determined not to lose her composure. Somehow they had gotten through the nightmare of the crowd forming, the routine imposed on them by a callow mustachioed policeman who took them down to the station to fill out endless forms. By the time it was over, Mary Catherine had invited her home for coffee, the insurance company had gotten her a new front fender, and they had become friends. Unlikely, but bound in some way.

Mary Catherine, who had been alone one year longer than Deborah, had the edge in terms of self-sufficiency and independence even though perhaps in some way the two were equally vulnerable. But Deborah came to rely on Mary Catherine's friendship, she felt she could tell her anything without being disliked. She was kind. And Deborah didn't meet many people who were kind. Abe had been kind in the beginning years and her father had been too kind. He had spoiled her with kindness, stuffed her sprayed her gorged her with kindness. When she was a little girl he would buy three dolls instead of one, gave her charge accounts at every department store in New York, wouldn't let her go to work like the other girls when she was sixteen because he had had to work since he was twelve and no daughter of his was going to work. Period.

Joshua Gold had had one dream and that was to see his daughter married to a rich man who would keep her charge accounts going, was Jewish, and would play golf with him on Sundays.

But Deborah had turned out to be an old-fashioned girl. She had been kneaded and molded, pressed into cookie-cutter shape, by the intrigue of illicit sex early. All her relationships with men were doomed, and she wore her masochism like a mink stole.

She adored the unattainable, the married man, the man congenitally unable to give. The ultimate in romantic love, she lusted after the father, she supposed, in her muddling Freudian way, who unfortunately already had a bedmate. Actually, she never enjoyed the affairs she had had before Abe anyway. She wasn't a very sexual woman. Abe was the only man who gave her an orgasm, accusing her periodically of frigidity.

She had met him when he was married, when his wife was pregnant as a matter of fact, and Deborah had somehow spirited him away. She had been very beautiful then, full-cheeked instead of hollowed out as she was today, results of Stillman, grapefruit, Atkins, tomato juice, water, whatever was in fashion diet, slim finally after those sallies into starvation.

She had been a compulsive eater all her life, gorging herself on any chocolate-covered cookies, crackers and Cracker Jacks, Hydrox she could get her hands on. Sunday nights in high school were the worst, the violent times when she would have what she called the gloomy Sunday madness where a hundred chocolate-covered peanut squirrels would pop into her mouth as though someone else's hands were doing the popping. She would not take responsibility for the gluttony, the insanity of eating a hundred chocolate-covered peanut squirrels. But somebody downstairs in that kitchen gorged herself, stuffed herself until she had to crawl to the bathroom on her hands and knees and pull off the jeans, tight-rolling over her rear, and pull on a gown, a loose, very loose one, over her swollen body. She would eat until she couldn't push the chocolate up to her mouth anymore and her belly would be hard and she wanted to vomit, but took an enema instead the next morning to purge herself of her excess, to rid herself of her sloth.

"I'm going into New York Monday, can't you show the house then?"

Mary Catherine's voice returned out from the shadow of Deborah's reverie; so many things to remember.

"How can you get off work?"

"I'm working Saturday this week."

"Have you made any more plans about the wedding?"

"Mary, I don't want to talk about it now. Essie will be here tomorrow, and tell someone else in the office to show the house. She'll be here till five thirty. Mary, I've got to go to work. It's after nine."

"Deborah, are you sure you're all right? You sound very weird. You said you were going on the wagon."

"Well, I didn't. Mary, I've got to hang up. See you tomorrow. I love you. 'Bye."

Deborah hadn't the patience to get into anything now. She hadn't decided whether she was going through with the wedding. She just couldn't decide, and it was three weeks away. Her indecisiveness had become a permanent state of being. As far as Sam was concerned the wedding was on, the party a week before on the twenty-second. As far as she was concerned she might be in Peking, Persia, Pocatello, Idaho, by that time. But she wouldn't think about that now. She would go downstairs, get some coffee, feed the goddamn cat, glance at the paper, and try to make it to work by nine thirty.

She grabbed her bag and glanced at the bed, rumpled. Her robe was in the middle of the floor, as were the boots she had worn yesterday. The cat had upset the wastebasket, and the brandy bottle on the night table still had a few sips in it. She poured it into a glass and dropped the bottle into the basket, sipping the drink. It felt hot in her stomach.

Downstairs, the dinner dishes were still on the kitchen table. The ketchup was sticky in a congealed red, the salad looked limp. She couldn't face it, and moved them into the sink. She would wash them when she got home. No, Essie was supposed to come sometime today. Where was that woman? Never there when she needed her.

The fat that had dripped down from the steak she had cooked herself the night before had hardened in the broiler. It made Deborah sick to her stomach.

Oh, God, Essie, please come in today, I can't stand this.

She put on some water to boil, poured some hard cat food into the dish even though she knew the cat preferred the soft canned stuff, went out to get the *Times*.

Thank God her roomer had left. She would never take in a roomer again. She had had marvelous fantasies about some brilliant newly divorced stockbroker who would rent the garage room to get a little extra money in, who would help put up the screens in the summer and come over for dinner during one of those aching February nights, smoke coming out of other chimneys, cars going into other driveways, dusk falling over other lives. But she had had no such luck. Don Baum had arrived all jolly and compliant, delighted to get the room and bath, fresh from a separation from Donna. Don and Donna, that must have been a pair. At any rate Don used to get out at about six thirty in the morning, before Deborah got up, and would read her *Times*, crumple it up and leave it a leafed-through nonchronological mess. When she asked him about it —"Why don't you get your own paper, for heaven's sake"—he looked at her incredulously. "Well, Donna never used to mind."

That had been the last tenant for the spare room and bath over the garage because almost the only people who ever answered the ad were men on their own for the first time in twenty years who couldn't go downtown and put their clothes in the laundromat or shop in the supermarket by themselves. Don had been the third tenant, and all of them seemed absolutely thrown by the loneliness.

A few young girls also applied, but she couldn't bear their beauty. It was simple as that. It had come to that, she couldn't bear being around people who were younger than she, prettier. She never told anyone that, even Mary Catherine or Lolly, because it made her sound so terrible, so small, so . . . but it was the truth. At the shop she could handle it because somehow being business it didn't count.

The kettle whistled and she made herself some instant coffee, black. She didn't have time to eat, she would catch a bite at lunch downtown. Flipping to the theater page, she glanced at an interview with a star in a Broadway musical. The familiar blond rosy glow lunged out at her from the paper. "My husband and I," she read the star saying, "are marriage partners, not friends. That's why there is a taboo in our house against discussing politics and religion." They've been married fifteen years and never discussed things. And they're not friends, how can you live with someone all those years and not be friends, Deborah thought. She needed a manicure; the cuticles were shabby. When were you and Abe ever friends, she thought.

She couldn't get into all that now, she had to go to work, so she threw the paper on the counter next to *The New Yorker* and *House and Garden,* got her coat, and ran out the door.

She could still smell the grease from the steak.

Chapter Five

After Mary Catherine had left Dr. Stander, she tried to put her life back in order. Carlo had taken his clothes, his shoes, his World War II souvenirs, his three hundred 78's including some Billie Holliday and Artie Shaw records, his power tools, and the hundred-dollar bound and illustrated copy of *Leaves of Grass* that Mary Catherine had given him for this thirtieth birthday.

There was always the possibility, she learned soon after he left, that she wouldn't know what to do with the freedom, with Carlo out of the house; the point of aggravation diminished, she might sit at home and stare out the window. He had been such a point of irritation for her for so long, leaving his clothes up and down the stairs, dragging along an old briefcase to work every day, getting drunk almost every night, pontificating about the virtues of the Republican fiscal system, insisting on wearing plaid high socks with his Bermuda shorts of twenty years ago, letting his paunch go. Why had that bothered her so much, his paunch? The way the flesh had become flaccid, a cow's udder, an appendage, almost unattached to the rest of him. She had thought he was so beautiful once; and now he had a paunch, and veins were beginning to form a ticktacktoe pattern along the sides of his nose.

Now he was gone. Francie missed him desperately and Mary Catherine was relieved. She had a room of her own, to do with as she pleased. She was free. But at the very beginning she was paralyzed by the headiness of it all. The terror of it all. She was the head of the household now. She might have been the more efficient one when Carlo was around, but it didn't matter, after the divorce papers were signed, and the bills started coming to the house with just her name on them, after the last vestige of him had disappeared, she realized that what remained was indeed just her.

She was now the one responsible for every decision affecting their lives, every purchase, every choice, every alternative, every option was hers. There was no one anymore to consult, to argue, to comply with, to compromise with. She was it. Head of the household, as it said on the income-tax form.

Mary Catherine had always been one to respond to a challenge, and this was the most compelling of all. But loneliness had set in, and that she had not been prepared for. It transcended dinners with friends, comforting glasses of wine with Lolly and Dave, always concerned, always caring about her. Lolly was just about the only one of all the women she knew who, when they heard about the divorce, would have her to dinner more than once. The others were never to be heard from again, because, she supposed, Dave was just about the only husband of all the women she knew who didn't ogle her in a provocative way, ask her for a drink in New York, a lunch in Eastville, a cup of coffee, a loaf of bread, and her.

Dave was as affectionate, as warm, as loving to her as ever, having already made his pitch in front of Lolly, saying that he thought Mary Catherine was probably one of the most attractive divorcées newly arrived on the market but thanks but no thanks, he loved her as a friend and loved his wife as a friend and lover and wanted to keep it all that way.

It was a relief. She pointedly stopped calling or receiving calls from some of her single friends. Their inquiries had become probings, their concern, curiosity; their information, gossip. If Women's Lib was supposed to obliterate competitiveness, being over thirty and suddenly single exaggerated it. She became wary, self-protective, selective about who she told what to.

Unmarried women were definitely worse than the married ones, who weren't too good either. But the divorcées, the widows, looked at her, she thought, as some kind of threat, as someone who was going to lure away whatever poor, hopefully still functioning male they happened to have in tow. They didn't call. They stayed away as far as they could. But when the current boyfriend disappeared they were back calling again, hoping she had some spares, some new prospects.

Mary Catherine put herself on a strict regime. She was up early, got Francie off to school, cleaned the house, prepared a stew for dinner at 7 A.M. that was finished cooking by 8:30, got to work by 9. She had three women working for her now, and one young twenty-five-year-old man who wanted to learn the business. Real estate had been slow because land and houses were going so high and there seemed to be so little money around, but somehow she made enough to support herself.

When she had taken the real estate course five years ago and passed the state test to her utter amazement, it had liberated her. She felt if she could do it, anyone could. Her talents did not move in the direction of business; she would rather read, stare out the window, dream. But she had worked since she was sixteen at all kinds of jobs to make money, and hated anything that was confining, that would keep her chained to a desk from nine to five. It was playacting for her, taking people out in her car, showing them houses, sizing

them up; putting people together with an ambiance
and a place to live. She appeared sweet and soft and
people responded to her, she remained friends with
clients long after the purchase was made, but she was
shrewd in her own way, the way that came from an
increased knowledge of herself. She had learned that
she could be manipulative, act expediently and be soft
at the same time. She didn't quite know how she had
managed that, Carlo had begrudgingly admired that
quality in her, that she could get people to come around.
"You really can get along with anybody," Lolly always
used to tell her, too, and sometimes she didn't know
whether that was a compliment or not. She was aware,
though, of a talent, come from sheer expedience, of
having to make her way herself, of not being able to
depend on anyone. She had just taught herself how to
get by.

But, there were no men.

"I've got eight single friends," Olga in the office told
her, "and every one of them is having an affair with
a married man."

What a bore, Mary Catherine thought.

How many times had she said it when Carlo was
still there? I'm going to just take off someday, just disappear into the clouds, and you'll miss me, oh, how
you'll miss me. She had thought about it every time
she got in the car. And they'd laugh and never take
her seriously and of course she knew that it was a
childish seeking of affirmation, like when she was little
and would pray to God, make deals with Him if He
would get her good and sick. That would show them,
that would show them, as she lay there like Shirley
Temple in *The Little Princess* under a satin quilt on
the top floor of a cornice-roof house gasping for breath
as the Angel of Death hovered. And everyone would
be praying or kneeling all around, and she would peek

out from the secure swelter of the quilt and smile and
smile at all those people not wanting her to die.

It was the same thing when she would threaten to
leave. That would make them sit up and take notice.
Forty-three years old and by God she had never moved
her wings for heaven's sake, and here were all these
Women's Lib ladies and *Cosmopolitan* ladies both on
the opposite ends of the page and by God they were
all flying.

The *Cosmopolitan* ladies started out from above their
silk jersey tops, their breasts peeking impudently off
the supermarket stand. They were busy getting their
man, those ladies, seducing him with aphrodisiac re-
cipes and slinky lingerie. The *Ms.* ladies were there
too with their sense of confidence and poems praising
their wombs and menses. All those women's eyes sur-
veyed her, staring out from the supermarket shelves,
the ruddy Redbook cover girl, the unbelievable cool
of the classy lady on *Town and Country*. She had
always been sure that those ladies Mrs. So-and-So on
Town and Country from chic places like Gross Point
(yes, taking off the *e* would make it a Jewish, not
Gentile, watering place), she was convinced that those
women on those covers, so trim, so finely honed and
painted and plucked, never never went to the bathroom or took with them the funky thick smell of sex
after.

One night, coming back on the Long Island Rail
Road from an evening with her Aunt Eleanora, who
had invited one of her many eligible males, each more
impossible than the other, to dinner, she met someone.

Dark mustache. Long, thick, dark-brown curly hair.
He picked her up on the midnight train. He had said
something to her at the newspaper counter, to which
she just nodded. Then he walked behind her as she
went to find her train. He sat down next to her and

she pulled out the *Harper's Bazaar* she had just bought and turned to the horoscope. She was sitting in a three-seater, so he wasn't too close, but she could feel his eyes on her legs. He was offhand, she was tired and unattracted, but still they chatted and it ended up by her halfheartedly giving him her phone number. It was 1 A.M. by now and she found being flip easier than being nice, and he seemed to like it.

So he called her a few days later at five o'clock one night at work and asked her if she would meet him for dinner in an hour. There really are no more rules about this like in the old days in high school, she thought, when you had to have at least three days in between someone asking you somewhere and the actual date.

She had said yes to see what would happen. She had to start somewhere. She had to do something about herself. All those feelings and she didn't know where to put them. The just doing something to see what would happen. How far could she go without being hurt or molested. (She was determined to put herself in risk, as Dr. Stander had suggested, to push herself to limits she never dreamed existed. She would do anything except hurt Francie, she had decided.)

He didn't attract her, even though he looked all right: dark good eyes, a small build with small hands. He was wearing a brown leather coat and a tan suede shoes. She never did like men with small hands, and everything was slim except he had a protruding belly like Santa, like barrels of beer, like Carlo, and he was so crude, so outrageous in his speech, in his skillful chance-taking courting of her, that though she protested and sat stiff and straight on her side of the car, she knew that the vulgarity of him would get to her and that if he put his hand on her breast she was lost. He did and she was.

She would burn to a crisp in hell, Beatrice and Tantalus and Michael rowing his boat ashore, they were all there in her head, but it wasn't her head that was reacting.

"Fuck me and I'll eat your pussy," he said. He kept saying "pussy," which semantically interested her in a mild way, as she sat, fascinated at his twentieth-century wooing only an hour after they had finished dinner after knowing each other just a few hours. "I love to eat pussy. I love the taste," he said, and she kept ignoring him or saying, "You're crazy," but somewhere inside her still knowing that she would go to bed with him just to see what it was like. As simple as that.

He started kissing her and exploring the inside of her lower gums, moving his tongue back and forth, feeling the bumps below where the teeth roots were, and his hand went below to her leg and slowly massaged her calf. "Wild, what wild legs," he said, "it's what made me sit down next to you," he said. "What really gets to me," he murmured, as he moved his fingers up her leg into her crotch, "is in the summer when girls have bare legs, bare legs turn me on," he said, "and wear no pants at all. Do you ever go with no pants and bare legs in the summer?"

How could she answer sitting in the front seat of his car, she had to contend with the involuntary movements of her pelvis; relax, the doctor had said, relax, it will come, when the baby was pushing, coming is so easy if I just stretch my legs out right here in this getting to be hot sweaty front seat and if I just loosen my thighs for one minute and let his finger creep into me I could come and come and come. He was whispering more into her ear, trying to get her hot and succeeding. She fought him all along the way, waiting to be mysterious, trying to be unattainable, while the space between her legs got wetter and wetter.

"Take it," he whispered, "take it, move my finger into you," he said, and she complied, taking his Magic Marker of a finger and placing it on the magic clitoral coital carnivorous spot, and he touched it and touched it and groaned, and he felt its heat, and its wetness made him throw his whole body on top of hers, and there in the car in the restaurant parking lot underneath a streetlight with the radio blaring Symphony Syd's Spanish music they came and they came.

"Wild," he said, "wild; let's go somewhere, we've got to go somewhere. I've got to make love to you."

"I love to make love," she managed, sounding foolish having to say something. "You like to fuck," he said and started up the car, and the hearse of it, the huge Cadillac unnecessary space of it lunged onto the highway and she leaned back her head and decided not to think about anything. To see what would happen.

And what happened was a motel.

"This place is a whorehouse," he said matter-of-factly, authoritatively. "You have to know the rules." The place looked like a cross between a prison and old English boarding school. All fading brick and monotonous repetitive doors and windows.

"You stay in the car," he ordered. "They've got it down to a science so girls don't have to be embarrassed. Here, read the paper," and he threw the New York *Post* at her.

In a moment he was gone and she sat in that huge hearse watching the cars from the highway whiz by, watching the little windows with the perfect little curtains shading them, little doll-houses, boxes, little boxes.

She watched him returning from the desk, the key in his hand. It was as natural as picking Francie up at school, her being here, she thought, sitting here in this alien car in this alien place with this alien man who in one hour had found her out, would find her out more. Like falling off a log.

He took her arm, he wasn't much taller than she, and apologized for not getting a room closer to the car. "They're pretty filled up." And he walked her through the gray-brick corridors with the disinfectant smell till they got to the room. Signs saying "ice" with arrows were pinned to the walls. His step was so sure, as though he were refilling footprints he had left the night before, and putting the key in the lock, it was as though he had done the same thing for at least a thousand and one nights.

Musty, with the oversize bed and the TV set overhead, and the glass in cellophane and the flowered wallpaper, and the double dresser. She liked it, seedy.

He mistook her silence for being ill at ease. He mistook her sitting in the one upholstered chair for nervousness. It wasn't that. She was two people experiencing this all at the same time. The person who was going to get laid, and the person who was fascinated by that person being there in the first place.

He chattered as he began undressing, but her aloofness put him off. He played with his tie, and sat down next to her and rubbed her leg. "Have you ever had your big toe sucked?"

She roared. She laughed so hard the tears came to her eyes. They slept an hour perhaps and then began again. The more he touched her the more she came, the more she held him the harder he got.

The orgasms came like pebbles against the window. They didn't stop, her body was a slot machine, pull the lever hit the jackpot. So many jackpots so many lemons so many grapes, the world was her oyster, the world was too much with her, the world was the way of the world, ninety-eight ninety-nine that my dear was mighty fine. He was so boastful, so corny, so full of sex stories about his exploits and his prowess that all she could do was laugh. At him, at herself, at her need.

But fuck her he did.

And his exuberance, his admiration of her, his constant talking before, during, and after utterly delighted her. Even the sucking of her big toe worked. It sent shivers up and down her back, and when he furrowed his head into her and ate and drank of her, his mouth pushing into her, his fingers found other orifices to delight her. "You're beautiful," he said, looking at her head finally resting on the pillow. He praised her body and kept kissing her inner calf.

"I've got a winner," he said, as he entered her and would not let her move. "No, no," he whispered, "let it stay quiet for a moment, let me get to know you," and she laughed again. A winner she was, across the finish line, all she could think of was the trotters, the jockey skillfully, gingerly reining the sleek animal in across the finishing line. A winner, that's what she was.

"Your eyes scare me," he said, "you look like a witch," when he stared into their darkness after she kept responding to his touch and coming. She knew it. She felt their brightness, she felt it all. She felt like a witch.

The man didn't have a sip, she thought, he didn't have to anesthetize himself to touch me. He's no bargain, she said to the Carlo in her head. But he touched me and touched me and didn't have a thing to drink.

"Would you go to bed with me and a friend, I'd love to see you with another man." She looked shocked, and somehow knew that someday she might do that too.

So she had learned about herself sexually from Seth.

He was thirty-five, married, a chiropodist. He certainly was no one to bring home to Mother, but he had introduced Mary Catherine to Mary Catherine. He had seen it, the sleeping person waiting to be aroused. She had accepted some of the business the nuns had told her in high school. And after a while it became clear that no matter how you sliced it, the main thing that would send you to hell the fastest would be sex. Married sex was O.K., which was why Carlo the beautiful Carlo had scored, had convinced her to do it, how else could she get sex without being married. There was no way. One nun had told her that being kissed was all right "as long as he kisses you like the priest kisses the altar stone during mass." One boy in high school kissed her like that all through the junior year and she was convinced she was frigid. But Carlo and she, what did they know? Oddly, the minute she had decided to get the divorce, every fear, every restriction the nuns ever told her, which had burned in her, disappeared. Just like that. It just didn't matter anymore. Seth saw that behind the lady, the chic gray streak, the little pearl earrings, and the wide pale eyes was a voluptuary. She had just never known it was there.

She remembered once long ago, on one of their expensive trips that they could never afford, she and Carlo went to Mexico. They had been in Acapulco and there was Lana Turner with the man who later got stabbed, Stompanato, and Lana Turner had on a pink tailored slack suit. There was candlelight, the native boys were diving down, down into a little hole of water for pennies, and the balmy evening and hot food and Spanish sounds hypnotized her. She watched Lana Turner that night and thought, she has to have that, the romance, the someone kissing her fingertips, the someone nibbling and whispering into her ear. It seemed dizzying to her that night, just watching the excessive beauty of the two, the excessiveness of the hot Mexican evening, the excessive sounds of the guitars. Her groin hurt, as though the actress's pleasure, all that atmosphere, no matter how contrived, entered her own body.

But at that time her sensuality had been only touched on, referred to in passing, in repose. She wasn't able to identify it, give it a label, exhibit A, you see, ladies and gentlemen of the court, this woman had a cunt and a body and she never really knew they were there before, and Carlo who at the beginning did love her, did delight in her sweet small body, somewhere along the way got more interested in impressing everybody and small-town politics and pretending. He got caught up in the pretending, and scotch helped, and that took care of Mary Catherine because her body ceased to be for him. Such delight he used to take in her, but as the years went by and the booze flowed and she became stronger, he couldn't cope. He couldn't take her, either standing, or sitting up, lying down. She would lie silent, resentful, in their oversize bed with the mahogany headboard. Her clitoris might well have been a needle in a haystack, a grain of sand at Malibu, as much as he explored it, was curious about it, wondered where it was that would give her pleasure. If she didn't come vaginally, he would turn over. That was that. Anything else wouldn't do. Carlo belonged to the old school.

There were girls she had gone to school with who went crazy once they finished with convent education. Men all the time, because they decided that it's just all or nothing, that you can't cheat in confession anyway, because it just doesn't take. So actually once you've hit the point sexually where it's clear you can't even kid yourself into believing you're going to abstain until you get married, there's no reason to stay with any of it. You're in the state of mortal sin. You can't go to confession because you're going to do it again. You can't go to Communion because if you receive Communion in mortal sin that's just another mortal sin. So, to save their sanity, they just stopped believing in all of it.

With Mary Catherine it took longer. Sex hadn't yet overwhelmed her. She had been confused by love, the stars in her eyes got in the way, they were blinding her. She never knew how voracious she was till later.

Seth helped. He began his own little campaign.

"You're sexy but don't know it," he would tell her, and within weeks after they had met he would lie with her in daylight, the curtains pinned across his window facing the junior high school, facing the Western Union office, facing the shoemaker. Life went on outside at two to three in the afternoon, and schoolchildren would be walking home, and Francie would be going to a friend's to bake cookies, and Mary Catherine was in between clients and from two to three in the afternoon or four or five, or whenever it was, there was a lull in the day's occupation. Seth would begin the education of Mary Catherine. He would have the radio on, and Mary Catherine would walk into the office, usually the secretary's day off, and past the whirlpools, past the cabinets filled with plastic feet, past the shelves of thin little tools for fixing feet. She couldn't imagine how he could look at feet all day. After locking the door, they would lie on the narrow couch in his waiting room and he would instruct her in the art of love. He would make her touch herself, a luxury she had never allowed herself. And some days he would take a Coke bottle and insert it inside her, so she could feel something "a little different," another day it was a banana, so she would understand the extent of her powers.

Seth wasn't very tall and he was losing his hair and

his nose was too long and his eyes barely had any lashes. He talked too loud and chewed on a cigar a lot, which made Mary Catherine a little nauseous. He was not elegant. But she liked the way he moved, slowly, deliberately, shoulders hunched up a little, and under his white foot-doctor's coat he would wear things like a black turtleneck with a peace-sign necklace. He was boorish, unlikely, but he understood the animal in her, and for the time being served his purpose. They served each other's purpose. His wife was a college teacher, very bright, he said, and he had two brilliant kids. But they liked to "experiment with alternate life-styles." Mary Catherine imagined him setting up his practice in a commune, treating all the athletes' feet, but she never said it.

He talked about sex a lot. It excited him. He was in heat. For example he told Mary Catherine an outrageous story she couldn't believe about a patient of his whom he met when he was practicing in New Orleans, a six-foot Amazon. "She was from a good family," he told her, smoothing her back, down to the buttocks, "and she had come to New Orleans from Minnesota with her fiancé. They met a black man at a bar and were drinking with him. Then they went back to his apartment where he wanted to make love to the girl, and she said, well, you had better ask my fiancé, whereupon the black man took a gun and shot his head off." Mary Catherine's eyes were wide. "He then proceeded to make love to the girl in front of the bleeding headless torso. And you broads are all the same, I swear you are, do you know what she told me?" What did she tell you, Mary Catherine said to the Seth in her head, you shaving off the corns with your manicured fingers with the shiny nail polish, what did she tell you as you fitted a bunion pad around the round lump growing out of her left foot.

"She told me she enjoyed it, imagine, enjoying fucking him right in front of her dead and dying fiancé. She said she was afraid and excited all at the same time. She helped him get rid of the body and stayed in bed with him for a week. The black guy went to jail and he's getting out soon. She sees a psychiatrist every single day. Actually, we got very friendly and once my wife and I went to the beach with her. Now she's six feet tall, remember, and built, and, Mary Catherine, she wore such a little bikini and all the unshaven of her showed, all that flesh. It was something. She's really very intelligent."

Mary Catherine began seeing him once a week. She had no idea how much longer she would continue it. It was all so unladylike but she took joy from it, after all those years of so little sex, such silent grunting evenings with the heavy malt odor mingling with the musk oil she had splashed over herself.

The next one was an Arab. She had met him at one of Aunt Eleanora's Sunday afternoon salons. Aunt Eleanora collected people like charms. The Arab had been on the Olympic shot-putting team or something when he was young. When he opened the door for Mary Catherine to his apartment all he had on were a pair of brief track-star shorts and a T-shirt. His body was overly developed, with thighs like giant andirons much too short to support the bursting chest. He was losing his hair, but, unlike American men, did nothing to hide the thinning or the burgeoning bald spot. No combing forward into little dips, no Zero Mostel slivers of bangs. The nose was straight and long and there was a scar, a beautiful scar from his ear down across his neck. A duel? A saber fight? Who knows, but Mary Catherine asked once and he wouldn't tell her, so that was that.

A short neck on that big body. He had a little pot belly too with it all, but he was allowed. He was forty and wasn't a shot-putter anymore, but a playwright. He helped her off with her coat and breathed down the back of her neck, putting little kisses there like whispers, like wind through olive trees. She leaned back and let him. And through his little satin shorts a hard thing crept out and her hand moved from one texture to another, to the smooth shiny shorts, to the warm firm living thing between her hands, to his hairy thigh under that. Three textures at once, three for the price of one, and he squeezed her so tight she thought she would lose breath. He kept kissing her, her eyes, her ears, into the throat, and she hadn't yet taken off her coat.

She kept holding his penis and stroking it and a pearl earring fell to the floor and he finally, somehow, got her coat off and drew her to the bed. The bed was a mattress on the floor in a cave corner of the one room. He had maneuvered her onto the mattress without a murmur from her, without conversation. He was a sultan, a pasha, a sheik ravishing a willing handmaiden, a sultaness, or whatever you call her.

He bit her nipples till she cried out and she almost swooned as he lay all his weight on her. He knew just what to do and his mouth found her and stayed on her. It moved up to her mouth and his tongue fluttered in her like an anteater in a Disney movie. As he entered her, his free hand moved up to her throat and he pressed tighter and tighter as he began to climax and she thought calmly as she looked up to the tower of a tent he had fashioned above the mattress: I will die on this spot, this man is a Bedouin, his camel is waiting outside, his spear is in the bathroom, his headdress hiding in the corner, he will choke the life out of me, and I don't know who he is. And he tightened in her and outside of her and finallly came and let her loose. The danger had passed.

"Go well, stay well," he had said when she left. She throbbed for hours after leaving him.

Mary Catherine had been determined to live and her body responded. It's everybody, it's not just me. What is it with everybody, she thought. Everyone she knew seemed to be in some kind of turmoil. Marriages were shaky. Was it forty? Was it that magic number forty? Was it that they all were suddenly realizing that perhaps half their lives were over, wondering what they had to show for it? The children were all growing up and out, the dinner parties kept going over the same ground, everyone seemed to be restless, something beating at them with the ominous rhythm of those drums in the distance in Late Show African movies. Was it the Women's Liberation movement, holding out the promise of the gold-plated streets of the New World, allowing all kinds of license but not telling them at the same time what to do with those men and husbands who lived with them before the revolution? What was it? Kids and casseroles and car pools had lost their sting. And they were, those ladies of Mary Catherine's acquaintance, struggling with it, and their restlessness seemed to be aggravated by Mary Catherine's new freedom. Because that wasn't her problem. She had just recently divested herself of an encumbrance. The millstone. The weak one. For Carlo had become weak through the years. Perhaps because she was strong, because she had to be, perhaps because she had watched her mother quietly reduce her father to the skeleton of the man he once was, perhaps because she had in some way destroyed the thing she wanted most, a strong man, one who would indeed dominate her, know more, be decisive, perhaps because of all this she and Carlo had disintegrated.

Aunt Eleanora said, "Why is it that strong women who really want to be dominated then proceed to cut off the balls they want so badly? Why do we do that, Mary Catherine?" Aunt Eleanora had been married three times, was now working on the fourth. Mary Catherine loved her. How she and her mother could have been sisters was beyond her. Her mother, austere, took pitiful refuge in a religion that left her with little solace anymore. The guilt crippler, Mary Catherine called her. But Eleanora, born of the same hardworking Irish mother, Eleanora who had to wash the same steps and clean the same toilets as Birdie, got out of South Boston fast. When she was sixteen she took off, got a job in New York City in a department store, discovered a flair for decorating windows that excited the store manager, and by the time she was twenty was sending more money home than her father had made in a year. She was about sixty now, and looked forty, and it didn't matter that she had had a few tucks taken in here and there, she was smashing.

Mary Catherine was convinced that Eleanora was the secret of her sanity. The savior of her humor, the source of her sensuality.

"Do something about that house," Eleanora had said right after the divorce. "Get rid of signs of him. Let it be you, from the song of the same name." They had been sitting one day in Eleanora's sunny town house, the legacy of husband number two, rich and doting, who still came to Thanksgiving dinner, along with his wife, husbands numbers one and three, and whatever children were home. Potential husband number four was also some kind of tycoon. "It's the only kind to get, my dear, not having money is like being on an airplane without wings. I love being rich. I just love it."

And it showed. Her house was filled with beautiful things, artifacts from India and the Far East, a tasteful and wildly framed collection of paintings and sculpture, the floors were always highly polished, and the moldings on the ceiling and doorways were delicately carved, probably at the turn of the century. She always received in the afternoon after work, for she still went to the office every day, eschewing a cab or limousine for the subway, since it was so much faster to get down to Thirty-fourth Street, where she now had her own designing firm. She wore massive American Indian jewelry and red taffeta gowns with ballooning sleeves, and gold-threaded saris made from fabric she had bought in Ceylon. She, like Mary Catherine, was small, energetic, very female in a way that was going out of style. There was an adorable quality about her that made men want to go to bed with her and laugh with delight at her.

And she had guts.

"Remember, change the drapes, paint the toilet seat green if you have to, but change the house. Make it yours, don't fool around with being someone else anymore. Listen, Mary Catherine, after Herman left I went through a whole thing of re-covering the furniture. Some of the fabric he had chosen, and dumb as it may sound, it wasn't me. That's important, to be you. I'm not saying go round for God's sake beating your breast about I've got to be me, I'm saying that where you live has to do with who you are, and you and Francie are now alone and there's no man there for a while. God, I can always tell a divorcée's house a mile away."

She got up, ran across the room, and started pulling off some dried leaves from a begonia plant. She put the leaves in her pocket. "There's always something frayed.

The house just smells of no man being there. Don't you dare, don't you dare let that happen to you. Flowers on the table for you and Francie, don't you ever in your life buy a TV dinner, and you cook for her as though the Duke of Marlborough was coming to dinner. The furniture always needs covering, and the stove hasn't been cleaned in months. Get a man in to do that, and do the repairs, don't let the shutters fall apart, and paint the house, get the lawn cut. I can't stand a divorcée's house that looks as though the rats had deserted the sinking ship. You can manage all that better than Carlo ever did, anyway. Just do it. Don't let this slip."

"Eleanora, that all takes a fortune."

"Bullshit. You earn a good living. I'm telling you, I'm giving you good advice." Moving back across the room, she patted Mary Catherine's head. "I always thought you should have dyed that streak in your hair when it first started coming, but now I see you were right. It's gorgeous. Suits you. You've got your own style at last. You're marvelous, Mary Catherine, and you don't give in, and by God, that's what it's all about. Are you staying for dinner?" She leaned over to smooth her hand absently on the rounded buttocks of a black marble nude sitting on the table. The nude was crouching, extending the flanks. "What an ass this girl has, never a day goes by without my feeling her. All right, so you know what you have to do. Clean it up. Don't give in to the feeling crudhood."

"What?"

"Being cruddy. Don't feel cruddy. Make your home a happy place. Even if you have to have candlelight dinners for you and the kid. I'm telling you, Mary Catherine, I know what I'm talking about. Keep things up. At the beginning you will revel in having him the hell out of the house. And I know old Carlo and I know what a slob he was. So you'll get your bearings and keep on working and buy some paintings of your own choice, it's just as well he took those awful prints you had hanging in the hall anyway. I wouldn't give you two cents for them. Look, I want you to be happy and you'll find someone and you'll be happy. You've done a damn good job with the kid. She's terrific, you're working and you'll get by. And, Mary Catherine. You'll get very lonely, and you'll get horny as anything and even a snake will do, but you'll get by because you're a survivor like me. We survive. We live. I don't believe in people who don't live."

"Eleanora?"

"What?"

"Please don't fix me up with any of your tycoons anymore. Please. That last man I met here . . ."

"Who? Oh, Eliot Rubenstein. What a charmer."

"Oh, he wasn't a charmer, he was awful. He kept putting his hand on my knee, big puffy hands with star sapphires on them."

"He liked you."

"He couldn't have. I was petulant, bored, and drank too much brandy with him so I wouldn't have to be aware of what was going on. He took me to task because I lived in a town that was busing in blacks from the inner city and how could we permit this to happen, he kept saying, when even the blacks didn't want it either, and after all he would spend millions on cleaning up the black schools but what good would it do to take just forty-five little kindergarteners and shove them into the lily-white of our neighborhoods. I thought I would take the arroz con pollo or whatever it was and push it into his face."

"I can't believe it. He's very liberal, contributes to all kinds of causes. I got a lot of money out of him for Cesar Chavez during the lettuce strike. Well, it doesn't matter really, after all, it was just someone to have a pleasant evening with, you're not so anxious to get married so fast, are you?"

"You know I'm not."

"Well, good. But I wouldn't wait too long. You must strike while everything is hot, you know. You're in good shape now, petite and pretty and sexy, but there is a whole batch of twenty-year-olds waiting in the wings."

"I can't stand that line of reasoning."

"Stand it or not, you will just have to face facts, and the facts are that it's quite a jungle out there and you are just as much one of the animals as anybody. You're as good as anybody, better, and you deserve a good man for once."

"What's a good man?"

"Aha, that, my dear, is the question. What is a good man? It's different for everybody. With me he's got to have money. Power is nice too."

"I don't care about either."

"Bullshit."

"That's not a nice way to talk, if my mother could hear you now."

"Forget about your mother, that poor woman took a life and threw it out the window. Did you remember pictures of her when she was young? All down and golden she was, with great shining eyes. She's dead now. The walking dead. I can't talk to her. I can't, I cry every time I think of it. Anyway, she's used to the way I talk and behave. She clucks a bit, but she's all right in her way. Anyway, a good man is hard to find, as they say, but you've got everything, it shouldn't be hard, but who are we kidding, it will be. I've never seen a world with so many terrific women and so many mediocre men. You see it all the time: successful, warm, exciting women, who for the security of a pre-

dictable bedmate will put up with boring, ineffectual
men."

"I don't know, I think . . ."

"It's true. Take my word for it. Most women of my
acquaintance are just more interesting than the men.
It's as simple as that. Maybe it's because they have had
to fight so much harder once they got out from under
the shadow of the dishwasher and Joy and Tide and
it has made them more curious, more alert to whatever
it is out there that's exciting. God, it isn't really that
I like women better than men, I don't. But if I'm
really being honest about it, I would say that I find
them richer in their interests, raunchier. God pity the
poor men of the next generation with all this new breed
of strong girls coming up. You know, at the Hearst
estate in San Simeon there is a thirty-five-hundred-
year-old statue, 'Sekhmet' it's called, and I remember
the guide saying that she was the Egyptian goddess of
war. And in great detail he told about how a woman
with this delicacy of body and litheness of limb had
the face of a lion, a true indication of the essence of
woman, the most beautiful, the most dangerous of all."

"Well, I don't know about that."

"Just listen to me, I know what I'm talking about.
We're strong and resilient and when we're not we're
Rediwhip, fluff, no substance. And we're prey, we're
prey to man, to these people less interesting, less re-
liable than we. I want you to fall in love, I want you
to have a good life, but I don't want you to throw
yourself away with nobodies."

"What on earth is a nobody?" Mary Catherine was
tempted to tell Eleanora of her excursions into the
flesh, of her discoveries, her collection of nobodies.

"Just don't waste yourself. You're special. I want
you to find the right man who will appreciate you and
give you a great life."

"I make a good living. I wouldn't make money one of my priorities."

"Don't knock it, don't you dare knock it. Brandy?"

"O.K. These glasses are beautiful."

"Herman."

"Eleanora, I love you."

"I love you too, that's why this is going to be an important time for you. A very important time. Just thank God you've got your job, that you've got a whole world that doesn't depend on the love of a man. You've got to have one eventually, we're nothing without it. And sex doesn't hurt either, believe me. I'd lose my looks tomorrow if I didn't have sex every night."

"You're kidding."

"I am not kidding, it's true. I love it, once a night is even sometimes not enough. The morning's nice too."

"Eleanora, you're sixty years old."

"Naïve. Naïve, just like everybody. What do you think, it's all going to dry up? You're wrong. As long as all your plumbing is intact and it doesn't hurt for some mysterious reason, you watch, it gets better. Why on earth should it stop? Why on earth should it ever stop? It's life-giving, it's a force I couldn't live without."

Eleanora poured herself another brandy and took an apple from a silver bowl. On one of the china plates sitting next to it on the marble-topped table she began slicing pieces of the tart green with a rococo-trimmed fruit knife.

"Apple?"

"No. Just keep going, explain to me . . ."

"How about some cheese?"

Eleanora sliced some fontina with the steel cheese knife, and put the yellow stuff on the apple. Green and yellow makes blue, the nuns had said in fifth grade. Mix the colors and a whole new one emerges. She bit slowly into the merging colors. She licked her lips, dabbing at the corner of her mouth with a lace-trimmed napkin. Her eyes glistened.

"Food. How I love food."

"How do you stay so trim?"

"You know, I exercise all the time. All the time, never a day goes by that I don't. God, this cheese is fabulous. Mary Catherine, you have to have some." Her tongue didn't stop, like a windshield wiper in a downpour it had its own steady rhythm.

"Look, I know what I'm talking about. Being alive. That's what it's all about. Getting excited about things. Just don't you ever get bored. Just you keep going."

It was infectious, her energy. The life poured out of her. Mary Catherine couldn't help but feel comforted. Yet she couldn't tell her about the men now, the new living her life at random, episodically. The motel rooms. The corridors and disinfectant smells, and night managers and elevator buttons, flowered rugs and gilt-edged mirrors in hushed halls. She couldn't tell her, or anybody for that matter, what was becoming one two three four five in one week perhaps, the one two three four five in one week whom she couldn't separate anymore one from the other, whose names chests and rumps all merged into one face, one member. That was the kind of year it was. A year of the flesh. Catching-up time, getting-hers time, life-will-never-be-the-same time. Mary Catherine was coming of age in suburbia. She hoped it wouldn't take too much of a toll.

Chapter Six

Mary Catherine loved her job.

She tried to explain, to cajole, to convince Deborah how important it was for her to have something all her own that she did well, that paid, that gave her a sense of herself.

Of all the people she knew, Lolly understood the best. Lolly could hole up in her studio for days when she was working on something; the kids, Dave, everything became muted, faraway. To that day Dave didn't really understand. Lolly would confide to Mary Catherine that it was a great sadness to her that deep inside him he didn't really understand. Intellectually he did, he wanted her to have something that fulfilled her. It wasn't as though he wasn't sympathetic to bright women pursuing their talents. He had always encouraged her to finish her master's degree work. But when she started free-lancing and writing, getting deeply absorbed in her work, late into the night, weekends, mornings, he was resentful.

"I know part of it is that really he's just jealous of my excitement about my work; he doesn't have it anymore from his. He isn't challenged by it. I've told him that, and part of him admits it, but really there's nothing either of us can do about it. I've got to keep going."

Mary Catherine envied Lolly a little; having a loving man, albeit one who felt that a woman could fulfill herself all over the place and as much as she liked as long as it didn't interfere with his meals on the table, his suits at the cleaners, his ego not ever ever being ruffled. The fact that she felt so loved, that she knew this man loved her, made her immensely attractive to other men. Somehow she intuitively knew that if one man loves you, many will, the scent of love being on you. It gave Lolly a comfortable lushness, a total delight in her own attractiveness.

And yet Lolly careened between a gnawing curiosity about other men, the obsession that finally ended her up in Dr. Stander's office, and a free-floating insecurity about holding on to Dave.

"I'll admit it," she said to Mary Catherine one day at the real estate office where Mary Catherine was waiting for a client. "I want it all ways. I'll admit it. I know he loves me. And I know I look it, but I'm not that secure and knowing he loves me means so much to me. Frankly I could use some of these extra nights during the week for my work, but I don't take them. He doesn't really have other interests for those nights and I know, or think, that he's been faithful all these years and I'm not strong enough to think of that crumbling. Mary Catherine, it's the commitment, the building on it that has kept us together all these years."

Mary Catherine understood. And she, in an odd way, envied Lolly for her dilemma. In some way it was a more simple one than hers: hers was a body in search of itself. It was so much simpler years ago when a woman's place was in the home and that was that, and she cooked and raised the family and the man went out to hunt and he never had time for screwing around, and discovering his sexual nature or what have you. To survive and to live out your established sexual role was prescribed. No sweat.

But the challenge for Mary Catherine and for Lolly, as they often discussed, was to be able to do both.

God, to do both. To be in bed wrapped in a lover's arms, that in a way was as much a place to belong as the workshop. The studio for Lolly, the office for Mary Catherine. Why was it so hard to have both?

"We've both learned different lessons, the two of us have," Mary Catherine said; sipping her coffee, absent-mindedly watching the third snow of the week fall silently outside the window.

"You've learned that you can't go to bed with a typewriter and be comforted by it, nor can it wrap its legs around you, and you've learned that you're incomplete without Dave and without the typewriter too, so you're constantly balancing and manipulating to fit both those forces into your life."

"Right. That's true. Sometimes I wonder if you really can have both."

"Me, I've learned that my vitality, my curiosity, my energy, my intellect, my soul are all connected to my sexuality. Does that make any sense to you? My sex is a ball of string that, unraveled, multiplies itself. It's like a worm who, if you cut him in half, becomes two worms, he multiplies himself and so do I. Lolly, does this sound crazy? I have found that it is the source of me, perhaps because I discovered it so late, maybe because Kinsey says that this is our time sexually, when everything comes together. I don't know. I just feel that this sexual sense of myself makes me comfortable, gives me a sense of power, a sense of self that always replenishes itself. I've never put it into words before. But it feels right. I don't know where it's all going to go, what it means, and it scares the hell out of me. I only know I've got to go with it. Maybe I'll end up some horny old fifty-year-old cruising bars for twenty-year-olds. I don't know."

"Oh, Mary Catherine, I envy it."

"And I envy you. I envy you a man who adores you."

At that moment, brushing the snowflakes off his Burberry, Malcolm Holland stamped into the office.

"Mrs. Romano?"

"That's me."

"Hi. I'm Malcolm Holland, we have an appointment at two. I'm a little late, but the snow held me up."

"Is Mrs. Holland with you?"

"Not this trip. She had to go south to visit her mother and she left it to me. I want to rent a house for the summer today. I don't want to have to come back. I've got her permission to pick whatever I want, as long as it's near the water and the train station."

"Fine. This is my friend Lolly Bernstein, Mr. Holland."

"Malcolm. Your town certainly looks beautiful when it snows."

"Have you ever summered here before?"

"Farther out. In Easthampton. But it's too far for us now, so we would like to be a little closer to the city. I'll stay in New York and only come out weekends, so I'd rather not have that long trip. I wonder if we could go now. I'd like to get back to the city before the snow gets worse."

"Of course. Lolly, I'll call you tomorrow. Perhaps you should get in touch with Deborah this afternoon. I haven't talked to her since the beginning of the week."

O.K. I'll call this afternoon. Good-bye, Mr. Holland. It was nice meeting you."

"Malcolm. Good-bye. If you two are any indication of the attractiveness of the ladies in this town, it would seem that we would have a delightful summer."

There it was. Charm. The bullshit. Palaver. Mary Catherine was a sucker for it. It's what had swept her away with Carlo, it's what got her every time. Charm. She was a pushover for it. Once she became involved with the charming man, she would then proceed to try to break it down, chip away at that combination of confidence and cockiness, innuendo and ease. She would try to break down that which attracted her in the first place. This man had it. She could tell.

"We'll take my car."

"Fine."

Malcolm was over six feet tall and looked about forty-five. His eyes were very blue, a crisscross of lines under them—the only sign of age on his face.

"What do you do, Malcolm?" she said, settling in behind the wheel of her car.

"I sell insurance."

Just like Carlo.

"I like the way the light hits your eyes," he was saying. She almost went past a red light. "You are really something else, Mrs. Romano. Do you know that?"

No, she didn't know that, she was something more, but she decided not to go into it. They talked about Bertolucci and Bach, both of whom he liked very much, Magritte and Mozart, and in between he would compliment her. She could see through everything he said: the lavish praise of her, the way his eyes moved smoothly to her breasts and her legs without skipping a beat. He had it down to a science. He had a New York apartment, four kids, a wife with whom he had a "comfortable and boring" relationship, and charm.

She took him to see five houses and he decided on the first. A one-story ranch house, with lots of sun, a block from the beach. The owner's wife was a painter and the house was filled with her warm colors, hung on whitewashed walls. "This will be easy for my wife to keep," he said as he wrote out a deposit. "Would you like to go for a drink before I go back?"

"Yes, thank you."

"Where's a good place? I don't know the town at all."

There really was nothing charming enough for all the charm oozing out of him, Mary Catherine thought, but since they were near the beach she took him to a little place that served clams in the summer. The bar was open.

He was an Aquarius, he told her, brash and full of it, and, as Mary Catherine was well aware, had it perfected, The Chase. He never took his eyes off her and seemed to thoughtfully examine everything she said to him.

They sat, sipping their drinks, watching the snow fall on the sand through the picture window. The ocean seemed an unwilling floor for the snow's blanket. She was attracted to him.

At one point there was a silence and she watched him look at her. She couldn't pull away. She stared, didn't blink, and he stared back. It was a contest who would move whose eyes first. She was magnetized, his eyes didn't move from her face and it seemed as though he was touching his lips to the inside of her thighs. Her chest was heaving up and down and she couldn't control it. She could think of nothing but his eyes on her.

Finally pulling away, she stood up. "We really should get back if you don't want to be caught in the storm."

"Right. I'm not going to call, you know."

"What do you mean?" As if she didn't know. Mary Catherine couldn't fool anyone, much less herself.

"Look, I'll level with you. I find you very, very attractive. I'm trying to stay close to the hearth these days. I had a longstanding affair and I almost left my wife for, and now I'm back trying to keep on the straight and narrow."

She didn't know what to say.

Sally. She couldn't get Sally out of her head. Sally,

who worked for her in the agency, who drank too much and had a history of breakdowns, who, when she would break down, would pick up firemen and sanitation engineers. Mary Catherine would see her at lunchtime, in the dark corner of a bar restaurant in town, an exaggerated look of concern in her eyes as she devoured her table partner. She would end up in a motel one day with a knife or an ice pick in her heart, Mary Catherine told her the last time she went off on a toot.

That prim, tight-lipped lady was wearing hot pants over her fifty-year-old rump that time, replacing the long skirts and loose-fitting clothes. When she was all right and in control, she was the best, did the bookkeeping for Mary Catherine, kept track of the thousand details she wasn't able to. Efficient, computerized.

Perhaps I will end up like that, she thought, with an ice pick in my heart in the throes of a John Garfield death, asleep, then dead in a lover's arms. The flashbulbs will pop and my child will be mortified as it splashes across the front page, "Real estate lady slain in bed with shoe salesman." Patent leather pumps perforated with pointed bullets.

She wondered if it showed. If Malcolm could see the desire in her eyes.

"Do you understand what I'm saying, Mary Catherine?"

"Of course."

"On the other hand, do you ever get into the city?"

"Occasionally."

"Well, perhaps we could have lunch."

"Oh, that doesn't make much sense, does it?"

"Probably not. What do you say?"

Malcolm had to make his position clear. In a way he was putting the onus on Mary Catherine. He didn't fool her one bit. Chemistry, thy name is idiocy.

"When do you think you'll be in next?"

"Possibly next week."

Tomorrow, yesterday.

Back at the office, she drove him to his car. They got out, and in the shadow of an overhanging sign from the travel agency next to her office he pinned her gently to the wall. Cheryl or Nancy or somebody was asking to be flown and Mary Catherine leaned against her eyes, flattening the nose.

"Here's my card," he said. "I mean it. Call me next week."

Chapter Seven

Six o'clock. It started to snow harder, and was getting cold. It was a hard time to get through. Mary Catherine went back into the office, straightened up, locked the door. It still got dark so early this time of year.

Everyone, of course, was going somewhere. Going to whatever it was behind their curtains, their shades, their lawns, their porches. She wrapped her coat around her and took her mittens out of the pockets, forgetting where she had parked her car. Was the chill in the air, or was it part of her? This time of day, the sky was black, this time of day when stores closed, parents picked up children from swimming classes at the Y, those little ones, who, defying the Asian flu, diphtheria, and the common ordinary everyday cold, would come streaming out of the brick building with damp hair and unzipped jackets, this time was calm, a letting down, a strangely pensive, melancholy time. She had trained herself not to give in to it. Dusk, you shall not master me, she would think grimly. Dusk, you will not swallow me up and make me sad. I will not let you.

Finding her car, the orange beckoning like a lighthouse beacon, Mary Catherine saw that it was coated with thick ice. With a sigh she turned on the motor, got the de-icer out of the glove compartment and the pole with the rubber scraper out of the trunk, and went to work. Winter wonderland.

She couldn't get up her hill. Low didn't work. High didn't work either. Ice had formed on the streets. Mary Catherine thought, there is a battle of wits, this commando course between me and winter, who is going to win out. Me or him. It. That old man with the icicles in his beard and snow forming on his scythe. Or was that Father Time? It doesn't matter. How was she going to get up the hill?

She couldn't. She left the car at the bottom of the hill. She was in no mood to combat ice as thick as tar. Last winter she had slid down the hill for about three minutes. Just slid. Saw her whole life in front of her just as they say you do. Nothing helped, she just slid. Don't use the brakes, the books say, don't panic, the safety pamphlets warn, don't anything, just slide. She did, three minutes' worth, landing in an embankment, only to cajole the irritable inhabitant of the nearest house to dig her out. That's no fun.

Walking in a winter wonderland.

Walking up the hill, Mary Catherine saw the moon through the snow. A cold moon, icy. Looking up, she thought she was a crucifix there. She thought she saw the graceful lethargic crucifix she had stared at every Sunday ever since she could remember. Staring at her. What was He doing up there? His body was a little more relaxed than usual, the face a bit more benign, but it was Him. He all right. Jesus from Saint Peter's on Hanover Street in downtown Boston. What was He doing up there in a Long Island sky, especially when she needed something to make her feel warm. Jesus up there surrounded by a few stars and a sliver of a cold winter moon was no help at the moment. Dusk would get no quarter from her. There would be only Francie home. Maybe she would have made a fire. Perhaps dinner would already be started.

It was hard to grip her boots into the street and its ice quilt. There was no sidewalk. She kept sliding. Sonja Henie would have manipulated the whole thing magnificently and John Payne and Don Ameche would have come along with their little Tyrolean hats and would have taken care of everything. But they were nowhere in sight. She would have to do it herself.

Looking up again, she saw He was still there. Smiling in a loving way. He had scared her when she was little. All that blood coming out of His palms.

And on Saturdays at 4:30 when she would go to confession, sitting in that little mahogany box, not much air and sort of charged, not unlike an orgone box, not unlike a coffin really, when you think about it. She would tell him (he tried to hide it but she knew it was Father Feeney) who was he kidding when he kept asking about who did what to whom.

Well, how dare he. Just how dare he. Mary Catherine would have none of it anymore. She knew who it was behind that curtain for God's sake, she knew that it was Father Feeney with his pink cheeks and blue eyes, three carefully placed wrinkles at the corners. She knew it was Father Feeney with his long black gown and starched white collar, the little hat covering his premature bald spot.

There was no danger of her admitting any masturbation to him anyway, because there was none. Her clitoris might have been her appendix for all she knew at that point. Father Feeney had nothing to worry about.

Finally getting a foothold on some snow on the far side of the road, she was able to walk more easily. "Jesus died for us" one of the icons nailed to the wall in their little church had read under the picture of Him being worshipped by two adoring women. That was a heavy responsibility, she used to feel. For me He died. How good, just how wonderful do I have to be to earn that sacrifice, she would think. It was a lot to bear. Perhaps that's one of the reasons that when she decided to throw it all over it didn't hurt much. Not much.

She got images, though, even now occasionally of Sister's paleblue eyes behind those rimless glasses. How she would have loved to have seen Sister's body in those days. What secrets lay under all that cloth and folds and white bibs? Yet sometimes she had to admit when she was lying quietly in her bed, she would see it, Sister's face, that soft white full-cheeked face, shaking her head. Just shaking her head. She wasn't bad, but she always made you feel so terrible if you even looked at yourself when you took a shower for heaven's sake. I suppose it isn't that way anymore, she thought, I suppose the reason I've got some kind of reasonable grip on myself is because I had something to break away from, someplace I knew I had to get to. "I have sinned through my own fault in my thoughts and in my words and in what I have done"; the penitential rite was still tattooed to the inside of her head, and that really wasn't playing fair. After all, that was a little like Big Brother is watching you, she thought, even then she had this streak in her that was desperate to keep her thoughts to herself.

Once when she was very little and it was a hot day, a very hot Sunday, she had passed the holy water and put her fingers in it, hypnotized by all the coolness just sitting in that cistern. Her mother was horrified and raised her hand to spank her, but her father, who, she remembered, was still drinking then, with a half smile just took her by the hand and led her out of church.

Looking up, pulling her scarf around her neck she looked up again to the moon. He was still there, but now He had the face of her father, thin, angular, when you looked at him full face it was as though you were looking at him sideways. They had taken refuge in each other, she thought, and if there is anything that has to do with my nerve it was because of him. Carlo always said that too. But he was so shy and when she was little would just bring her a book to read, Swinburne's poems or Robert Herrick's works, she couldn't understand but when he would read them to her it didn't matter, since he would come tuck her in, hear her prayers, and recite the words. When he went on to AA he became quieter than ever, since he had been a silent drinker anyway, but the two of them would sneak down to the kitchen late at night and he would fix her a Dagwood sandwich and they would talk.

So many people living someplace in her head. Dad, Dennis. She hadn't heard from Dennis in weeks. Her baby brother was not quite thirty, still lived home, worked at the same job for years. He didn't get out in time. Once a year ago she had met him in Boston and they were drinking beer in a place they had known since they were kids. Dennis was still handsome, turned-up nose, deepset green eyes, such a handsome Irish boy he was. But he drank too much and couldn't get away from home. Never got serious about a girl, stayed at his job with the computers, got melancholy. He had told her that time about how Father Feeney had made him feel so bad, when he was fourteen, when he told him he had masturbated. So bad, he said, and now after the ninth beer he could still remember the feeling, his eyes brimming with tears. He wasn't strong enough to get out from under. Someday. Someday he will.

Grateful home. She smelled the chops on the stove, the fire was blazing. That Francie.

Chapter Eight

On their first time she and Malcolm stood in his friend's room, looking at each other. She took off her raincoat, shaking off the wet, throwing it on the chair.

His friend's apartment was small, just one room. It had the look of being a place to make love in, catch a bite, but never to read, think, or feel at home in. There was dust over everything, even on the expensive hi-fi resting in the corner, and the bed took up most of the room. It was round, covered by a brown and white pony-skin rug. There was wine in the refrigerator, Yugoslavian, three bottles of ketchup, some mustard, two already opened bottles of quinine water and club soda, some cheese hardened by exposure to the air, and some salami, curling.

Mary Catherine picked up a magazine from the coffee table. *Réalités*.

"My friend has a French girl friend."

"How long has he been divorced?"

"He's not. Just separated. He was married twenty years and just fell out of love with his wife. She got fat and uninteresting to him, so he started taking up with stewardesses."

In my next life I'm going to be a stewardess, Mary Catherine thought. Sleek and svelte and irresistible to lonely, on-the-make businessmen bored out of their skulls by those wives who put in their growing-up time, supportive raising-children time. Forty-five-year-olds terrified that that's all, folks, that's all there is, the wife at home, the bridge games on the 4:52, the kids getting into dope, the having to cope with it all, the having to get it up at night when your wife's flesh has lost its appeal, when months of swimming at the Y and modern dance classes and gymnastics still can't tone the body to the taut crispness of a young thigh, a twenty-five-year-old upper arm. The sight of a breast, looking as though someone had let the air out of it, resting weakly, limply on a rib cage, or an ass looking like a tire with the tread worn off, the stretch marks running wild over the buttock map, would make them impotent, she supposed. The buttock, fallen, like Jell-O before it hardens, swaying. Some men could do it, love it still, she supposed, as the indignities of middle age infringed upon their women, the respect and the sharing, the basic compatibility transcending the inexactitude of the flesh.

"Would you like some wine?"

"It's eleven in the morning."

"So?"

"O.K."

She was excited.

She became reserved suddenly, sitting in a straight-backed chair, crossing her legs primly, folding her hands.

"I feel odd."

"Why, because it's eleven in the morning?"

"Maybe. Maybe because this room is so antiseptic."

"I knew from the first minute that there was something between us."

Is this one of the remarkable lessons learned in those years of freedom? To give off messages? It had gotten so that she could tell in an instant whether a conversation was going to lead to a physical exploration of each other.

So far she was not yet depleted. Inside, for some reason, despite the number of penises that had been inside her, despite the listless, lustless, lustful arms that had held her, she was still very much intact.

It had been very conscious, the seeing what would happen, the putting herself in risk. She had written to herself: "As a divorced woman I would like to behave like a divorced man. I would like to hop on a plane and wander. Just wander, move from airport to airport, talking to people sitting next to me, finding out who they are, what they are to me. And when I get there, wherever I am going, I would like to wander some more. And if men want me I will be there and I will do what I want to, have to do and I will not be debilitated, the essential Mary Catherine will be intact. I will find out what it's like out there and who they all are to me.

"Because although the naked eye might not be able to figure it out, I am too contained. I am tired, as a matter of fact, of being too contained, of holding it in, the flying. Because that's what I want to do. Fly. Move. Go. See. Find out.

"I find, as a divorced woman, that married groups, suburban gatherings, are, without doubt, dull inept ways to pass the time between eight and midnight. Staying home, as I do often, the divorced woman with a child, this nubile teen-ager who is stretching and yearning herself in her own way, is not an eventful way for a woman who is trapped by her own gonads."

And she had discovered that her body was a never-ending source of pleasure for her. And her lovers, sadly, she thought, had become nameless, numberless, and whenever she could find them, she met them head on. Unquestioning, never consciously searching for the one, everyone else seemed to be looking for Mr. Right, perhaps she was looking for Mr. Wrong instead, because that's what she was finding. She wondered about her quest. She truly didn't know what it was that she was looking for but she continued it, that nameless numberless journey.

What for heaven's sake do we look for in our lovers, she thought. What? Do we want them to think we are beautiful? Do we hold our stomachs in as they caress us? Do we tighten the muscles of the thighs as they run their lips softly over them? Do we need desperately the words telling us how lovely we are?

When she was young and would neck (neck, why do they call it neck, she used to think, why not call it ear or hip or toe on the couch in the parlor) on the love-seat, appropriately named, of course, in her parents' living room, their room was right over it, they would have to be so quiet, she and the boy.

And as they struggled, brassiere hooks stuck and breasts yearning to be touched, same thing, she would suck in her plump round belly (and that was hard to do; that is, be passionate and not breathe and worry about pimples under his fingers all at the same time).

So is that what we want as we tempt them, she thought, the lovers. Show them how skilled, how loving, how sexy, how orgasmic, how womanly, how fashionable we can be. Is that it, is that why we make hotel rooms our hostels, our resting places, our watering places? Is that why we make TV sets and closed curtains, ice-makers in the hall and heavy bedspreads our playthings, the accouterments of our days and nights?

Malcolm was taking off his jacket, loosening his tie. He moved over to the radio and turned it on. Swing, Benny Goodman in the middle of everything, their period. He sat down on the bed and took off his shoes, pulled off his socks. His feet were very white, thin, elegant in a man so tall.

He hung his tie up on a hanger in the closet and started taking off his shirt. It had thin blue stripes on a white background. He walked over to her, strangely vulnerable in an undershirt, and held out both hands. "Stand up, Mary Catherine."

She stood up, a small child obeying her daddy, a little sister looking up to her big brother.

He put his arms around her and kissed her. She liked to kiss. Carlo had moved on from her lips too soon. He had never lingered, and none of them, those men out there, had loitered, paused long enough at the depot, the stopover place.

She put her arms around him, caressing his back. His body was warm and she could feel a roundness pushing against her breasts.

They leaned back and looked at one another.

She put her hands on his chest, feeling his nipples. He winced.

"What?"

"My nipples are as sensitive as yours. I've always had swelling where the breasts are. In locker rooms at college, they used to kid me and there was never anything I could do about it. I'm overweight now, when I'm thinner it goes down."

He started kissing her again and unzipped the back of her sweater.

He was careful and tender. When he kissed her breasts she moaned and he looked at her, blue eyes wide.

"I'm so glad you like that," he said.

The significance of that was beyond Mary Catherine. Either his wife didn't like it, or other lady friends. Mary Catherine was very responsive, and was not curious to further the comment.

After it was over they lay with Mary Catherine's arm around Malcolm, his head cradled on her shoulder.

"I'm so glad your body is still good," he said. "I was so afraid it would be . . ."

"Old?"

"Yes. Is that terrible?"

She didn't answer. Sure it's terrible. You get to be forty and if your breasts aren't as high as an elephant's eye and your stomach isn't flat anymore you might as well skulk away, turn in your fucking card. Turn your face to the wall.

He was the only man in her life at the moment who moved her, stirred her in any way, and most of their time together he spent talking about other women. Stewardesses, "lollipops" from his college days, models met at business conventions.

"Is that so terrible? Don't be mad."

"Who's mad?"

"I mean it's always a challenge, and Pat and I, well, the sex isn't so bad, I suppose, but we never talk anymore. The other night I hit her at dinner in front of the kids. I could have kicked myself. Went off my trolley but she aggravated me so much I couldn't control myself. She whines and complains—she drives me to distraction. I went out, took the car and didn't come back till after midnight. I was going to call you but I knew you were out of town. Mary Catherine, what are you thinking?"

She smoothed the hair back from his temples. His skin was unlined. He had told her he was fifty, but his eyes still shone and his hair was thick and curly. She liked to touch it. He shut his eyes as she felt his scalp undulating under her fingers. With one hand she caressed his cheek.

Eyes closed, his hand on her belly, he said, "I don't run around a lot anymore. Sometimes, though, I think I'm not such a hot lover. Maybe I don't really satisfy a woman, so I go from one to the other to make sure, to make sure I hear the moans and groans, see the relief in the eyes."

He opened his eyes, looking at her.

"Can you understand that, Mary Catherine?"

She moved to the fleshy part of his shoulders, massaging. She wanted to protect him, hold him, not let the bad men get him.

She was staring out the window at rooftops. They would have to go soon. Rendezvous at dusk, morning trysts, sex in the afternoon. Intact. She was intact.

Chapter Nine

Mary Catherine was dozing. The 4:52 into New York lurched and rolled with a lulling regularity and was putting her to sleep. There was gray heads in front of her, just grayness, no shoulders, bald spots. In the seat across the aisle, a black woman with a sleek wig was holding a baby. She had a folded-up stroller and three shopping bags.

She was talking loudly to the world at large.

"If God didn't want you to be white he would have made you . . . listen, conductor, you help me with the baby, O.K.? Everybody looks at me like I'm crazy. Listen," she said to the baby, who had started crying,

"Dada don't do nothing for you, you calling Dada. Listen, did you know that when you lose your mother you lose your best friend? Thank you, mister, why can't all conductors be like that? You white, now my mother told me don't smoke." She was making smoke rings, and the conductor was trying to get the baby out of blowing range. "Don't bother, I'm not drunk. I'm feeling good. A man is shit, well, not all men. Right on. I ain't drunk, I ain't worried about money. Shit, I work hard. Everybody lookin' at me like I'm screwy. How de do," she trilled to Mary Catherine, waving three fingers.

"My mother told me you treat a person good, white, black. Listen, miss, you look like you bite on your fingers. My mother told me it's not the color, it's who you are, your personality. My mother going to raise hell for drinking. I'm tired tonight." She put the baby on her shoulder as she prepared to get off the train. The conductor came by and helped her with the bags and stroller. "You lose your mother, you lose your best friend." She tripped with the baby in her arms and the conductor lunged forward to help. "Conductor, everything's all right. The baby's all right. Good night, everybody," she called as she stepped gingerly down the steps.

The conductor came back into the car. "The baby's all right," he told the world at large.

Mary Catherine spied Ellen Spinoza coming back from the ladies' room, if one could dignify it by that term, it being never clean, the windows, like the rest, encrusted with dirt, always lacking in toilet paper, soap, always smelling fetid. She looked quickly out the window, but she was caught. It's not that she didn't like Ellen, a petite portrait painter whose work was achieving some prominence in New York, it was that this time to herself, this train time, was cherished minutes for thinking. She hated to share them.

"Mary C., I'm so glad to see you, can I join you, I'm sitting ahead?"

There had been times when Mary Catherine, absolutely incapable of getting a civil or coherent word out on a morning train, would mumble that she had some paperwork to do and would the person mind terribly if she wouldn't talk. But this time was different. It was afternoon, she had more energy.

A handsome woman, Ellen was even smaller than Mary Catherine (it was glorious, she almost felt tall beside her), not quite reaching five feet. She had wide eyes, and no chest. Her front was as flat as a boy's and she always wore narrow, little-boy shirts that made her look even more like a little boy. Her hair was blond and she wore bangs that were old-fashioned but suited her, and always long, dangling silver earrings. Ellen was widowed two years ago.

"How are you, Mary Catherine?"

"Fine, really fine, Ellen. How's it going?"

"Oh, things are all right. I'm having a show at the Madison Gallery in the spring. I'll send you an invitation." Ellen was wearing an enormous silver ring that almost dwarfed her whole hand. "The twins decided to go to different colleges finally, which relieved me, because they both got early admission to Brown, but I really felt it would have been the wrong thing, and Todd finally agreed and is going to Tufts. So at least they won't be too far."

"That is the first year they'll be away?"

"You have no idea how empty that house is going to be. I don't know what I'm going to do." Mary Catherine took her coat off, suddenly a blast of heat in the car made her sticky under the arms. "But listen, if I could get used to Jack going I guess I can get used to anything."

Ellen's big eyes still grew moist at the mention of him. Mary Catherine stayed silent. She knew Ellen wanted to talk.

"It's that bed, you know, that big double bed that hurts. Even after two years. I really should get rid of it." She stared out the window. It was beginning to rain. "It seems silly, doesn't it, to make such a fuss about one big mattress, but that's been the hardest thing. Sleeping alone. I just wish we'd had some more years."

"I know."

"Look, if you want to read, Mary, don't let me bother you. What are you going in for?"

"I have a dinner appointment with Carlo. Just some business."

"I used to meet Jack in town every Thursday and we'd go to the opera. I'd get all dressed up and feel like a fool on the dirty train with my long gown and opera pumps. I sat with the coffin, Mary, did I ever tell you that, just like Ethel Kennedy I took him home in a coffin on the train.

"But you know what," she sighed, "a strange thing happens, you learn you can love again. I had a thing with a speed freak for a few months, he was half my age. Can you imagine. He has a studio next to mine on the Bowery. It was fine, I was alive, I learned how to be alive again, at least he taught me that. But I had to end it, it was crazy, pulling me apart."

The train jerked forward and Ellen's bag fell to the floor. "You know," she said, bending down to pick it up, "the thing that you learn, I don't know if this has been your experience or not, but the thing you learn is that men are deficient. There are so many more interesting women than men. That's scary, isn't it? Be-

cause that's all that there leaves, us women. [...]
into her eyes. Ellen patted her arm. "Don[...]
dear. I'm not becoming a lesbian or anyth[...]
getting wise and mature and learning to co[...]
widowhood. Black, black," she mused, "[...]
wear black ever. Black is the color of my [...]
heart."

"What do you mean?"

"Oh, nothing. Nothing, nothing. All I kn[...]
I now throw myself into my work. I wo[...]
fifteen hours a day, in my New York and [...]
studios. Sometimes I sleep over in New York[...]
come home for days, the boys can take care[...]
selves. Work is one answer. Don't you think[...]
Catherine."

"Yes, Ellen, yes I do."

The restaurant was dark.
The tablecloths were red and white the[...]
candles on the tables.

It was the first time Mary Catherine had see[...]
in six months. Francie would take a train into New
York to see him, and when he was in Eastville, he
would rarely come to the house anymore.

At the beginning, when they were first divorced, he
was not in good shape. He was drinking heavily,
cracked up his car on the Long Island Expressway.
But then, as business began picking up, when it appeared that there were women out there who found
him attractive, personable, he revived. He went
with three women in the first six months of the divorce.
Sometimes, at the beginning, when he would come to
see Francie, he would bring his dates to the house. He
always had someone in the car. A blonde, a redhead
perhaps, sometimes with her own children with her.
He would come in the back door, come through the

kitchen, a source of irritation to Mary Catherine, but she never said anything. She excused the back door, but refused to chat with, pass judgment on, or greet his succession of ladies.

Ideally, she felt a friendly divorce would be the best for Francie. And Mary Catherine tried, for appearance's sake, to keep it that way. Francie liked to remember when her mother and father loved one another. And Mary Catherine tried never to say anything about Carlo to Francie that would jeopardize her daughter's good feeling for him, but when there were things about which she disagreed strongly, she spoke her mind. Like the girls he brought to the door, for example. Who needed that, she thought. And said.

But she had called him about some papers she needed his signature on, and he had told her he was not going to be on the Island for several weeks, but if she wanted to meet him in New York he would be glad to see her. First he asked her to come to his office. But Mary Catherine, reacting less maturely than she would have liked, did not want to see him on his turf. He, sitting behind his desk, she sitting opposite him, legs crossed, as though he were interviewing her for a job. No, she told him, let's meet for a drink. Midtown, he suggested, but then he couldn't stay too long since he had an appointment. What about dinner? So she agreed. Going to meet Carlo after six months.

And she looked at him, this ex-husband, this old lover, this college chum, this father of her child, this new man about town.

She had wanted Glenn Ford in *And So Ends Our Night,* the innocence and sweetness of him, the lean earnestness of him, that's what she thought she had wanted all those years ago, and what she thought she got.

He looked better than she had seen him in ages. He

had lost weight, much of the paunch was smoothed away, his eyes showed their glow once more, and even though there was a long, thin line moving from his nose to his chin, he was still attractive, and she had to admit to herself she got a twinge when she saw him.

Carlo had been adopted by a hardworking Italian family when he was a baby and the childless couple had rejoiced in the beautiful baby. He had blue-black hair and clear blue eyes and was the darling of his parents, spoiled, coddled. He had learned early in life always to take the easy way out. And his fresh dark looks helped.

A soft bulge pressed out of his sweater where his belly was. He got up, pulled her chair out for her when she entered. Smooth, he was smooth.

"What will you drink? Scotch as usual?"

"Yes please."

He was assured, she thought. Smoking leisurely, eyeing the legs of the miniskirted waitress; he had acquired confidence. He also had a pocketbook strapped over his shoulder. She noticed that the sneakers had been replaced by black leather pumps, and a trim-fitting pair of black-and-white-checked pants showed out from under the table.

She looked at his hands; the fingers were long, the nails half moons. He had taken to getting manicures. She couldn't remember those hands on her. Eighteen years and she couldn't remember what it felt like, making love to him, this man opposite her. Lying in bed with him, what was it like, watching Johnny Carson with him. Reading, eating apples with him, apples and cheese, ice cream and butterscotch sauce with him, grapes and oranges with him, in bed at night watching Johnny Carson with him.

"That new?"

"No, it's last year's."

"The color is good for you. How's Francie?"

She misses you. Why don't you call?

"She's fine. Her school work has improved incredibly. She got an A+ on a report on Lamartine for French."

"Who's he?"

"A French poet."

"So what's new?"

The waitress came and brought the drinks. She handed them the menus.

Mary Catherine ran her finger through the candle. Carlo was looking at her crossed legs.

"I brought the papers from the tax man and the lawyer."

"We don't have to talk about that really right now do we?"

Yes, I'd prefer it, yes, I don't quite know what to do with all these feelings of regret, anger, remorse, wasted time. Maybe that's the prevailing feeling. The wasted time. So much else I could have been doing.

"What will you have, Mary Catherine?"

"A small steak and salad will be fine."

"How about some wine?"

She wasn't going to have a thing to drink at all, she had promised herself before she came. She wanted to have all her faculties, she wanted to be civil and cordial and sophisticated about all this but she wanted to be on top of it. No scene, certainly, no fights. Maybe, just maybe they could still be friends. She had never seen it work, though, being friends. Only Eleanora had been able to pull it off, the keeping in touch with the husband, the continuing of relationships on other levels. But of course all Eleanora's ex-husbands were still in love with her. A little bit, anyway, so no matter who they married after, or what kind of lives they continued, she still managed to be a part of their lives.

Otherwise, in her observation, it was impossible. Being friends. The emotional investment on either end was too great, so that when it was over, the residual bitterness or passion dissipated itself. How wonderful never to have to talk to your wasted years, Mary Catherine thought, how wonderful never to have to peek at your past, how wonderful never to have to confront your mistakes, your weaknesses. But it couldn't be that way, certainly since they had a mutual child. A child mutually. Certainly not when there were papers to sign.

"Fine. Red. Is that all right with you?"

"Great. I'm having lamb chops."

"How's the agency?"

"Fine. There still seems to be tight money. People don't seem to be buying."

"Francie told me you've joined a new firm."

"A big New York firm. It looks like a good deal."

The waitress brought two large salads.

"How about another scotch, Mary Catherine?"

"No, no thank you. The wine will be fine."

"I'll get it now."

"We haven't seen each other in six months."

"I know.'

"Are you feeling all right?"

"Yes, I'm fine."

"You look fine. You've lost weight, haven't you?"

"About twenty pounds."

"Carlo, how did you do it?"

"I stopped drinking for a while, and I don't know, it just dropped off, the weight. Having to cook for myself, that may have helped."

"Have you learned how?"

"Well, I throw things together. Taught myself how to make Jell-O."

You used to pass through the kitchen, never stopping, you never boiled an egg in our house, you sat

*there waiting to be waited on as though I was your
mother, as though I was the housekeeper, even though
I worked as hard and as long as you did.....*

"It's fun, it's not bad—the cooking. And I have
people help me."

*I don't want to hear about your women. I'm de-
termined not to hear about your women.*

"Do you spend much time alone, Carlo?"

She was on dangerous ground, but the few glasses
of wine she had drunk gave her a feeling of invin-
cibility. That she would pull off this dinner. That she
would be the stronger of the two when it was all over.

"What do you mean, alone?"

"I mean just sit in your apartment and read, listen
to music. Think."

"You mean without a woman there?"

"What I mean really is have you ever just really
spent some time alone since the divorce?"

"It hasn't been necessary. I don't like to be alone."

Knock it off, Mary Catherine said to herself.

"I've found, Carlo, that that's been one of the best
things about being alone, that I've learned how to think
to myself. Just get to my feelings."

"You were always like that. You don't mind being
alone."

"I don't like it all the time. It's just that I think we
all should be able to spend time fruitfully alone."

"I know. No lectures today, Mary Catherine."

Touché. One point for you.

The bottle of Chianti was empty.

"How about a little more wine, Mary Catherine?"

*Sitting at the kitchen table talking politics. Carlo
shouting. An intimacy of sorts. The preliminary. The
protection. The prelude to love. In vino veritas.*

"All right. I really can't stay too long."

"Where are you going from here?"

"Back to Eastville. Back home."

"Did you drive in or take the train?"

"The train. I took the train."

Mary Catherine excused herself and went to the bathroom. She took a dime out of her purse and called home collect.

"How's Dad?" Francie asked.

"He's fine, love. He asked for you. He'll probably see you in a week or two. He's awfully busy with his new job."

"When are you coming home, Mom?"

"Are you all right alone? You should have had someone sleep over."

"Hilda's here."

"Oh, good. I feel better.'

' "How does he look?"

"Thin. Really thin. Very good."

"When did he say he was coming up?"

"A week or two, honey. He's going to call you tomorrow. I'm calling from the ladies' room."

"Did you ever read about Sacco and Vanzetti?"

"Yes."

"That was so sad. Did you think they were innocent?"

"Francie, do we have to talk about that now, over the phone? I won't be home too late."

"I'm going to do my term paper on them. Do we have any books on them?"

"Yes, in my room. The bookcase next to the television.'

"That was so sad. I just know they were innocent, Mom. That's what I'm going to try to prove. Say hello to Dad for me."

"Yes, dear."

"He didn't by any chance ask you to marry him again, did he?"

"You're really a panic."

"Just wondering."

"Francie, do you have food for dinner? I did go shopping and the refrigerator is full."

"I already ate. The plumber called. He said it would cost $200 to fix the tub in your room. It's all very complicated, but I have his number."

"Two hundred! I don't believe it."

"He said it as though he was offering us the biggest bargain of the year."

"Oh, God. Well, I'll call him tomorrow. Go to bed early. I love you."

"Me too. Say hi to Dad for me."

"'Bye, my love."

"Bye, Ma."

Carlo stood up again for her when she sat down at the table. He was almost finished with his meal.

"This place reminds me of Angelo's, where we used to go in college, Remember?"

"On Spruce Street."

"Yes. They had marvelous spaghetti with clam sauce. We sure polished off bottles of Chianti in those days, didn't we?"

"Yes."

"Remember you used to make fettucini on Saturday afternoons that summer before we were married, when your folks used to go downtown. We'd sit in the kitchen eating, drinking the wine, and listening to the Metropolitan Opera rebroadcasts coming from New York."

"I remember."

You sit opposite a man, she thought, a man who you woke up with every morning for the past eighteen years, and all of a sudden it's yesterday's business. Now you wake up and don't remember what it felt like when he kissed you, this man you woke up with every morning for eighteen years.

"I guess I'm more sentimental than you, Mary Catherine. I always was. I remember things like that. It's true that we've grown away from each other, and the divorce, I think, is the best thing that we've done. But still I remember those days. You used to wear those long Mexican muumuus or whatever you call them, and I would walk into your house on Saturdays and smell the garlic coming from the kitchen. And I would be singing on those Saturday mornings as I was shaving. Can you imagine, singing. I was so excited to be spending the day with you."

There were tears in Carlo's eyes.

So many years ago you used to look at me with tears in your eyes, Mary Catherine thought. It's one of the things I fell in love with, that I could move someone to tears. Well, this is the first time in over twenty years you've cried again. Cried because of me, anyway, because I moved you. Even the remembrance of the moving you.

"I remember, Carlo."

"I'm not saying that we didn't do the right thing. We did, getting the divorce has really been the right thing, but it was so loving at the beginning. You were so beautiful. I haven' thought about those good times in a long time."

"It's a long time ago."

"I know, I know. There's a lot of water under the bridge, isn't there."

"Yes, Carlo."

"Well, where do you think we went wrong?"

"Carlo, there's no point to this really—there isn't."

"Yes there is. Yes there is. I want to know now that part of it is over—what happened, where did we first start going wrong? Was it because you had to work, that I couldn't support us completely? Was that it?"

"Carlo, you know that wasn't it, that was never it.

I didn't mind working. It was important for me to work. I would have liked to go back to school. Get another degree maybe, do more with myself. But I didn't mind the working. Let's not rehash all this all over again."

I'm not ashamed, he thought. I'm not ashamed of these tears. The feelings were so intense in those days, I've never replaced them. I wonder if I ever will. Is it because it was a first love, is it because we were so young? I don't know. I will not be worried about my sentimentality anymore. She scared me, that's what she did. There was a ferocity about her, a wildness I didn't know what to do with. And God, was she perfect. God, she thought she was so perfect. Who can live with that. Who can live with somebody who keeps rubbing it in that she's helping to support the family when you've lost a job, two jobs, three jobs. Nobody, no self-respecting man. Ever. I'll never forgive her for that. She deballed me in those days. So soon. So fast she made me feel like shit. I had to protect myself, I had to be strong somewhere, somehow.

"Do you remember Anne Pointer in Michigan?"

"Of course."

"She wanted me to divorce you and marry her.'

"What do you mean?"

"We had an affair for over a year, before we moved to Eastville."

Why tell me now. Why oh why tell me now.

"We would meet in Ann Arbor once or twice a month and she would cry and carry on; she wanted me to leave you. She was on the verge of leaving Herb when we decided to move to Eastville."

It doesn't matter anymore.

"Why are you telling me that, Carlo?"

"I don't know. I somehow think you ought to know. She was your friend."

"Herb was your friend too."

Show off. Boaster. Whoremaster. How many others I wonder, just how many others. You had to fortify yourself with a drink to make love to me, and then took on Anne Pointer sober, I'll bet.

"I felt unessential to you."

"What do you mean?"

"I don't know. You made me feel that I wasn't necessary. When we were in bed I used to feel you could be with anybody. That I was just an instrument."

"Carlo, what are you talking about? You've had too much wine."

"No sir, no sir. I didn't feel important to you. You would put me down, God, would you put me down. I didn't feel like anything."

"Carlo, I thought you said you had stopped drinking?"

"This is the first time I've had this much in a long time. What's the difference what I've had to drink. It just seems so strange that eighteen years go by and we end up over a bottle of red wine in a restaurant with red-and-white-checked tablecloths just like we began."

I will not get sucked into this. I will not fall for this.

Mary Catherine pulled her large purse up from the floor, unzipped it, and took out the papers her lawyer had given her for Carlo's signature. She handed them to Carlo. Their fingers touched.

"Do you have a pen?"

"We used to lie out in the meadow in back of the outdoor swimming pool on campus, remember, Mary Catherine, we would kiss for hours."

She would run out of there if he touched her again.

"Carlo, please don't go over all that, especially since you just gave me the news about Anne Pointer. You had me there. I never knew."

"Does it bother you?"

He was leaning forward, blowing smoke to the side.
No satisfaction for you, buster.

"What do you think?"

"I don't know. I'd like to think it did."

Mary Catherine looked at him; his eyes were becoming bloodshot, he was lighting up another cigarette, pushing back a lock of hair that had fallen over his forehead.

"You know, Carlo, when you visit Sarah Stans two blocks away, and don't come to see Francie, she sees your car outside Sarah's house. She knows you're there."

She wasn't going to say anything about that.

She wished she could be funny. She wished she could pass this whole thing off with good humor. Get him the hell off her back. She did not want him to affect her, and still he did. She was glad she had divorced him but knew that the investment was made too young, when she was too vulnerable, and she knew somehow that some way he would always be able to affect her one way or the other, that he would irritate her, and in spite of it all she wanted him to want her. Still. She marveled at the perversity of her.

She wished she was funny. She wished like Rosalind Russell or Eve Arden she could be arch and witty, quick. But she couldn't. She wasn't tall enough.

She had sworn to herself she wouldn't say anything about his tactlessness, the way he was hurting Francie, but, as usual, she couldn't help it. And she certainly couldn't pull off being funny about it.

"Forget it, Carlo, forget I said anything about it. It's your life now. I have nothing to say about it."

"You should have been a nun, Mary Catherine." He smiled. "You are without a doubt the most self-righteous person I know. I guess it's the thing I have against you most. You talk and act as though you are the most perfect, the most infallible person in the world, and really you're just like the rest of us."

"Who ever said I was perfect. I just lived with a slob of a man who didn't pay his bills, who forged my name on checks, who made such a fuss about keeping up with not only the Joneses but just about everyone else on the block—"

"What the hell are you getting so mad about? It's all over. We're divorced, finished. Right? So why are you yelling, for Chrissakes?"

She was shaking.

"Who never held me, who fought off my kisses, how about that, Carlo. What about love, what about making love?"

"You scared me. Some times your voraciousness just put me off. A woman shouldn't be so wanting."

"Oh, God, did you hear that. Who said a woman shouldn't be so wanting? Should a man be wanting? Should any of us be wanting? Making love is life-giving, holding back is like dying."

"Bad, Mary Catherine. Bad metaphor."

"Forget it, just forget it, Carlo. I couldn't talk to you then and I can't talk to you now."

Loving we were, sitting around the dinner table. Francie all got up in her red tutu doing her Jane Froman number as she was clearing the table, all ebullience and energy, crashing up from the first course, pausing only to loop herself in his lap, her daddy's lap, placing a kiss behind his left ear where it was beginning to show a hint of baldness, the pouting, panting, stretching herself into the kitchen only to dump the dishes in the sink.

How he loved that. How he used to love that, his daughter and her energy, her abandon, her sultry Dorothy Dandridge, her June Preisser freshness, her painfully awkward seductive ways, that nine-year-old, that daughter of his. Whom he loved.

Over. On to the next.

"Carlo, I've got to go. Please sign these."

"O.K., Mary Catherine, O.K. We should be able to be friends."

Go fuck yourself.

"I'll try, Carlo. I'm trying."

"Let's at least for Francie."

Please go fuck yourself. Leave me be.

"I promise. You're right, Carlo."

"Just let me pay the check and we can go. Tell Francie I'll call her this weekend. Maybe we can do something. No, damn, I've got to go to Cleveland."

"Maybe next weekend."

"Sure. Tell her I'm sorry. I'll call the first chance I've got."

"O.K., Carlo."

Mary Catherine gathered up her bag and her shawl, catching a glance at herself in the plant-lined mirror in back of them. Her face looked like a mailed manila envelope.

Outside, on the street, Carlo gave Mary Catherine the papers back. A soft wind was coming up. People were holding their coats around them, plastering their hats on their heads.

Carlo put his hands on her shoulders. She couldn't decide whether he was trying to steady himself or caress her.

"I don't live far from here, Mary Catherine. Do you want to come for a drink?"

For a split second, a fragment in time, she wanted to hold him, let him know everything will be all right, darling, after the nightmare is all over; for a split second, a fragment in time, she wanted to make love to him, hold that oh, so familiar face in her hands and feel the eyelashes flutter against her cheek.

"I'll miss the last train. I've really got to go. Francie's alone." A lie.

He didn't remove his hands from her shoulders. They were playing a dumb game, she knew, but was hypnotized into wondering how it was all going to turn out.

"Are you sure?"

She felt the heat of his hands.

"Yes, Carlo."

He moved his hands down around her back, and embraced her. Her face was in his chest, her hands around his back. He was maneuvering her into the kissing position.

She found herself patting his back as though burping a baby, comforting a child, keeping an ex-husband away. She felt his ribs.

"You really have lost weight, Carlo," she said.

A taxi drove up, she extricated herself from his arms, and opened the door.

Chapter Ten

Mary Catherine dozed on the train home. She kept trying to remember what Carlo looked like. The new one. The thin Carlo with no paunch and a pocketbook over his shoulder. She couldn't. The Carlo she had lived with for so long took precedence in her mind. As the conductor shouted "Eastville," she jerked awake, her mouth tasting dry and sour. She drove home from the station, put the car in the garage, and unlocked the kitchen door. Francie had left every light on in the house. The electric bill would be astronomical.

She locked the house, took off her shoes, and tiptoed up the stairs. She didn't want to wake Francie. Standing at the doorway to her room, Mary Catherine caught her breath.

Francie, my love.

Francie was asleep. Her nightgown had moved up over her thighs, almost to her throat. She had thrown off the sheet and blanket. A puff of soft hair, golden, was under the arm flung over her head, and strands of yellow hair lounged over the pillow. The pubic hair was blond, quiet tufts, and a golden down glistened on her belly in the glow of the nightlight. Her breasts were high, with the nipples spreading the width of them like the taut neck of a giraffe. Francie's waist and torso stretched long.

Mary Catherine, woozy from the wine, her own groin moist still, stood in the doorway looking at her daughter. The cat was curled at the bottom of the bed, and a Tampax box, open, rested on the desk, next to the panda she had slept with since she was two. The bear was shabby by now, the rump had been sewed many times to prevent the cotton-ball intestines escaping. Tampax and pandas, breasts and comic books, pierced ears and nightmares, little girl blue, little girl yellow, little girl, my little girl. Mary Catherine leaned down, kissed the damp face of her child; she felt warm, and the cool beads of perspiration spilled into her temples, which were wet. Mary Catherine smoothed the hair back and forth, back and forth.

Francie, my love.

Still asleep, the girl put her arms around her mother's neck, holding. They stayed like that awhile, Mary Catherine feeling her breasts pressing against those of her daughter. I will give you my strength, she thought, I will give you my power, my motherliness. Take it, take my body, my warmth, let it move into you, let it feed you, Francie, my love.

Tears were on Mary Catherine's cheeks. She hadn't cried in a long while. Where did they come from, the tears? I am just holding my daughter. In her sleep still, the girl held tight to her mother.

Breasts, Mary Catherine thought. Breasts. This child, this person, this woman-child lay at my breast and suckled and I looked down and saw the lashes, sleeping lashes they were, as lips pursed pure hunger at me. You lay there, my Francie, and I looked down at your sleeping lashes and felt your softness, your roundness, your bottom, and felt you sleep suckling at my breast and desire came into my groin. You suckled and I felt the power of it in my groin. My child at my breast made me limp, full of desire, the nipple, its new mysterious tiny bumps were all erect always ready to give the milk, and the odd liquid, thin, not quite white, would come forth from me into you, my child, my Francie, from me into you. Not only did I bring you forth, push you out of me, push, Mary Catherine, push, Hail Mary, praise the Lord, Francesca Alice Romano is born, and out from that hidden place you came. I pushed you out, push like moving your bowels, push, Mary Catherine, push out the life the new person out of your body and there you were, bloody and wrapped in cellophane or Saran wrap or whatever it was, Francie, there you were out of me. Life. A living thing.

I gave you life and I reinforced it. I gave you succor, my breast, that nipple, that little pointed thing with enlarged little bumps like warts, like little hills in your mouth touching my own breast pushing the nipple into your mouth, I gave it to you. Sometimes Carlo, when he was drunk, would put my whole breast in his mouth, she thought. He would have swallowed it, chewed it, and thrown it to the lions if I hadn't stopped him.

Mary Catherine's face was wet with tears as she removed herself from Francie's embrace. She pulled the covers over the child and tucked them in, and bent down once more and kissed her.

In a flash she remembered her dream. Finally. And it chilled her. She had come into the house and had gone into the bathroom. There were bubbles from the bubble bath up to the ceiling, on the floor, in the sink, in the toilet. When she went into the bathroom she saw a small figure, naked, lying on the floor. It was three-year-old Francie. Mary Catherine pulled her out, panicking. Her heart had stopped. She put her mouth on the child's, kissing her back to life. Live Francie, live, live, and the eyelids fluttered, the long eyelashes moved like a bird's wing, daintily, and the eyes opened. She lived.

The emptiness of the dream feeling returned and Mary Catherine leaned down one more time to smooth away the damp hair from Francie's temples.

Maybe why Francie meant so much to her was that before she had a child she never really knew what it was to love, what it was to really care for someone else in an unselfish way. Slowly it happened—the love. Not all at once. The magic of the little thing was too intimidating for the love to take over too fast. But it did. Without Mary Catherine, Francie would die. She used to think that if she didn't feed her or change her and let her lie there in her salty wetness, then she would die. It was up to her to make sure she survived. And out of that being needed so desperately came a fierce love and an overwhelming tenderness. Whether it was intuitive and the maternal instinct, if there was such a thing, Mary Catherine couldn't tell. Before she had fenced and toyed and mouthed and played games at love. First with her parents, who talked about love and duty in the same breath, later with Carlo panting, breathing heavily into her ear. Promising promises, promises, promises. None if it had made sense and the LOVE, the Robert Indiana giant red and blue and green letters flashing on and off like the Great White Way, had been letters signifying nothing.

Belly land. Remember belly land when the stomach swelled and the breasts were spread over your chest and were so sensitive to the touch. Wonderful mountains they were, those breasts and that ridiculous profile, that pointed thing, that round thing that turned out to be a person. That was where you were, that was what mattered. It had meant so much that Mary Catherine couldn't think about it. Too much. Too important. Too deep.

But it was where she was. It meant a lot and she couldn't understand how people who had children who died could stand it. How do you bear it, she often thought, little coffins, little people put in the ground. I will not think about it, like Scarlett O'Hara, she would think about it tomorrow or the next day or never.

Mary Catherine knew someone who had carried around a dead baby inside her for months. It was dead because of the Rh blood business. What does it feel like to carry around arms and legs and a head with hair that is a dead thing and not breathing? She didn't like to get morbid about it, but she did think about it periodically, how sad that would be, how very sad.

Why did it mean so much to her, the giving birth, the feeling life, she thought about that. She wondered if it was good for Francie or not, this feeling, this otherness that she felt about the whole thing, this deep connection to her own body. She could never figure it out, especially since the priests and nuns had tried to convince her that, really, having babies was, in a way, close to the idea of accepting the burden of God was going to stick you with. The theory was that by doing God's will you'd get all sorts of fulfillment and joy at the end, but that was coupled with the other theory that the more God loved you, the more pain and suffering he gave you. She had never accepted it. Never.

Good night, Francie.

She closed the door softly.

It was 2 A.M.

The phone by the bed shouted at Mary Catherine, waking her. It seemed so far away, in another place. She struggled to get to the phone world.

Feeling around the night table, she threw her book and cup of half-filled tea to the floor. She found the light.

"Hello." The dark voice was her own.

"Mary Catherine."

"Yes, who is this?"

"Alfred."

"Alfred, what time is it?"

"I have no idea."

"Is everything all right?"

Alfred was a man she had been to dinner with twice. And by a tacit agreement, both had acknowledged that there was nothing worth pursuing. The formerly marrieds have a language, a rhythm all their own.

"Sure. I just wanted to call."

"Alfred, it's two in the morning."

"I know. But I know you always stay up pretty late."

"How have you been?"

"Not bad. Took my kids to Florida for a week."

"That must have been nice."

A little cough.

"Well, it was dull. They had a good time, though. Playing tennis, and we did a little golf."

Silence.

"Was there any particular reason why you called?"

She pictured him sitting with his feet on his desk in his Park Avenue living room. She had had a drink there once before they went to dinner. The price tags were still on the lamps. The cellophane still on the back of chairs.

He had gotten something expensive just so both his children could have their own room when they came to visit. His pocketbook business was bad now, so he had difficulty affording this luxury. He hated his wife, with whom he had been in litigation for two years now.

"I think I called because I'm lonely. I don't like to be alone."

He didn't ask to see her. She was grateful for that.

"Oh, Alfred, but at least you can admit it. You'll meet someone."

"And, Mary Catherine"—it all came out in a rush—"I'm worried about my daughter."

"What happened?"

"She's eleven, you know, and I think just got her period. I found two pairs of stained panties and she denied they were hers. How old are they before they start to use something?"

"She should be using something now."

"What, Kotex or Tampax or something?"

"These days they have smaller Tampax for kids. It's nothing."

"Then why isn't she using it?"

"You really ought to talk to her mother about it."

"I can't. She is a monster. I haven't talked to her in months."

"Can't you talk to your daughter?"

"I can't. She gets all embarrassed. Maybe I should speak to her teacher."

"Alfred. You've got to be able to talk to your wife. For your daughter's sake."

"Forget it. But why would she deny that the panties are hers?"

"I don't know. Except that it's not an unusual thing. I've heard of kids acting that way before."

"It depresses me. I'm not reaching her. Mary Catherine, are you sleepy?"

"I'm up now."

"Well, I just called because I was so damned lonely."

"I know, Alfred. I'm your friend. Call me anytime. I'm always up late."

"Thanks. I'm your friend too."

"I know that, Alfred."

"Good night, Mary Catherine."

"Good night, Alfred."

She turned out the light. Finally.

Chapter Eleven

Walking down the street these February days, Mary Catherine would find herself aware only of her own breasts. She would clasp her fingers around her waist to feel the bones, move up to the roundness; the better to feel you with, my dear. She challenged every man she saw. Toyed with every glance, seduced every direct gaze. She felt ennobled, purified, enhanced.

But if they had been drinking and smelled of smoky

bars, had stumbling speech and groping hands, she would have none of them. No more. No more Carlos.

And of course none of them moved her, those lovers, none of them made her cry. Still, she could love them all with her body, her untiring arms, her relentless calves, winding themselves around muscled, long, short, hairy, hairless legs after legs. So many legs.

She would love them all, all honorable or not so honorable men, and lying with them, stroking their backs and smoothing their temples, she would feel as though they had known one another always. The intimacy flowing from palm to skin, the care, the concern, full of feeling all maternal heaviness would sustain her all night long. It wasn't necessary to truly love them, of course, it was easy to touch them and make believe that something important was happening.

It was a wonderment how she could extract out of those late lovemaking hours, and the afterwards, such anonymous feeling of tenderness.

Instant intimacy. Twentieth-century wooing. How easy to get used to them. How quickly. Men in showers, men in baths, men shaving, men brushing their teeth, men jingling change on the dresser, men folding their pants, keeping the crease, men simulating love, pretending years together, capsulizing marriages, six-hour lifetimes.

With Seth the chiropodist she enjoyed a bizarre, totally sexual interlude. They never went anywhere, meeting only in his office or in motel rooms. He showed her his collection of pornography, even nude pictures of former girl friends. One was a voluptuous blond Swede with enormous breasts and straight blond hair. He had a picture of her rubbing her vagina on the corner of a table.

Browsing, browsing in bookstores like some peeping Tom, like some secret silent masturbator on Forty-

second Street skulking into the back of the store peeping at peep shows, nonchalant, cool, all aplomb, she
would watch them go in, the secret silent masturbators,
satisfying themselves on their lunch hours, feeding
some secret silent place. She would watch them, envy-
ing them, how she would like to be a man and un-
ashamed poke about at the peep shows, watching the
girls lying flat, the black stockings and garter belt, thin
slits of heels puffing out their thighs, legs spread as
some unknown man puts himself on top of them. In
the magazines the girls had pimples and bruises, great
strawberry marks or jagged black, blue, and purple
marks stretching across their thighs and buttocks.

At fourteen and fifteen her forays had been erudite,
circumspect, browsing, browsing in art stores, bookstores, the photos so proper, so artistic, so prurient, and
she didn't even know that it was giving her pleasure to
look at them, she just felt compelled to. She hadn't
even known that the bodies excited her; art books and
paintings, she would stare endlessly at them. There
would be guilt and her heart would be beating so fast
and somehow she knew that it would be something she
should be confessing to the priest about, but she refused, she would not share it and didn't remember the
feeling until viewing Seth's private photographic collection.

One day, walking on Forty-second Street, she saw a
sign pasted to a window on a peep-show storefront.
"Hi, fellows, I'm Jody the original life-size inflatable
doll," it said. "I was molded right down to the last
detail by a famous sculptor. I'm lifelike in every detail.
My body is formed from soft smooth flesh like vinyl
that has humanlike features and feels like the body
you'll love to touch. I'm a playmate for the modern
playboy, soft, pliable fleshlike feel. I'm five feet four

inches tall, 37, 24, 36 measurements, and flexible. Can I be your living companion? I'll live in your home, travel in your car and even swim with you. I float. By actual test my skin is three times thicker, heavier, and more durable than any doll on the market. For the ultimate enjoyment of me, order the complete set of interesting accessories, including wig, bikini, etc. Inflatable breasts to cuddle up to in the evening, inflatable buttocks, with skin three times thicker, heavier and more lifelike than any doll on the market."

The doll was in the window when Mary Catherine saw it. It was only $9.95 and was wearing a peek-a-boo negligee. It came with two wigs, a blond and brunette.

Tht same morning, riding into the city on a train, she clipped out a story from *The New York Times* to show Seth.

MAN SHOT IN 42ND ST. MOVIE THEATER

A patron in a Times Square movie was wounded, apparently accidentally, by a ricocheting bullet from a gun reportedly fired by a man sitting behind him, the police said.

Arsenio Campomanes, Jr., 41 years old, was shot in the Harem Theater, at 249 West 42nd Street. The bullet went through his upper back and throat. He was in fair condition late yesterday in Polyclinic Hospital. Papers found on his person indicate that he lives at University Hospital in Saskatoon, Saskatchewan, Canada, the police said.

The police searched the 30 patrons in the theater and said they found a two-shot derringer pistol, with oue bullet expended, in the possession of Jacob Fensterszaub, 25, a waiter, of 888 Montgomery Street, Brooklyn. Mr. Fensterszaub, who was arrested, apparently had been playing with the gun when it fired, the police said.

"What was he doing playing with that gun," Mary Catherine asked Seth later that night. "Poor Mr. Campomanes will never indulge himself again. God punished him. But what was that other man doing playing with a gun?"

"You're a dirty girl," Seth said.

No I'm not, she thought. He doesn't understand that it was catching-up time for her. Devil-in-the-flesh time for her.

He said he would take her to a strip joint. She had never seen a striptease.

Malcolm, on the other hand, always called at the last minute, or never called when he said he would.

Rub-a-dub-dub, two men in a tub—she had two men and many more, and none of them, not one of them was hers. None of them, even Malcolm for whom she had all the symptoms straight out of the pulp magazines, the knots in her stomach, the visceral response to his voice on the telephone, his handwriting, none of them touched her. Something had happened to the feeling machine. She could see Malcolm in the afternoon, and if in the evening Seth would absentmindedly put his hand on her breast, in seconds she was aroused, in seconds she could be supine and mounted.

How, tell me how I can be faithful ever again, she thought, when if a man brushes up against me in the subway my nipple stretches out to him.

How, tell me how I can be loyal to one when another rubs my nipple ever so gently protruding out of a black jersey dress I have worn with nothing underneath because truly, even though I am not attracted, I want him to want me. All of them, those men out there dancing on their phalluses, supporting their weight on the stilts of those cocks.

She couldn't believe now that up until a year or so ago she had only known one man in her life. The nuns had said, of course, that not only was sleeping with men you weren't married to putting yourself in "the occasion of sin" but having unmarried sex was a mortal sin because it was fornication. So anything that seemed even likely to lead up to screwing was a mortal sin because you were putting yourself in danger.

She thought now of how she had bought a lot of that when she was young, how in a way the whole ritual and structure had given her some comfort, even though intellectually she had seen the loopholes. It had all made sense until she started going out with boys. Nobody had told her what to do with those feelings when they came near her. Because even if she had done anything that would slightly indicate it was leading up to sex, in confession she had to say "the Act of Contrition sincerely to be forgiven." And that last sentence, "I firmly resolve with that help of thy grace to sin no more and to avoid the near occasion of sin." That was the rub. That near occasion.

There had always been some conjecture about actually how far you could go with a boy before it was considered a mortal sin. Different priests had different theories, and Mary Catherine had to shop around for one who wasn't too strict. Her mother, unknowing, would always want to stick her with Father Feeney since he was comforting and gave her succor, but Mary Catherine had heard about another priest on the other side of town who wouldn't interpret French kissing as a mortal sin. She figured out a way to get there.

Of course, now later in the after-Carlo years she realized that none of that meant anything anymore. The thing she kept thinking about was that she had discovered her own body and was trying hard to be responsible to it in her way.

Malcolm was so elusive with her that she became obsessive in trying to harness time and energy with him. She was drawn to him, yet always knowing that he was giving her nothing. As far as understanding the dynamics of it, she was one step ahead of herself, yet plunged headlong where she knew she shouldn't be in the first place.

She never felt secure with him. It was all right while they were in bed, touching, there was some kind of connection, but after, dressed, talking became stilted. Men do that, she thought. Initiate the postcoital *tristesse*. A woman could let a minute last forever, could make love forever, could be admired forever. With Malcolm a minute never lasted more than a minute.

Yet she moved with ease in and out of the outrageous with him. One night they stayed overnight in a hotel off Sixth Avenue. There were no towels in the bathroom and paper in the tub to step on when you took a shower. They fastened the double lock on the door.

He liked to smoke pot when they went to bed. Mary Catherine, cool in her role as libertine, smoked with him even though it made her want to throw up. They got into the big bed and played the name game. It was a game they had invented after nights of making love in hotel rooms with television sets in them. Black and white sets, color sets, it didn't matter.

"Allen Jenkins."

"Very good."

She would listen again, eyes closed, and guess whose voice it was in the late-night movie. This was a hard one.

"Walter Abel."

"Fantastic," and he would lean down and kiss her,

the smooth sweet smell of pot moving into the room. Mary Catherine, challenged by the game, always beat him; even though he was older and had seen more films, her ear was better.

"This is easy, she's unmistakable."

"Claire Trevor."

"Sheldon Leonard."

"Eugene Pallette."

"Ann Dvorak."

"How on earth can anyone in his right mind remember the sound of Ann Dvorak's voice."

"I just do. The movies were my life. I used to go to two, three in a day."

"You'll never in a million years be able to get this one."

"I give up. Wait. I know, I know, Lynne Overman. He was in *Northwest Passage* with Robert Preston and Preston Foster. They were always together in films and Paulette Goddard, who was beautiful, was the girl."

"Mary, you're just a lot older than I am, that's all it is."

He put a leg over hers. The toes were cold. It was not a spontaneous gesture, but one designated to stimulate intimacy. The marijuana had loosened him. He was more affectionate when he was smoking, she noticed, but a leg over hers, an embrace, even a kiss on the bottom lip often tight against his gum would be tentative. Malcolm's lovemaking was always tentative, as though there was a train to catch, people to see, a life to be lived, somewhere else.

She had called Francie that night, lying in bed, the sheet draped chastely around her. Malcolm was watching her. And as she said motherly things into the phone, her feeling, her immersion in her child showing, his features softened.

She hung up, assured everything was well, and said

to him, after a long look, "You are warmed when you see me in a different role, aren't you? You see me not as this lady, this sex lady in bed with you, but as a mother. Another Mary Catherine."

She got up, went into the bathroom, and put some of his toothpaste on her finger and rubbed her teeth and gums. She looked in the mirror. It was just after, and, like pictures taken when she was twenty, shiny she was, like Garbo and Dietrich in Karsh or Steichen pictures where the light just catches the white of the eye. Bright, wet. And her skin shone beneath the surface, and the look was one of power. There was no mistaking it. Power, imperious, winning. The completions had made her important. The finish, the so many finishes had granted her the queendom. Queendom for a day. If that.

Still, her state of being in heat was a source of delight to her, she was involved in her own sensuality. Here I am, over forty with half my life over, and I am in heat, she would think. She somehow had learned how to live only with the person with whom she was at that moment. Among the rules she had set for herself was never to let a thought of another's odor or touch enter her head.

Malcolm's wife was away Thursday, so he asked her to a performance of the *Saint Matthew Passion* at the Park Avenue Church. They had been sitting in the back on bridge chairs because they had come late. The man next to her kept looking at her. He knew the music better than she did, she could tell, bobbing his head, taking off his glasses, staring at the large chandeliers hanging from the ceiling. Malcolm was sitting at her right and she was flirting with the man on her left.

He had on a checked jacket and a brown turtleneck sweater, and kept taking his glances on and off to read the text. When they were off he would look at her legs.

She wanted to go home with him, touch his hair.

She liked it better when the soloists did not sing. The full chorus filled the nave of the church.

He took an old theater ticket out of his breast pocket and looked at it. Then at her.

She licked her lips. Malcolm was barely noticing. He was conducting the score.

The man did not take his eyes off her legs. *"Befiehl du dreine Weh,"* the chorus sang, *"Und was dein Herze Krankt, Der allertreusten Pflege Des der den Hummel lenkt; Der Wolken Luft in Wi den Gibt Hege, Luf un Behn, Der wird auch Wege finden, Da dein Fug gehen kann."*

If she were courageous, she would put her name and phone number on the program and pass it to him. But she wasn't that courageous.

She shut her eyes as the voices of the boys' choir (blond hair, red hair, bluejackets with emblems on the right breast, freckles and wide-open mouths) merged with the full chorus.

The man got up and stood at the back of her chair. She was very aware of him and somehow shared the music with him rather than with Malcolm.

She was having inappropriate thoughts. Are, after all, we women really whores, she thought. Is it in our natures to be true to the one we think is of our choosing when there are one, two, or three whose physical presence makes the palms grow moist, when all we want to do is smooth back a lock of hair, rub a broad back, take a hand and kiss it tenderly.

To put it more succinctly, am I indeed a whore or simply incapable of keeping my cunt out of my head, looking at an attractive man as, just that, someone who happens to have features that please me, a body, a walk, a fingernail that for God's sake for some reason excites me. The presence, of him, that other one, who

is always, by the way, an unattainable, who has a
string of ponies, a stable of forget-me-nots, and I,
knowing full well that I am so extraordinary, certainly
don't want to be part of a school of dolphins, but the
teacher, right?

And rationally I know that these ding-dongs or
whatever one calls these goodlooking creatures of the
hard on, cock of the head, cock on the walk, cock of
the cock type man, they are the ones who tempt me,
tempt me.

Am I unresurrectable, am I Sadie Thompson with a
red satin dress sashaying through life? Am I unable to
be true as Eleanor Parker was all dewy-eyed and faithful forever to Dennis Morgan in *The Very Thought of
You?*

Am I a wonderfully sexy broad, truly just a whore,
or in truth an immature little girl who cannot be true,
who cannot be true, be true, my dear, be true to you.

When the concert was over she was exhausted. They
both took off their glasses, the man and Mary Catherine, looked into each other's eyes, and Malcolm led
her down the stone steps onto the rain-soaked streets.

Chapter Twelve

Saturday morning, February 15, was bustling, almost
like Christmas in a way. Mary Catherine would meet
people she hadn't seen in a long while on Saturdays,
in the grocery, the bookstore, the cut-rate drugstore.
And the well-starched white-collared dark-jacketed
Black Muslims from the neighboring inner city would

be selling their newspaper on the street corners, careful never to offend, moving in and around casually clad suburbanites with a courteousness and civility, thinking God knows what. The newspaper cost a dollar. High school girls would laugh with them, break off into discussions about free lunch programs, then run off to the record store to buy the latest Carol King. Small-town, in a way. Good to know a lot of people, Mary Catherine thought, going into the bookstore. It was one of the best things about the town, she thought, Saturday mornings. In the winter it was a bond, a warming thing buttressing against the raw wind, that familiarity, that nodding and smiling at faces seen, faces not known, but each bringing with it its own frame of reference: from PTA meetings, political rallies, the library, people not indigenous to the fabric of her life, but comforting peripherally. In the summer they had on tennis clothes, or bathing suits, the people (covered now that they were older), with caftans over dimpled thighs or shifts slit up the sides, and it always took a long time to do the errands because, leaned up against a telephone pole or curved into a store window, she would stop and chat, get caught up on news that meant nothing but some kind of our-town continuity.

February was the worst suburban month of all, unless, like the lucky ones, one could escape, returning from the Bahamas or Puerto Rico with russet faces yellowing in the white winter air, peeling and scaly, flaky, drying from the gluttony of excessive suns. February was a naked month. Everything exposed. The trees, stripped, the pale pallor of skins washed out, dried out by steaming radiators, heart aching for some green, some kind of growing. February killed the spirit unless one was mighty inside, unless one had wells of summer stored up inside, unless one could be comforted by orange flames in the fireplace shooting hope

into the room. Getting through February, slogan of the
month for Mary Catherine.

A few years ago when the drug scene had been at
its height downtown, Saturday mornings were dreary,
the great American dream turned into a nightmare
right in front of everyone's eyes. Kids remembered
from Brownie meetings, cookie-baking in someone's
kitchen, little beige people with bows in their hair,
little brown caps with tiny points at the top, little
brown belts and white gloves in the Memorial Day
parade, glasses and two teeth missing and freckles and
little gold pins over the left breast pocket. Little brown
ribs pressed close in a hug, the little brown people had
turned into strangers.

String hair and army jackets, bumpy pimpled skins,
blank looks locked into blank look. Sitting in "pot
alley," a little miniature park next to the movie, they
would sit and eye the parent people on the sidewalk.
The Brownies would hang on to some skinny olive
drab arm, excited, talking loud, or, silent, stare out
into the street. You could see the pushers then, anyone could tell who they were, but the police had to
catch them in the act to make an arrest, and the underground, the subculture, had turned Main Street into an
armed camp. The Brownies were druggies and they
were angry, those kids in the alley, hostile sullen stealing pitiful sick. Our town had become their town for a
year or two then, and Saturday morning had become
the marketplace, the buying and selling place, and no
once could do anything about it.

But today they were gone for the most part. Seeking solace elsewhere; wine was cheaper, with less hassl-
ing, pills easier to get, peace of mind available with
meditation, ontology, a guru who would dispense the
knowledge that would give meaning to it all. In the
city the Hare Krishna children sold incense, stopped

you respectfully, shaved heads gleaming, in the suburbs the children tried in their own way to make sense
out of the plenty and the privilege and their place in it.

As Mary Catherine swung the car around the Revo-
lutionary War statue presiding in the center of town,
she saw Joey walking, as he always did, a bit into the
road, a bit on the sidewalk. He had turned gray overnight, Mary Catherine thought, slowing down her
orange Datsun so she could squint through the sun-
studded windshield at him.

Joey was the town drunk. An anachronism perhaps,
a town drunk in a town where most people drank too
much; at parties, on the 5:13, at the restaurants and
bars, at the station where the men poured off the train
like gin gurgling out of a bottle. The drinking was
standard operating procedure. Joey was the bottom of
the bottle, the Bowery bum in the middle of all the
chic understated affluence, and no one paid much attention to him.

He used to frighten the children until they got used
to him. Like some giant Lenny he lumbered through
town, always, walking, always shaggy, dressed in whatever he could find. He had been a gardener, people
said, and lived with a maiden aunt who gave him
money for liquor. Periodically, when the spring began
and lawns needed liming and bulbs planted, some land-
scape gardener would give him a half day's work here
and there. And Mary Catherine would see him, here
and there, hunched over someone's greenery.

In the seven years she had lived in the town, Mary
Catherine had never once gone up to him and said a
kind word. She felt badly about that. When Francie
was ten, she had come home, shaken, because Joey,
looking like some Abominable Snowman, had leered
at her and then shouted at her unintelligibly at the
candy store. She wanted to say something to someone,

but knew deep down that he was harmless. He couldn't do the social amenities. That's all. He scared the children but never hurt them, so there was a tacit agreement between him and the town; we will leave you alone and you will remain lonely.

But Mary Catherine couldn't bear his loneliness, especially in winter when he walked the icy streets, some threadbare thing wrapped around him, his hands looking like bricks.

She was exhausted. Trying to find a parking place on Saturday had been like being in the middle of the roller derby. You just kept going around and around because, like suburban musical chairs, people played the Saturday game, waiting, hovering, ready to pounce on a spare parking place.

Driving home, she swerved into the driveway, thinking that she had better fill up those potholes before Aunt Eleanora came for Deborah's party next week. She understood her aunt's point, though, it would be so easy just to let things go when there was no one there to nag about taking care of it.

Bringing her packages into the house, she fixed the door so it would remain open.

"Francie, please help me with this stuff."

"Mother, you won't believe it, you just won't believe it."

Francie was on the phone, her hand cupping the receiver. At sixteen she was taller than her mother, "well developed," as her grandmother said. Unlike either her mother or father she was very blond, even-featured, with long straight hair and brown eyes. She looked more Nordic than the Irish-Italian in her blood.

"Now what."

"It did it again. The septic tank. It is so disgusting and revolting down there you will die. It's gross, just gross. I'm calling the guy now."

Last year the septic tank had overflowed into the basement and it was one of the least attractive days of Mary Catherine's life.

"Mother, you talk to him."

"Mrs. Romano, this is Bill."

"How could that happen again, Bill?"

"We cleaned it out just six months ago."

"I know, can you come over right now?"

"Well, I've got a few other jobs to do."

"Bill, we can't live with this now."

"Well, late this afternoon. Listen, don't flush any toilets."

She hung up. "That's all we needed."

"I'm going to throw up."

"Stop it, they'll fix it."

"How come nobody else's tank overflows?"

"Of course they do. It's not the thing they talk about in the cafeteria at school. Help me with the groceries please."

"I'm running off to Hilda's."

"We were supposed to go shopping today."

"Right. I'll be home in an hour and we'll go. What are you going to do about the shit man? How on earth can someone make his living that way?"

"I guess someone has to do it. God, what a lifetime profession. Francie, help me with the groceries."

"You have a habit of repeating yourself."

"Because I don't see any movement, any action, any indication that you heard me, and are in any way thinking of clearing out the back seat of the car."

"O.K., O.K., I'm going."

They put the groceries away. They had a deal that Francie never had to wrap the meat. She couldn't bear looking at raw meat. She had been a vegetarian for about three months once and still periodically went on meatless diets, but it was mainly the way it looked that got to her, the blood on the packages, the moist slithery texture upset her. Standing there in the kitchen, the two of them, putting away lettuce, yogurt, cheese, fruit, very few sweets (they both watched their weight carefully but often met at the refrigerator late at night after good-nights and lights had already been turned out). They had similar habits. Looking over at her daughter as she was piling tuna fish and salmon in the cupboard, Mary Catherine got a rush of feeling. She brought over the wax paper and silver foil to put in the drawer next to the cupboard and put her arms around Francie. Her hair smelled like babies; her cheek was warm.

"I love you."

"Me too, Mom. I'll see you in an hour. Good luck with the turds."

"Honestly."

Francie spent most of her time alone, or with Hilda, her best friend. They had been friends since the Romanos moved to town, and were both bookworms, loving to spend a Saturday curled up in either one of their living rooms or bedrooms, listening to music and reading. They had tried pot together, talked endlessly into the night together about sex, cried together when both their parents' marriages split up. That probably was the greatest bond of all. They were both only children, and they had both seen their fathers leave.

Yet, Francie knew and Hilda agreed, that as much as they'd missed them, things were better with their fathers gone. Sometimes Francie missed Carlo so badly she would stay in her room writing poem after poem to him, letter after letter. She never mailed them, never showed anybody the poems. But they reminded her how she felt, when she would take them out and reread them. She knew it was better now that he was gone; no more shouting, no more 3 A.M. tears, or 4

A.M. door slams when her father would zoom out of
the driveway going God knows where.

One good thing, if it was a good thing at all, was
that she wasn't alone. Half her class had divorced
parents. It was a congenital suburban symptom, and
although she was resigned to it now, she would never
get used to it.

She would never get married. Ever. Well, maybe if
she was dying to have a child, but she didn't even think
she wanted one at this point. It was hard to tell. At any
rate, the divorce had brought her closer to her mother,
with Aunt Eleanora always hovering in the background.
Francie—when she was in the fifth grade she had written the teacher a long letter begging her to call her by
her rightful name. "Francesca is the proud Italian
name my father gave me and I would like to be called
that, please." So that teacher did, but everyone else
insisted on calling her Francie and it stuck. Her mother
lovingly dwelled on "Francesca," since Mary Catherine
loved the name. "Francesca Romano, you will be an
opera singer, you will debut at the Met with that beautiful name, or you'll run a restaurant on Mulberry
Street, one or the other," her mother would laugh, hug-
ging her.

Her mother hugged her a lot. Even now when she
was sixteen, Mary Catherine would come in and lie
down with her and rub her back the way she did when
she was a little girl. Then it would always be preceded
by a story. She loved it when her mother read lying
there next to her. *Alice in Wonderland* when she was
little, Bible stories sometimes, and as she got older,
sonnets by Edna St. Vincent Millay. She never understood them very well, but loved the sounds of the
words. She had gotten the habit of writing poetry from
Mary Catherine, who herself took solace in pouring her
feelings out on paper in poems. She couldn't ever think

of times when her mother wasn't very busy, but always sensed a kind of loneliness about her. When she was younger she would come into her mother's office every day after school and Mary Catherine would give her money for ice cream and they would talk for a while. Mary Catherine would stay late often at the office, and somehow Francie knew it was just to keep on having someone to talk to there. The year before the divorce her mother and father never did anything together, and Carlo, gruff, awkward in his bear hugs, his evenings spent on the telephone or going out to town meetings, seemed to move further and further away from Francie.

She loved her mother, worried about her, and swore that when she grew up she would never be like her. Since the divorce she could always tell if she had a man, somewhere. Her mother never had to say a word. She would never be like that. When there was someone someplace who loved her or made her think that he loved her and cared about her, Mary Catherine could be light and funny, capable of rushing into her room like a teen-ager herself and tackling her down on her bed, plastering kisses all over her. When there was no one, when the phone was silent, when the house had no sound, she knew, Francie did, that the man or men, whoever they were, had gone away or didn't care anymore. It was as simple as that. No man, no spirit. No man, no full-time mother. Mary Catherine would put in the time then; Francie would call her on it.

"Your heart certainly wasn't in this meal," she would say, tasting the drab undercooked chicken Mary Catherine had thrown together for dinner.

"No, my love, it wasn't. I'm miserable."

"What is it this time?"

"Francie dear. I'm sure you don't want to hear the whole boring story. Suffice it to say I can't stand the silence in this house. Except for your calls and your kids, this house is a morgue. I want lights, camera, action. I want adventure."

"Do you want me to go to a movie with you?"

"What a love you are. Have you finished your homework?"

"I only have a little more to do. What's for dessert?"

They had sat there, the two of them, with candlelight, the good dishes, since Aunt Eleanora made such a fuss about the necessity of their not getting to be slobs. They were two girls together, two ladies coping, each in her way.

Francie's grades had fallen drastically the year before the divorce; she had smoked at lot of pot, started hanging out with girls she didn't really even like. She had to do something, the tension in the house was awful and it just seemed that all anyone ever did was drink, deep into the night.

Finally, after her father moved out, Mary Catherine had become her old self again, spending time with her, going shopping, taking her to lunch on Saturdays. How she loved that.

During one of those elegant lunches Francie admitted that it was best that Carlo moved out. But, she had added wistfully, "I still love the thought of having two parents who once maybe really loved each other."

Chapter Thirteen

The phone rang.

"I'd like to suck your cunt."

"Mom, it's for you."

Francie had decided not to take him seriously any-more; the breather with music in the background had turned into the obscene caller and Francie was not to be intimidated.

Mary Catherine, unsuspecting, picked up the phone and he went at it, his usual spiel. Clarence, as they had dubbed him, started in about how many things she could do to make him get a hard on. Mary Catherine hung up and wrote down "1:30 P.M. Saturday" on a page by the phone.

"Very funny."

"Did you call the phone company?"

"Three times. The woman said to continue keeping a log on what times he calls, and if it keeps up they will change our number and we can have a free unlisted number."

"So why don't we do that?"

"Because I keep thinking he will go away and we can avoid the inconvenience. He gets me so mad I could kill him. Now he really has been tapering off. The last notation here is a month ago, but look, again on a Saturday afternoon."

"I guess he's got other customers during the week. Mother, I'm nervous about him, though he always calls when he's sure you're home. I'll bet it's someone we know."

"That doesn't speak very well for the class of people in our acquaintanceship."

"Well, I've got to go. I'll see you in an hour."

Mary Catherine went to the cellar door. The odor of feces was strong. She went upstairs, put on a pair of jeans and a shirt, some heavy boots, old leather gloves, and went to the basement to confront the mess.

They were floating in the basement. The turds. And the odor made her gag. It was stale and fetid and she worried about the clothes in the washing machine. She put the kerchief she had brought over her face and, wrapping them in newspaper, started putting them in a pail. If she didn't, she was convinced they'd all die of bubonic plague or something. It seemed to her at that moment it would have been nice to have a man around the house, as they say. But she had to admit she didn't know a man in the world who would go around picking up turds in the basement anyway. She wanted to die on the spot. But she didn't and cleaned out some of the excrement as best she could. Going upstairs, she ran for the back door and went outside to breathe, taking the homegrown fertilizer and putting it on a hardened flower bed hiding under winter's cover.

While she was in the bathroom washing her hands, now wearing a long hostess gown so she would feel female again, she heard a car pull into the driveway.

Looking out the window she saw a sleek Cadillac. Yellow. And out stepped Central Casting's least likely applicant for the septic tank job.

"Mrs. Romano." He tapped on the back door.

"Come in."

"Good afternoon, I'm Ralph Frate, from Official Septic Tanks."

"Where's Bill?"

"This really sounds more serious than just an overflow since you were cleaned out so recently, so he asked me to come look it over."

He handed her a card—Ralph Frate, Supervisor, Vice-President.

Wow! What service.

Ralph wore black suede shoes. He had a star sapphire on his pinkie and pomade on his hair. He had a shirt and a tie and a tiepin. His septic tank suit.

"Would you like some coffee?"

"Love it," he agreed readily, "two lumps, no cream, please. Now, while that's heating, do you have a spade?"

"A what?"

"A spade, a shovel. I have to go in the backyard and see where the blockage is and find out if you have enough leaching fields."

"You wouldn't like to see the basement, would you?"

Why should she be the only one who should suffer. After all, it was his business.

"Do you mind if I ask a question?"

"Shoot."

"You don't look like someone in septic tanks."

"People always say that. I was the accountant for the firm and saw that they needed overhauling, so that's what I did. The trick is to give as personal service as you can. I'll be right back."

He returned in a few minutes, a look of concern in his eyes.

"This may be a big job. A very big job. That's gushing like crazy. I think there's some blockage in the line somewhere. We can fix it for you temporarily, but in order to do a total job, to make sure it won't happen again, we may have to dig up the whole backyard and put more leaching fields in to make it drain."

"You're kidding."

"I'm not kidding, Mrs. Romano. That's what it sounded like when Bill got the call in the office."

"What does something like that cost?"

"Well, wait, I haven't told you everything. The other possibility is that the septic tank itself is cracked. How old is it?"

"I have no idea. I never knew I even had it until the shit hit the fan, so to speak."

Mr. Frate's face showed disdain.

"Well, the other possibility is that it's cracked and, if that's the case, you'll have to get a new one, which would run you maybe one or two thousand dollars."

She started looking at Ralph Frate with more respect. No wonder he was putting the company back on its feet.

"When will I find out about all this?"

"Well, we'll know better by Monday morning, to see if it holds after the men come. They should be here very soon. Look, on the other hand, it just may be a blockage and they can fix that with a snake."

"A what?"

She wasn't too up on the vernacular. "When does your husband get home?"

"He's away on a trip, and he's certainly not going to like the one- or two-thousand-dollar misunderstanding."

"Well, let's just hope for the best. I'll be over bright and early Monday morning to check on it. Then we'll certainly know better."

"Mr. Frate."

"Yes."

"Do you think it would be possible for your men when they come to sort of clean up the basement? I tried to do a little but I'm sure I didn't do enough and I'm afraid of the health hazard. Is that part of your service? Would they do that?"

A sweetness, a lilt to her tone.

"Well, it really isn't part of our regular service, frankly. But I'll leave a note for them to do it. It may cost you extra."

"That's all right. I just don't like the idea of them there, you know what I mean."

"Of course," he said, solicitous. "Well, thank you for the coffee. And I'll see you Monday. Bright and early. Good luck."

I'll need it, she thought as he drove off. Who needs this. I don't, that's for sure.

"So what happened, Mother?"

Francie walked in the door, carrying three Cat Stevens albums, a bag of oranges, her guitar, and a book on suicide.

"What are you reading?"

"Suicide. Hilda lent it to me. He tried it himself, you know."

"Who?"

"Alvarez. There's a whole thing all about Sylvia Plath in there—how he knew her in London and feels so badly because he didn't do enough to help her."

She took an apple out of the refrigerator.

"How come you have your guitar?"

"Hilda had borrowed it. I'm giving her lessons."

"How's she doing?"

"Mother, what did the guy say about the septic tank?"

"Well, you missed it. He stepped out of the pages of *Esquire* or *Playboy*. He was snazzy as anything and seemed to know his business, using terms like leaching and snake it out and everything. I refuse to worry about it till I know for sure it's going to cost one thousand dollars."

"You're kidding."

"I don't kid about shit."

"Mother, what did he say?'

"It's not worth going into. Suffice it to say they'll un-block it or block it or whatever he was saying. I really didn't understand a word and we'll know by Monday. But I've got too much else on my mind to worry about something I'm not sure I have to worry about yet. So. Let me get some clothes on and we'll go."

"O.K., hurry. I'm having dinner at Hilda's. They're having roast beef and Yorkshire pudding. Her mother's having company and invited me."

"O.K., good. I'm glad you told me so I won't take anything out of the freezer."

"What are you doing tonight, Mother?"

"Home. I'm home tonight."

"I'll stay if you like."

"Francesca, don't be ridiculous. I don't mind at all."

"Well, why don't you call up Deborah? She looks awful these days. I saw her downtown at the cheese store yesterday and she looks like death warmed over."

"That is a ridiculous expression."

"What's the matter with her, Mother?"

"She's lonely and she drinks. That's it in a nutshell."

"God. I'm never going to touch a drop when I grow up, not one single drop. You're a different person since you stopped drinking. Do you think she's right to marry Sam? Doesn't her drinking bother him?"

Mary Catherine looked at Francie. Thank God, thank God I got myself together.

"I'll run upstairs and change and be right down."

Within minutes Mary Catherine had put on a skirt and sweater, combed her hair, put some makeup on, and they were off. Francie needed a dress for Deborah's party next Saturday night and the wedding, if it ever came off.

Mary Catherine loved to go shopping with Francie. She had loved it when she was little, like playing with dolls it was, buying little pinafores and patent-leather shoes, winter coats and bonnet hats, ribbons in her hair. She had loved the smell of her, the feel of her. She loved to touch her when she was a little girl and still did. She realized now that all that affection, all that warmth in her that Carlo could never accept or tap, had gone into so many other places.

After going to three stores and finding nothing, they ended up at one featuring Indian and Afghanistan dresses. Everyone was wearing them and Mary Catherine was getting a little tired of them, but Francie looked lovely in a soft coral cotton.

In the tiny dressing room Mary Catherine collapsed onto a small stool in the corner as Francie took off her clothes and put them on her lap.

She looked at her daughter in the three-way mirror. She never wore a brassiere. There was a long line of down on her back from her neck to her buttocks, and her breasts, full, womanly, were reflected in the glass. That woman there trying on a coral cotton dress came out of me, Mary Catherine thought. That woman, her body so sweet, so painful to see, came out of my body. Awesome. It was too much to think about. That beauty whose white long neck will be kissed and caressed by some man someday is my daughter. Almost, almost a woman.

They bought the dress and Mary Catherine drove Francie to Hilda's.

The house was a very quiet one to come home to.

Chapter Fourteen

A week before her party, two weeks before her wedding, Deborah was sitting at her desk, surrounded by a stack of envelopes. She had twisted her hair into a bun on top of her head, the blond halo the result of a nervous habit she had had for years. She was typing laboriously.

"I have gotten ten answers to my ad," she wrote to herself. "Ten people want to be my pen pal, my mail friend, my envelope lover. I am sitting here in my room and there are one, two cups of old coffee, one wineglass with a little vodka left in it, and one old-fashioned glass with a lot of vodka in it that I am still drinking. There is one bowl with the remains of some coleslaw in it, and another has orange peel in it. That is the kind of diet-type dinner—coleslaw and oranges —I have, and a few hours before that I had a phallic kosher hot dog dipped in elegant french mustard, Dijon it was. That's how I try to keep thin and it's not easy, believe me, but round and round I am in my belly and everything else is so straight and narrow. Anyway which one, which one shall I answer of these ten potential pen pals?"

Despite the fact that Deborah was supposed to be getting married in two-weeks, she had put an ad in the personal column of *The Village Voice*. She wanted to meet someone, despite the fact that Sam had pressed for her decision ("I'm not waiting any longer, Deborah dear," that's what he called her all the time, "Debdear," like one word, like one thought). And indeed why not, why shouldn't she marry him; certainly no one else had asked her, and so what if he was only five feet four, weighed 225, was shaped like a penguin and always looked as though he were leaning backward. So what if he repeated "Debdear" after every other sentence, he wanted her. Like her father, Joshua Gold, used to when Deborah was a little girl, Sam liked to show her off. Her taste was still intact, as was her ability to put together "coordinates." Her mother used to call them that when she would take her to Altman's and Russek's, De Pinna and Best's and put together beige skirts with beige sweaters and an off-white kerchief tied with a Scotch pin smack in the middle of it, and downstairs in the shoe department the pumps would be a warm brown and at the stocking department on the first floor of any of the stores she would stock up on dark-brown hose. Just so everything matched, her mother had said. And the training had paid off; stacks of cashmeres with matching cardigans still lined her drawers, and even today she could somehow get herself some appropriate coordinates that made her look, if not ultra-chic, certainly contemporary. And Sam liked that. He liked the thick gold loops she wore clipped onto her ears, and chains and charms around her neck and T-shirts under silk blouses. And no matter how much she had had to drink, she could always think clearly enough to be coordinated. Sam liked that.

But she didn't like Sam.

And he was all she had. Friends had tried to fix her up with men after Abe left. Even her son Roger had introduced her to a father of one of his classmates. But something always seemed to go wrong. She had been to a Parents Without Partners meeting and found herself feeling sorry for everyone there, herself included.

There were twice as many, perhaps three times as many, women as men there, and most of them looked younger than she did. She had had to fortify herself with two straight shots before she went, so terrified was she of finding scores of Deborahs in one room, with scores of Deborah-type loneliness and malaise. But she had met Miriam Sloat there, who had been Roger's fourth-grade teacher. Miriam was very short, had an enormous bosom (Roger used to say that for music she would wear a blouse that had violins and clarinets all over it and when she conducted the class singing of "Greensleeves" the instruments skittered across her bosom like mice in a maze). But Miriam was an old hand at this and came every Friday night that she didn't have a date to a PWP open meeting. "The smaller groups are more interesting," she told Deborah. "Sometimes the discussions aren't bad, and it's a little more intimate."

"Have you ever met anyone?" Deborah blurted right out. The point of the whole thing.

"Oh, some really nice men. But no one special. Really. One man I liked a lot, but his large alimony payments kept him so broke we never went anywhere. I would have him to dinner a lot, and he used to take Jamie, my youngest, fishing on Sundays, but all of a sudden it occurred to me that I was settling, you know what I mean, Deborah, settling. I was brighter than he was and had more vitality, and God, I was bored. So we sort of petered out. He was a good decent man, had custody of his two kids, but he was so dull."

A tall man with thick glasses had whisked Miriam away from Deborah that time and she had stood alone, sixteen again and too tall for the boys, sixteen again waiting for someone to ask her to dance, sixteen again and nobody loves me, everybody hates me, I'm going to go eat worms, big fat juicy ones, little fat skinny ones . . . Idiotic. Her children weren't small, so she didn't need men to help take them swimming or skiing or to have a barbecue with or go to a ball game with. She didn't need all these partnerless parents for that. She needed them to talk to and to buy her a drink and talk about Turgenev with. She had stayed, though, that time, and listened to a psychologist talk about "Dating and how it affects the children." She felt like everyone's mother. She wished them all well. She really did. But she never went back.

Which brought her back to Sam. Which brought her back to her last-ditch do-or-die effort to meet someone new before she started playing house with Sam.

"Tall, ex-Jewish princess," she had written, "well read, 40 [she lied a little], adores the theater, divorced, attractive, would like to meet unattached man who is curious of mind, intelligent, and who like me has already sown his wild oats." She would not be cuckolded again. She wanted the impossible. The faithful man. The man who would be faithful to her. A man who would not fall apart at the sight of twenty-year-old breasts, or melt in a breathlessly uncontrolled response to Elizabeth Browning's "How Do I Love Thee?". And since last week she had received ten responses. Four physics professors, two from upstate New York, one from Indiana, and one from Roanoke, Virginia. They all said they liked music, the reflective life, and as far as they knew their oats had been sown. Each one sounded quite whole, respectable. There was a yearning of sorts in each answer, except for the flip ones, the sexual ones ("I am well hung, and at your disposal for dalliance, if that's what you're after," one writer had written, signing it "Jock," and another, who admitted from the outset that he was not unattached but he and his wife had a very liberated view of marriage and he was forty-two, said "despite a rather heavy intellectual overhead, I dig grass, acid occasionally, the Stones, Dylan, Leadbelly, good bars, dogs, jogging, and I am a very good lover, not unusually vigorous or anything, just good").

A sixty-seven-year-old man answered who wanted the "psychic affection of a beautiful woman," and a dentist who said he was vigorous and loved horses. Three answers were mimeographed. Deborah hadn't realized what a business this was. Some, she supposed, having been through this so many times, wanted to weed out the undesirables fast. One mimeographed pen pal who said he was forty-seven, and five feet six inches tall, explained his situation right out. "I am separated, no kids, and am paying fifty dollars a week to my wife under family court order. At present I have given up hope of obtaining a fair dissolution of my marriage from within the United States and am planning to eventually cut my wife off financially by moving to Europe, probably Denmark. . . ." He went into great detail in the mimeographed form sent out in response to God knows how many letters. He made himself perfectly clear and even went so far as to protect himself from further hurt by writing, "I could only make tentative marriage plans with somebody who could adjust to these circumstances. Because of this traumatic experience, I would only consider remarriage after joint psychiatric examination of the prospective bride and myself." Poor devil, he was worse off than she was.

The fifty-year-old six-footer who had never married wrote that he wanted a woman who had a "high degree of intellectual and personal integrity, was honest and sincere and would be willing to get out and exercise her dead butt on weekends," since he played a lot of tennis.

Deborah had felt so foolish in the first place putting

the ad in, and now as she contemplated answering one she felt even more peculiar. Yet somehow she was compelled to do it. How I wish I were in love, she thought. Is that childish, is that romantic adolescence? I wish I were in love. I wish it would rain. Then there would be sounds at the window, sounds in the streets, cars splashing crashing through puddles, sounds against the pane, gray sounds, even rhythms. I wish it would rain.

There are no children in this house, there are no steps on the stairs and no music, no Cat Stevens and no Bob Dylan. No sound, as a matter of fact. A pump goes on in the cellar mysteriously or the furnace, dormant, suddenly swooshes on its own sound, pushing heat into the radiators. Or a dog barks. Or there is a laugh from next door. Maybe a telephone. Maybe a telephone should ring, no one in particular. The sound jarring to the walls. I will not turn on the television or radio. I will confront it, the silence this Sunday, silent Sunday. She could call someone, she could get invited, get on a train, sit in a hotel lobby, join a singles club, smile at someone's husband. Marry Sam. Yes she could do that too.

Or, she thought, sipping the last drop of vodka out of her glass, or, she could answer one of these letters and maybe he would come along, the man I love, and he'll be big and strong, the man I love. Maybe Monday, maybe Tuesday. Maybe never.

So she answered the only one who sounded as though he had a sense of humor. "I am very physically appealing," he wrote, "slim, dark, six feet, forty but look mid-thirties, better than just goodlooking. Responsive to Woody Allen and Mel Brooks. As far as sensuality is concerned, I'm very big on palm and toe kissing. Curiosity, after reading your ad, all-consuming. Virtues other than what you ask for: humility. Defects fully

NOBODY MAKES ME CRY

admitted: sloppy penmanship." That was for sure, since she could barely read his note.

So she called him up at the number he had included in the letter and they made a lunch date for the next day. Just like that. It wasn't hard. He seemed very much at ease. As though he'd been through this kind of thing many times before.

As arranged, he met her at the browsing book corner of the Museum of Modern Art. She came in, a bit breathless, and saw no one to fit the description he had given himself.

She saw a young man standing by the cashier. Blue jeans, open-necked blue-patterned shirt, a leather jacket with wide lapels and leather buttons. Instinctively she knew it was he. Let him come over to me, she thought, picking up a book on Paul Klee. Perhaps I don't fit the description I gave him about myself. "Blond hair, a beige coat. Good legs."

"Yes, you do have good legs," he said, coming over to her.

"You're taking a chance. I could have been someone else and not me," she said.

"True, but I knew you were the voice on the phone. But you're older. I pictured you as looking younger."

Thanks. Off to a flying start.

They walked out of the museum past the man selling chestnuts, past the pretzel man, and moved up toward Fifth Avenue.

"It's nice to meet you."

"Me too."

She knew immediately this was a false alarm. But would sit through the lunch. Pass the hour.

He found a small Italian restaurant on Fifty-third Street off Lexington Avenue and guided her in. He didn't look all that young for his age, she thought.

He didn't order a drink. She had determined not to

have anything but settled on a glass of wine. She ordered a chef's salad and he a bowl of spaghetti.

"You're attractive," he said.

"Thank you."

"I've never been to bed with a woman older than I. They are always younger."

My, he gets right to it.

"How old are you?" she asked.

"Forty. When I was thirty-nine I almost had a breakdown."

She picked at the swiss cheese lying neatly sliced in the middle of the plate.

"What happened?"

"I was going to be forty."

"But it happens to a lot of us.'

"I know. But I had always been so young. When I was in my twenties and thirties I was invincible. I felt I would never get old. And six months before I turned forty I started getting this panic."

"What kind of panic?"

"I would be sitting in my office and suddenly would be afflicted with every symptom of disease."

"And what happened?"

"I developed a hypochondria that paralyzed me. I was at the doctor's all the time. I called him up at all hours. I would break out into a sweat every time I thought about it. I thought I was going crazy."

"So what happened?"

"Finally the doctor sent me to a psychiatrist, and I've been with her for a year. I seem to talk more easily to women." He kept looking at her hands.

"Has it helped?" She noticed he was hardly eating, picking at his food.

"I don't know. I don't think so. Maybe. I don't know. I do have certain complexes."

The waitress, perky in maroon boots and short skirt, brought the coffees.

"I have this rape thing."

Deborah looked at her watch. She had known him twenty minutes.

"Yes, I like to feel I'm raping a woman. Not violent or bloody or anything, but taking her by force. And in with that are the hands. Hands really turn me on. You know, especially the hands over the mouth. You see, I like it done to me too. I like to make a pact with a woman. And with the pact and the fantasy, it all has to be justified, plausible, the rape, that's very important."

"I see."

"My wife and I had it worked out this way for a while, until she felt that she was just an object, she stopped getting a kick out of it. But it's exciting. I like it that way."

"I see."

"Hands. Hands are very important. They are very sexual. Don't you think so?"

"Well, I never thought much about hands."

"I really like to kiss hands."

"What about loving. Loving in sex?" She had to ask it.

"Well, sex has to do with lust and affection. The rape is the lust part, I suppose, the affection comes later, or before. It's a power thing. I like to overpower and then be overpowered. What about you?"

"I don't think of it that way. I must admit the rape thing leaves very little room for participating for a woman, or fun if she's busy fighting you off."

"I think one of the reasons I can talk to women about this and not to men is because it's titillating. But I do find that I hang around a lot with separated men these days and we commiserate, why the marriages are breaking up, and you know what? In almost every case, including mine, it's the wife that has outgrown the husband. It's the wife who wants more, and the men are paralyzed, they don't know what hit them."

"Do you think you could ever get back with your wife?"

"No. She still needs things from me, my literary interests, my passion for films. Funny, that's just the thing that attracted her to me in the first place and it's the thing that broke us up."

"What do you mean?" Deborah ordered another glass of wine and poured more oil and vinegar on her salad.

"I would come home from work and want to watch television. Watch the Knicks. I'm obsessive. I've learned to my chagrin that I'm an obsessive personality. I would be a voyeur in that sense, watch the Knicks, and if they'd lose, not be depressed for two hours but maybe two days. Things like that. The hypochondria, the rape, the Knicks. She just couldn't take it anymore."

"I see. Could I have more coffee, please?"

"What happened with you and your husband?"

Not worth the effort.

"We just never should have married. I really think that was it more than anything."

"I've never gone to bed with anyone my own age, always younger. It's like going to bed with your mother. But even though you're over forty, you still have a sexual quality about you. I can tell."

"Perhaps, but can I tell you something?"

"Sure. Would you like more coffee?"

"Yes, I would."

"What?"

"The rape thing really doesn't do anything for me."

"Well . . ."

"I mean, maybe in context or something. But frankly it's not my thing."

"Yes, of course, but still you wouldn't just write it off?"

"I'm afraid so."

"It's too bad, since we both like the theater so much."

"Yes."

She was smiling. So was he.

"So that means there's really nothing."

"I think so. This is a little awkward, isn't it?"

"Not really. I just like to make my position clear."

"Yes, I understand."

"Listen, hey, why don't you think about it?" he asked. "I'll leave it to you," he said, helping her on with her coat. "You call me if you want to see me again."

"All right.'

"We could go to the theater. I love to do that."

"Right. Thanks for lunch."

"You're easy to talk to."

"Thanks."

"I'm just learning how to talk to people and open up. It's taken such a long time. My wife used to always want to talk and I would walk out of the room. Like I did with my mother. My folks were monsters. What about yours?"

"Not bad."

"My father had high blood pressure and we were always afraid of upsetting him. I kept so much in."

"What about the rape thing?"

"I've had it since I was thirteen."

He paid the bill and led her out the door.

"Where are you going from here?'

"To the Third Avenue bus."

"I'll walk you."

His hand was limp around her waist.

When the bus came, he helped her up the high step.

"Well, you certainly do have good legs.'

She waved good-bye through the window.

Sitting on the bus, Deborah watched all the cowlicks in front of her. Cowlick. She thought how on earth did a bunch of hair standing straight up get that name. Lots of licking cows.

Is it possible, she thought, taking out her rouge, smoothing a bit under the eye and up the cheek, is it possible that Sam it is? Sam it will be; Sam who took her to Quo Vadis and dazzled her with red velvet walls and steak Diane; Sam who lived high up in a tower somewhere in medieval splendor in a penthouse in Fort Lee, New Jersey, because he got a tax benefit and "for just across the river I got the same view from the other side." Sam who got his money God knows how, investing in pornographic films, dropping the SEC into the conversation a lot, mutual funds, this deal, diamonds in South Africa, that deal, baseball teams in Texas. "Listen, Deborah," he would say, "I don't know why it's hard for you to understand this. You have a closing on this property there, and the government comes along and . . ." It was like that a lot. His wife had died, his children had grown up and gone, Deborah was fair in bed, drank a little too much, but he could handle her. Her father had good real estate contacts, and she was a high-class broad and that's what he liked the most. At fifty-five the twenty-year-olds meant nothing to him anymore, and Deborah, although a little distended in the belly, was tall and still had a good shape. He liked them tall. He liked it when she would put people like Vivaldi on the phonograph and read those books, books only for "vanillas." He would certainly never read that stuff, but he liked the fact that she did. She drank a little too much but she had class. That's why he wanted her.

After they had first met at Mary Catherine's Aunt

Eleanora's, he had courted her grandly: two dozen yellow roses, presents from Gucci and Pucci. And she loved it. Daddy all over again. But going to bed with him and listening to his business partners plan their million-dollar schemes, presiding as pseudo-hostess over his cocktail-time wheelings and dealings, all went against the grain. Once at one of the cocktail closings she had just taken the bottle into the bathroom after she did the necessary amenities and passed a little cheese around. They never missed her.

Well, she thought, Sam is the only way to get away from the Sunday silence. To escape the quiet house. Her father was tired of sending a check every time she got depressed or drank too much and called him on one emergency after another: a new furnace, a two-thousand-dollar landscaping bill, a whole new roof. He'd had it, and outside of her monthly allowance based on pre-divorce standard of living, he was a well run dry. No more money from that quarter. Have to look elsewhere. I'm certainly not going to make anything working in a bookstore and at this point that's about all I can do.

Which brought her back to Sam. Riding up Third Avenue, Deborah passed Bloomingdale's. She didn't have the stamina for that today. She didn't know where she was going. Somehow she had been convinced that her lunch date was going to solve all her problems, that this dashing college professor type who enjoyed the joys of kissing toes and the insides of hands would take her away from it all.

But of course he didn't. He went back to work and here she was left with the afternoon to kill, after lying to the store manager that she was too sick to come to work. Well, the first thing she would do was get a drink. At Seventy-ninth Street, in a flurry, so that she almost dropped her purse, she reached up and pulled

the rope for her stop. She tripped over the swelling
ankles of a tired-looking black woman, banged her
shoulder purse into the paunch of a sallow-faced man
carrying a briefcase, and stepped out of the bus.

She crossed over to Lexington, then Park, then to
Madison, and saw the modest spasms of fountains in
front of the Metropolitan shooting up. At least in
Europe the fountains are fountains, she thought, shooting their streams with gusto and elaborate geyser
bravado, but here, because of the water shortage or
something, the fountains were embarrassingly spastic.
Coitus interruptus.

The Stanhope Hotel was there waiting for her.

Sitting at the bar, she ordered a vodka on the rocks
from the waiter, who put some salted peanuts in front
of her. I try, I really do, she thought, but I get hung
up on expectations, that's what it is. All those lovers,
and yet when Abe came along I was sure it was forever
because that's the way it's supposed to be. Or was
supposed to be. I can't, she thought, I can't keep up
with the times. I try, but maybe Mary Catherine is
right when she says she can just see me in my room
when I was ten, all white-piqué-cotton canopy and
beautiful dolls sitting on the white satin pillow, and
the dressing table with a comb, brush, and mirror set
Joshua brought me back from Hong Kong. How did
she know? I denied it, she smiled into her drink, but
she was right. That's the way it was almost till I went
to college and that's the way I really always wanted it
to stay. I did so many grown-up things, screwed so
many men, got married, gave dinner parties, had kids,
but all I want to do is get back into that room with the
white-cotton ceiling wrapped in chintz and starch with
Joshua coming home with the paper under his arm. I
used to want to grow up so fast, wore lipstick and
stockings and put my hair up long before anyone else.

Why did I push it, for God's sake. Maybe it wouldn't be so bad with Sam, maybe she would have dinner with him tonight and put her head on his shoulder and bite his earlobe the way he liked, and maybe, just maybe, he would make everything all right. He had said something about Japan in the summer, and if she had stayed married to Abe for fifty years she never would have gotten to Japan, maybe it won't be so bad, maybe he'll lose weight, maybe he'll get taller, maybe I'll get younger, maybe I'll go back to school and get a Ph.D. in Chaucerian English, maybe I'll go get a facial.

Deborah got up a bit unsteadily, paid her bill, eyed the people sitting at the table eyeing her, and went to the phone. Sam wasn't in his office but she left a message with his secretary that she would meet him for dinner at seven at his office. She was able to get a facial appointment at Bendel's. This wasn't going to be such a rotten day after all.

Chapter Fifteen

Beautiful black girls all over the place, kneading and soothing Deborah. I am drowning in hot oils, she thought, in a moment I will sleep a deep sleep as the creams and textures and a variety of smells move in and around my eyes, on my throat, under my chin. A machine is swirling against my skin feeling like a frothy toothbrush and now myriads of lips are kissing me, sloppy suction kisses but kisses, and masks upon masks fall on my face, tingling, tightening, steaming. God, I can't breathe, this thing is over my face with

only two little holes punched out for my nostrils. I am
dying, I will die here in this dark room. "Ten minutes,
that's all, dear," and she taps the door shut silently and
the wet pads over my face are becoming hotter and
hotter. They are electrified, I think. I will be electro-
cuted in this dark room and no one will know. They
will come back, the silent lady with the airplane slippers and the silent hands, and there I will be off in a
poof of smoke, just my charred ashes remaining in this
chic, silent place. But I will take deep breaths. I will
forget the darkness, the pressure on my face. I am the
man in the iron mask. Louis Hayward is my name.
Click click, one two three, locked in a cage of no air
like being ducked under the waves. No air, no breath,
I will suffocate. Where is the air of yesteryear? Air. I
need air. I will die here. Help me. I will suffocate.

But I don't, no, I don't. I will fall asleep instead.
I will drift. I am seduced back by her moving hands,
loving me, tempting me, kneading me.

It seemed to Deborah when she went to pay her
bill that the puffs under her eyes were a little more
pronounced after the facial than before, but she felt
beautiful. Ready for Sam.

Sam Aronowitz always had aspired. Brought up in
an affluent suburb of Boston, he had caddied for the
rich men at the local Jewish country club. He had
always been short, and he would struggle grunting,
sweating, every summer vacation since he was twelve,
before he became a beach boy at fifteen, cleaning out
the lockers, moving smelly sweat socks out of the way
as he swept. His parents were the lower-middle class
in an upper-middle-class neighborhood, and he hated
it. He hated it and vowed he would be as big as those
slobs for whom he picked up golf balls. He told

Deborah that one of the finest moments in his life was when he bought out the bankrupt company of Hyman Cohen, the same Hyman Cohen who had called him a snot-nosed kid because, before the days of the caddie cart, he had not been able to keep up with the Cohen party at the seventh hole.

Sam carried a Vuitton note pad in his breast pocket, had three Vasarleys and two Lichtensteins in his office, which was on the fifth floor of a town house in the upper seventies, off Fifth. His secretary was twenty-three, blond, fair-skinned, and, as Deborah predicted, had an English accent. They were big this year, girls with English accents, in offices in old brownstones with marble fireplaces and beamed ceilings.

"Debdear," Sam cooed as Deborah walked past Miss cool, the English tit willow. "How about a kiss, babe?" She held her hands on his sideburns and brushed her lips to the top of his head. Bald, it was as smooth as the inside of a baby's arm. No wrinkle, no sign of the ravaging sun on that smooth pate.

"I just have to finish up a conversation and we'll eat. Help yourself."

Cheese and Danish crackers and three bottles of white wine graced the teakwood tray on the antique table in front of the fireplace. Deborah poured herself a glass of liebfraumilch.

It was always a bit disconcerting to watch Sam talk into the wall, into the window, into the fireplace, wherever, with that fancy phone apparatus that he had where you don't talk into a receiver. And the person talks back to the world. Whoever is in the room can hear the other part of the conversation.

Sam loved it. He loved to flick switches, put the stereo on, call Heather (what else?) in so he could sign some letters.

"Listen," he growled into the air, "I don't give a

damn what he says, you tell him the deal's off unless he comes through tomorrow. Nine A.M. sharp. Do ya hear me?"

Two hundred twenty-five pounds he is, Deborah thought. Can you imagine that, pounds on top of me; moons for fingernails, cuticles clipped and pruned, like an English garden all trimmed and even hedges of him. The roundness in his belly is all soft and overhanging, not very pretty, but the buttocks are small, the thighs neatly tucked in, but alas, the inner part gives way like a cow's udder depleted from the milking. He holds me and doesn't hold me, all two hundred twenty-five pounds of him embrace me, and nothing of him is there embracing, and his member becomes hard through the well-cut suit that hides the roundness, the Daks slacks that are buttoned and buckled in such a way as to minimize the belly.

Your generosity is vulgar, she said in her head to the bulging cigar he held in his fingers pointing at a Jim Dine for emphasis. "Don't you threaten me, you bastard," he shouted. His kindness is excessive. His taste is heavy. But he wants me. I give him class. And uneasiness. She knew that. She was a woman who made him uneasy; she made him feel less, and for some reason he liked it. Deborah knew it, banked on it. It got her a lot of free meals. She was getting that crass.

Sam stayed on the telephone for an hour and Deborah had six glasses of wine. She knew she would have to get up at six in the morning to catch the 7:07 back to Long Island to get to work by nine. She knew she would feel logy and heavy in the morning, but it didn't matter. It certainly didn't matter. She was going to marry Sam. She had decided. It was the only thing to do. Joshua would be jubilant, forgetting Sam's stature, Sam's paunch; his pouch was more interesting. Despite his baldness he would be the hair apparent. He could support his daughter, go to temple, and play golf with him on Sundays.

After dinner they drove across the George Washington Bridge, the lights as symmetrical as hundreds of straight pins standing up in the bottom of a sewing box.

The entrance to the apartment house was expensive. Marble floors and mirrored walls, plastic greenery, plastic flowers, plaster-of-Paris Grecian urns and Aphrodites. Upstairs on the thirty-second floor, a broad expanse of glass reflected a terrace surrounding the five-bedroom apartment. It had once been two, and the walls were lined with what appeared to Deborah to be very colorful, linear, very cold works by contemporary artists.

"I buy what I like," he had told Deborah, "and I like all this modern stuff. It doesn't bother me that I don't understand it. It's where the money is today and that's for sure. The stock market is kaput, real estate is too risky, and what's left is art, and maybe vineyards. I'm going to southern France in about a month to look some over."

They sat in the living room on an oversized beige sofa and looked out at the lights of the city. "All my life I dreamed about living like this," he said, putting his arm around Deborah and rubbing the back of her neck. "You know, I used to go with a girl in high school. Well, not really go with her, because it was all very platonic. I taught her to drive and her mother loved me and we would sit in the kitchen and eat cookies while she'd go out on dates. And they lived in this house there on a hill. High on a hill; her father was in the pocketbook business or something and had made a mint during the war and they had this house there that I just idolized. And I swore, Debdear, I swore I'd live like that someday, never wanting, being able to buy and charge any damn thing I wanted. I did

it, and I do it and I love it, the feeling of never having
to ask anyone for anything. Do you know what I
mean?"

"Yes, I do."

Deborah was drunk. She had consumed a lot of wine
at dinner and three brandies here at Sam's. How was
she going to get up in the morning and become a re-
verse commuter? How on earth was she going to get
up from this couch and get into bed? How on earth
was she going to make love to Sam, Sam the big fat
man who said he wanted her?

In Sam's marble bathroom, with its gold faucets
and marbelized toilet seats, Deborah threw up. She felt
dizzy. Opening the medicine chest, she saw ten little
gray jars all in a row, each had a typewritten message
on it—directions to Sam from his dermatologist. "Pat
on first thing in the morning," one said, or "Leave on
cream overnight."

Lying in his king-queen-prince-consort-size bed,
Deborah was astounded at how clearly she was thinking. Expedience, she thought, this is an expedience
lovemaking hour. Your body, dear Sam, means nothing
to me there on top of me, the folds of your stomach
pushing into me. You are off the beat, out of step, out
of tune. I look over your shoulder out the window and
dozens of sparkling lights are twinkling like *Tales of
Manhattan,* like Rita Hayworth and Glenn Ford dancing on the moon, like old romance in my head, such
promise, there used to be such promise, and here over
your shoulder the lights and moving headlights like ants
slowly building a hill move out there over your
shoulder and I feel nothing. You move me, turn me
over, lift me up, put me down, put your member in,
take it out, put your mouth on me, your hands are
unknowing, not like Abe, and it doesn't matter, it is
boring, it is not good.

She slept, and the last thought was one of flesh, like the time Roger came home from school and said that in biology they had seen a film showing the hysterectomy of a dog. And he described the flesh they took out from the belly, white fat he had said. All that. White fat. On top of her. But I'm going to do it, she thought, her arm outstretched as if to ward off a blow. I'm going to do it—marry Sam, that is.

Chapter Sixteen

Seth kept his promise about the strip show. He took Mary Catherine down to the Village somewhere off MacDougal Street. A hawker stood outside ushering people in off the street.

The posters promised dangerous delights, forbidden things. Life-size photos of lipsticked smiling girls with pompadours or long, floating hair. On their breasts, full, upright, were tiny pasties, the fifty-second state, a star in the flag of anatomy, a tiny leaf to cover the triangle. And they wore high heels, the highest they could find. All thin and tall, jutting the arch, the leg plumped out to its shapeliest, the calf curved, thigh firm. The hands were cupped behind the head, so the breasts would appear higher, and the little string around the pelvic area, meeting in the middle, covered the puffed-out center.

Years ago Mary Catherine's Uncle Joseph, who members of the family said had been thrown off the police force but nobody really talked about it, used to bring one stripper or show girl after another to Sunday dinner. They were Chinese and Australian, English and French. When she was about seven, one Chinese girl, perfectly formed, an Amazon in miniature, wanted to go to the bathroom. Mary Catherine had taken her upstairs and waited for her in her bedroom where she wanted to show her a Chinese doll she had, with fake silken hair and painted-on slants for eyes. The girl came in and was still pulling up her panties. She saw Mary Catherine staring at her and laughed. She pulled off her skirt entirely, revealing ice-white skin, bones for hips, and a hairless mound.

Mary Catherine couldn't take her eyes off it. She looked so innocent, her center looked just like Mary Catherine's. There was no hair at all. The girl explained that in her profession they always had to shave down there and frankly she thought it was so much more attractive, didn't Mary Catherine?

The girls in the posters were not very pretty and looked as though Bruno of Hollywood had posed them long ago and, as though "playing statues," they were atrophied into position, so outdated were the hairdos and the expressions. And they were yellowed, the posters were, as were the doormen who stood outside tempting people with the wares inside. It wasn't the same as the go-go girls or the topless ones who bounced their breasts into the chocolate cake as they leaned down to serve, it was down and dirty, old-time burlesque, it was pears and apples plucked from forbidden orchards, leftover titillation, visual aids, it was voyeurism veritas.

She groped for Seth's arm as she stumbled inside. She couldn't see. It was like walking into velvet. Slowly a dimly lighted stage could be seen somewhere far away. And a bar on the left started to take shape.

Shadows were standing against it or sitting on stools.
Their eyes were on the stage.

"Order a double," Seth whispered as the waiter led
them to the table. "They water the drinks here like
crazy." They sat at a table in the back, far from the
raised stage that was in the middle of the room. Seth
pulled the tablecloth down so it covered their knees.
Looking out, all Mary Catherine could see was the
reflection of the red and blue lights on a pair of glasses
across the way, the glint of shine from patent-leather
shoes beneath rows of tables. Faceless, they were. The
men with the raincoats wanted live action.

Seth loved it. He used to cut school when he was a
kid, he said. Take the subway for one stop uptown and
then turn around and go right downtown to the burlesque houses.

"When I was in New Orleans," he bragged, "I lived
with Tornado Monsoon. You know her. *Playboy* just
did a whole thing on her. Tits the size of an elephant's
rear." Charming, Mary Catherine thought, who would
ever want to get near the hind part of an elephant?

"She wouldn't let me out of the apartment. Asking
for it over and over. Sure, the red hair was dyed, sure
she was shot full of silicone, but she could hack it
and work up a guy better than anyone. Sure she was
getting old, and her neck had creases, but in the dark
who cared. She would smother you with those tits.
And drink. She could put it away. Bourbon. Bourbon,
she drank. She wasn't one of those strippers who tried
to pretend they were ladies. Class she didn't have. But
she knew how to work a man up, she knew it and she
loved it. I think she had an orgasm on stage every
time she did her act. She used to do this thing with a
feather."

He went on like that a lot, Seth did. When she was
little and the nuns would watch every moment to make

sure no one knew anything about the magic they had in themselves, she used to go to the dictionary and look up words. She was ten, maybe eleven. And the weirdest words gave her a thrill. *Breast.* Knocked her out. And *spank.* *Spank,* she would get the strangest sensations from a string of letters put together on a printed page.

Seth was awful, she knew that. How on earth did she with her black Irish sweet looks, tiny hands and feet, get mixed up with this boor? It doesn't matter, she thought in the darkness, squinting her eyes into slits, seeing only spots of light on the stage, not hearing the thumping piano player and the tunes designed to push purple passion from your toes to your fingertips. It doesn't matter, I will go the way the wind blows me, anything is better than nothing.

"Come on, Mary Catherine, the show is beginning," Seth said.

He had ordered a drink for her. He put his arm around her waist and touched her breast. "Why are you wearing a bra, you don't need it. Unhook it."

"Here?"

"Listen, kid, in the dark no one knows anything. They can't even see who's sitting next to them. They're only interested in the girls on the stage."

The female comedian came first. Old. Dumpy in gold lamé with tarnished shoes and hair the color of straw. Her stomach was one round circle, pushing like cambium layers on an old oak out of the skintight dress. Mary Catherine could see her belly button indented. She stood with her legs apart in the dress so that her hips and buttocks almost cracked the seams. She didn't have any underwear on. Her arms were old, hanging, and the fingers stubby, piglike, had rings on them. Her cleavage pushed her breasts together into fine prune wrinkles and her chest was freckled like large splotches of mud after a heavy rain.

As if that's all there is in this world, the humping she was talking about, the creases and crevices to get into, the obscene gestures, the sticking the microphone between her legs. She stayed on too long and the one table of visiting salesmen or whoever they were sitting closest to the stage was beginning to get restless. Who is she, Mary Catherine thought. Some old-time vaude-villian trying to survive with a raunchy repertoire of unfunny un-Rabelaisian repartee. She probably has a grandchild home she has to support. Seth absentmind-edly played with her nipples while the lady sang Sophie Tuckerisms into the microphone, which she periodically put down her bosom so they could hear her heart beat.

A Chinese gentleman sat primly at the next table. Mary Catherine could barely make out his features it was so dark. He was watching Seth move his fingers over her nipples. Seth put his hand into her blouse, and cupped her breasts. Mary Catherine turned and found the Chinese man looking into her eyes. Seth straightened the white tablecloth once again to make sure no one across the way could see him. He hiked up Mary Catherine's skirt.

"Seth . . ."

"Stop it. Try it, you'll like it."

"Seth," she whispered, "there's a man next to you. . . ."

"I know," he breathed heavily into her ear. "Let him get his kicks. I sort of like it that he looks at you. Maybe we can all get together later."

"Don't be crazy."

"Well, how do you like it so far?"

"It's dark."

"That's it?"

"I can't tell anything yet."

Another comedian took over. The natives were getting restless. "Bring on the girls," someone with short hair and tie on at the salesmen's table cried out.

This one was a big man whose rapid-fire delivery would make poor Jack E. Leonard roll over in his grave, Mary Catherine thought. "Listen, I'd shake hands with you"—he leaned down to a man at the big table—"but I see you're still busy." "Listen, if you had a hard on and ran into a brick wall you'd break your nose." "Listen, if you're looking for the toilet, you're in it." He stood deadpan, firing the words out to the crowd, defying them, begging them to hate him. He was keeping the girls away.

He turned to the left side of the stage to the few tables that were occupied. "Did you hear about the hippie who was picked up by the truck driver? He asked him, 'Aren't you going to ask if I'm a girl or a boy?' 'Well, it doesn't matter,' he answered, 'because I'm going to fuck you anyway'."

Seth laughed. The Chinese, no, he was Japanese, Mary Catherine decided, kept looking at her breasts. She kept thinking of her father. Wondering if he ever came to places like this, if he ever guffawed at jokes like that. When she was a little girl she would die if she was in the same room with him when Uncle Joseph would start in on one of his jokes. Her father would get a glint in his eye, and at the same time would be uncomfortable that she was listening. She was always somehow very aware that he was excited by it, knowing at the same time it was inappropriate for her ears. There was always a mixture of discomfort and titillation for her. Anything off color or naked was frowned on in her house, and yet early in the game she sensed that they really meant the opposite, her parents. That it was bad, those words and those bodies, that it was something dark. But it was something mysterious, tempting.

Once when she was fourteen she walked in on her father when he was dressing. It was the first time she had ever seen a penis. He had sat down quickly, his skinny legs and hairless chest shrinking from her gaze. She had retreated quickly, but the sight of that limp foreign thing had haunted her. She remembered thinking that it looked exactly like a Baby Ruth bar, surrounded by black snow. She didn't like the looks of it. It frightened her, and for years after they were married Carlo had to force her to watch him walk across the floor naked. It had taken her a while, but she got used to it. Now she was making up for lost time, she thought.

"Listen, they never would have impeached Nixon," the M.C. went on, getting a little social commentary into his act, "all they had to do was let Ted Kennedy give him a ride home." He put his hand to his head and looked out in great relief. "Whew, boy, you really scared me, fella, I thought you were sitting upside down." This one got a laugh out of everyone. By sheer doggedness he was bringing them around. "Bring on the girls," a man said, waving his drink in the air.

"Your wife has two assholes and you're one of them," the comedian retorted. Everyone roared. Seth squeezed her. She was getting very warm.

"Got to go to the john, fella? Don't try the pecker stretcher, it's a rip-off. You know, I know a girl who works for the telephone company. She's training to be a lineman and she can climb my pole anytime."

He was getting raunchier and raunchier and the men in the audience could smell it, the proximity, the perfume of the girl waiting in the wings. "How do you do, sir," he said politely, pointing to a young man at the first table, "I see you just got out of the army and are sitting there with your discharge in your hand." Everyone groaned and he moved in with "O.K., gents, I know you've all been titillated and transformed by my little repartee, but now I see we're ready to give you what you really came to see, the most luscious, the most lovely lady you've ever feasted your eyes on."

All of a sudden the deadpan Busten Keaton was turning into Phil Silvers in front of her eyes, Mary Catherine thought. The pitch had more flourishes, his voice more intonation. "Did you take your heart pill, Dad, because if you didn't you're really going to need it because we now present . . ."

And out from the wings to the accompaniment of the piano came not Carmen, but Lady What's her-name, the first comedienne. This time with a chair and a boa. Setting the stage. Looking a little sheepish, envious for a split second that the moments of anticipation were not for her, she cried, "Here she is, ladies and gentlemen . . ." Again . . . "Carmen, the curvacious."

And out strutted Carmen.

She was not beat up. She was beautiful, with a long biege satin gown clinging to her body and matching beige gloves up to her elbows. She had a bright red flower in her hair. Why not? She hadn't been named Carmen for nothing. Her heels were high and the slit on the side of her skirt reached to her waist. She circled the stage, swooping about the corners. She walked tall and straight. A lady, she looked like a lady, Mary Catherine thought. She moved about the stage with long, confident steps. A tiger. Circling. All those eyes on her.

Seth took a short cigar and puffed it between the first and third fingers. The smoke was making Mary Catherine sick. It became very hot in that tunnel, that underground place, and Seth's fingers were moving inside her blouse.

Carmen stared contemptuously out into the light. Obviously, she was above all this, the daughter of a

Castilian nobleman probably—she had horses on the pampas, perhaps she rode the bulls on Sunday. . . .

Finger by finger, Carmen pulled off the gloves. She never missed a beat. "Malagueña" was pumping away from the back of the stage, a bald head and cigarette smoke were all Mary Catherine could see from that direction. With a flourish, Carmen throw one glove over to one side, and started in on the other.

The music repeating the da da dumda da dum da da dum da dum deem dum, only louder now, hypnotized the sparse audience. Carmen had every eye. Off went the other glove and on went Carmen to the stool, licking her lips now as she leaned back to unzip her regal gown. Seth's lips were glistening from his tongue, his hand moved up and down Mary Catherine's nipples. Mary Catherine's eyes never left Carmen, who now assumed a fixed stare on one man in the audience. Zip went the dress, and Carmen stood up, the soft stuff falling to the floor, and Carmen, knees straight as though Simon says touch your toes, my dear, and now you may take two giant steps, my dear, flung the dress over to a corner of the stage and straddled the stool. Clad in frilly little panties and a sequinned bra, she started playing with the boa. She wasn't a lady anymore. The boa tickled her chest and inner thighs and Carmen smiled. Carmen didn't seem to be acting. Carmen was enjoying herself and everyone in the room felt it.

Seth moved his hand between Mary Catherine's legs. He stroked the inside of her thigh, softly, slowly. "The insides of your thighs are like velvet," he whispered in her ear. It was rather a poetic phrase from a prosaic man, she thought, feeling so many things at the same time. Not quite knowing what to concentrate on where. He is prosaic, his prose is prosaic, he is an elegaic prosaic. The words danced in her head. Mr. Tojo next to her was getting her very nervous as he hungrily watched Seth's fingers move deftly in and around her inner thigh. Why doesn't he watch Carmen, what does he want with me for God's sake, Mary Catherine thought. She couldn't muster up a good dirty look because she was too conscious of the growing tension building in her groin. Seth, who knew her body so well, unbuttoned her blouse, exposing her breasts. She pulled it together.

"Stop it, no one can see, who wants to look at you when that dish is humping up there?"

"He does," she whispered in a panic, buttoning her blouse.

"Leave it. It's so dark in here, you really have to squint. Mary Catherine, we're all the way back in the corner. Lean back. Don't worry about a thing. God, your tits are smooth." He had managed to unbutton every button on her blouse again, so that there she sat behind a pulled-down tablecloth, next to a lecherous visiting fireman from Tokyo, being handled by a foot doctor who was a sex maniac.

Seth kneaded her exposed breasts slowly, pausing to finger the nipples. The Japanese was stroking his penis. Mary Catherine took a long sip of scotch. She felt as though she were bathing in milk with rose petals soothing her skin. Seth kept rounding her breast, shaping it.

Carmen gyrated to the music. She wasn't very graceful, but she was bathed in a soft light now as she stepped daintily out of the panties, revealing a black lacy garter belt and black stockings. Like those dolls people bring back from Russia, Mary Catherine thought, a little peasant inside the bigger peasant. and a littler peasant than that inside the little one. Open the babushka and lo, another little one. Carmen kept peeling the layers of the onion off and under each one was one more flimsy piece of fabric next to her body.

Seth kept making little humming noises.

Mary Catherine straightened her legs under the table.

And Carmen. Carmen was involved only in herself. She had forgotten the leers, the stares, she reveled in herself.

She unhooked her brassiere and threw it out at the table nearest the stage. Her breasts were smaller than they had appeared under the boned brassiere. Shiny stars graced the nipples and she took each breast in her hands and rubbed it lovingly.

She shook her breasts and stood up again, still in time to the music, and slowly began to unhook the garter belt. Her fingers circled her waist as she fingered the catch. Deft. She was not scornful anymore, she was exciting herself. She sat down again and straightened out one leg, kicking off the shoe. The curved thing pointed at the ceiling as she unhooked the garter belt. She dangled the stocking. Shaking it to and fro. Seth kept rubbing Mary Catherine and she kept feeling it, thinking she would shout her pleasure so loud they would throw her out of there. Yet somehow somewhere still she knew that you weren't supposed to carry on this way in a public place.

Carmen was totally naked, the lights were crimson, the music was building and building to a crescendo now, and Carmen was leaning back on the stool, legs apart, head back, tickling herself with the boa. Purple, it was.

She shook her breasts as though they weren't attached to her. The lights played checkers on her body, running up and down her like a lover's lips. She put her hands over her breasts, stroked her nipples, slowly walked down to the edge of the stage, and kneeled down. She took one breast in both her hands and, stroking it, gave it to a bald man at ringside. He put his drink down and put his hand on it. Pull it off,

Carmen gestured, and the man, obviously an old hand at this kind of thing, removed her pasty. He put his hand over her breast, and Carmen laughed. She was missing two teeth. Her buttocks had stretch marks.

Seth moved into Mary Catherine with one hand. With the other he held one breast, then the other. The Japanese had taken out his penis. Seth touched her, all her places. Carmen put the man's hand into her breasts. She threw back her head and laughed. There was hair under her ams.

The Japanese man did not take his eyes off Mary Catherine. Seth fondled her relentlessly.

Carmen sat on the edge of the stage, her legs almost on two tables. She spread them. She licked her fingers. Touched her nipples. Made love to herself.

Mary Catherine came.

Seth took her hand and made her rub his hardness. The Japanese whispered something to Seth.

"He wants us all to go to a hotel," he said.

"No."

"Might be fun. He's very rich. A rich camera maker or something, I'll bet."

"Seth, no. No no no. He probably has a hara-kiri knife up his sleeve. Tell him no. Make him go away."

Seth whispered to him, as the music swelled into the finale. The man rose, bowed, and smiled. Thank God he was all zipped up, Mary Catherine thought.

Chapter Seventeen

Mary Catherine continued going out with men she met at parties. Who friends introduced her to. Tuesday night she had a date with Daniel; a blind date, a new one. It didn't work out.

Like many men who were just encountering the first flutterings of divorce, he was shaky, defensive, determined not to make the same mistake again, even if it was just over dinner with Mary Catherine. At the restaurant, Daniel spent the entire four courses, from shish kebab to potato pancakes to sour cream to fresh fruit to cheese, knocking his wife, what a sloppy housekeeper she was. How stupid. How she never read. How she hit the children. How they never had clean socks. How bitterly she was fighting for money, how bitterly he was fighting to give her as little as possible. A man in the process of getting a divorce is all cottage cheese, firm in spots, mostly mush, Mary Catherine thought.

Daniel was fiercely involved with his children, he told Mary Catherine, visited every other night, planned elaborate weekends and vacations with them. "We are really pals," he said, "and I don't want anything to change." Well, whether or not it would change as it did with Carlo, who for a dedicated father did a great disappearing act, she didn't know. But she had to admit, it did get to be pretty pat and predictable, the palaver. She could tell what they were thinking before they said it.

And romance, romance was the thing the men craved,

Mary Catherine discovered. I want to fall in love, one tall handsome actor Mary Catherine met at yoga class told her (they met when the teacher asked Mary Catherine to pick his legs up during his headstand). He had just left his wife, a statuesque beauty who was, he said, cold to him in bed. Mary Catherine had liked him, but his flaccidity, his tentative touch had made her turn away.

But he and some others she met had wanted the bells to ring, the flowers to fall out of the heavens. The heart to pound. The appetite to go away. Romance, Jeanette MacDonald and Nelson Eddy. Dante and Beatrice, Tristan and Isolde. Leopold and Loeb.

Mary Catherine wasn't fooled. She had had that. She had married with a beating heart and glistening eyes; it was going to be forever and love and caring would conquer everything. She would never touch another man. Ever. And Carlo would be the one. The one and only.

"My darling," she had written a year before they were married, "I am very much in love with you, the freedom of expression I feel, the exquisite tenderness and concern make me woman, make me as near complete as it is now possible, make me very happy.

"I will always love you, I will always respect your words and silences. We interact as one person. I meant it when I said that at times I almost feel as though your hands were growing out of mine.

"You are my man. I am your woman. I remember what you said about becoming frightened when I seem to love so fully. Sometimes it scares me to let someone mean so very much to me. Yet deep down I know that it could never be any other way with me, that I must love you completely in order to express myself as I should."

Whatever it was and no matter how bad and corny

the syntax, she had meant it at the time, she really had and was as romantic as Merle Oberon shouting for her Heathcliff on the moors. She may have become more cynical now, but still it was why the romanticism of the men moved her, their underlying need for poetry. Even though she saw the childlike expectation of it, it's what made her understand. And made her keep going back for more.

But she tended to create intensity where there was none. Fabricate charm and appeal, make it up, make the man up, so great was her need. He's soft, she would think, or he's kind or he's bright or he's sensitive. Most of the time none of it was true. She was terrible about making judgments about men. Not that it was the men's fault. It was hers. Her fault, because her ability to judge was impaired by an overpowering need to make someone be what she thought she wanted. Naturally, it never worked.

Daniel, who was tall and sharp-nosed, and whose blue eyes beamed at her, showed signs of his rigidity, his immobility shone through the conversation but she ignored it. He's bright, she thought, so knowledgeable on archaeological digs in Iraq. He knew the name of every Mesopotamian king from the beginning of Mesopotamian kings. When he told her he hated *Last Tango* because it was decadent and anyone who would take a woman from behind was a homosexual, she excused it in her mind. Fun to disagree. Opposites attract. That's good for the relationship. That mythical "meaningful relationship" everyone was talking about.

When he berated her for telling her daughter not to wait up on the second date because Francie would then know that they had probably gone to bed and how unfeeling that was of her, she did become a little wary. His marriage to a woman less accomplished, less bright, "not from a good family," had crippled him. He was precise, always on time, very neat, but she excused it all when he kissed her. Somehow the flesh relaxed, the tightness around his mouth loosened, and he held her sweetly.

It didn't matter because he never called again, anyway, after he took offense when she told him he wasn't spontaneous. Well, he wasn't, Mary Catherine thought, and she would be damned if she would lie. But she lied to herself, she knew that, all the time. Always hoping that this one was the one. The one who would, like the television commercials, take the ache away. She was smart, didn't have any illusions, but lied to herself anyway. Every time.

But Mary Catherine would pick herself up, dust herself off, and start all over again. Not too much wiser. But a little.

She went places alone too. After two years of it now, she dressed, put her makeup on, kissed Francie good-bye, left the outside light on for herself, put the garbage out, all as though she were two people. In the spring, going out at dusk, the air so familiarly fair, she would ache a little. Remembering that once there were two of them going someplace and she could almost sense the presence of Carlo. Not that she missed him. She didn't. She missed the shoulder, the suit jacket, the figure getting in on the driver side of the car. Now, coming home, she had to fumble for her key herself, struggle through dark country roads herself, beat the truck drivers at their own game herself if she was driving home late from New York. The Long Island Expressway spawned those husky tyrants of the road, demonically chasing her in her little orange Datsun; Tom and Jerry they were, and she was Jerry escaping their highway madness. Bright lights blinding her in the rearview mirror, honking goose guffaws as they wanted to pass, predators leaving her in a wave of their own dust as she cowered over on the right side, the slow side of the highway. She cursed them as they stared haughtily, imperiously, disdainfully down at her from their cabs perched on high, ogling her legs, shaking their heads in disgust. Lady driver, dumb broad, get a horse, she heard it all in her head. But they would not deter her; she would drive home alone in her orange Datsun undaunted because she had learned to combat those demons of the night, whether it be creaks in the house, voracious truck drivers, or those unspoken fears of getting a flat tire, blowing a gasket, an overhead radiator, all at two in the morning with no state police call box handy, with no kind Samaritan nearby. She got a little nervous, but in two years she had learned how to manage. It wasn't that she necessarily wanted to be so capable, at times she felt it rather unladylike of her, as a matter of fact, to be so handy, but she had learned through necessity to live expediently. Whether it meant smiling sweetly at the garbage man so he wouldn't charge her extra for four more garbage pails than usual, or having dinner with a dull man who could nevertheless get her two seats to Baryshnikov when he was in town, she would do it. Her wits. Whatever they were, she had learned to live by them. Calculating at times, she would call up a man if she felt she wanted one, her Arab friend, for example, who had she noticed pinned to the bulletin board of his tiny bedroom "You are one of many thousands." After a warming meal, some drinks in a neighborhood bar, they would make love all night.

In the morning she would rise before him, make herself some instant coffee, get dressed, and silently fold her tent and steal away. She would confront the empty early-morning streets, catch a cab, embark on the Long Island Rail Road and open up her office by 8:00 A.M.

It had served its purpose. An interchange. An expedient one. She had decided to extract her pleasure, her bang-whir, thank-you-sir hours; so it wasn't so glorious, so it wasn't the sound and the fury, so she wasn't touched, still her outsides were touched and she would just forget about her insides for a while. And however she might not like the odor of the stuff he put in his hair, and however it made his hair feel hard and coarse, there was indeed some pleasure, she would think. And she was renewed. How do I differ from a man, she thought. Nohow. It is the same. I can be harder even, more calculating, because my desire, I am convinced, is stronger.

Francie, at the beginning of the divorce, had been afraid when Mary Catherine went out. She was convinced Mary Catherine was going to get into a bloody automobile accident or that the car would overturn, pinning her underneath. She bombarded her mother with her fears. Secretly, she knew there would be no one left to take care of her. Her father had become a mysterious presence almost overnight. Now you see him, now you don't. He had moved on. Her grandmother was too sad and her Aunt Eleanora too crazy. She wanted her mother alive. But as time went on and she got older, she could stay alone periodically or have a friend come to stay when Mary went to dinner or to a movie.

Francie was sleeping at Hilda's Wednesday night, and Mary Catherine was going to Lolly and Dave's for dinner. Francie was studying for a test covering the Civil War to today. Lolly had told Mary Catherine that Herb and Alice, old friends with whom she and Dave had gone to Cornell, were spending a few days with them. Just they and the Tenzers were coming, Lolly said—"He makes a fortune making voice-overs for commercials"—and Frieda Latner, another divorcée. The Bernsteins took in strays. Lolly, who really would much rather have gone into her studio and done some work, still felt she had to have some kind of social life for Dave. She loved to cook elegant things that the kids would never look at, and she didn't like her single lady friends not to have a place to go. She liked Herb and Alice, who both taught college, and hadn't seen them in a while. She was amazed at how heavy both of them had become during the past year. Huge padded rumps on both of them. They had brought their sullen eleven-year-old with them, which Lolly could have done without. Her own children were sleeping out. Weekend guests were one of the trademarks of a town like Eastville, New Yorkers aching for some sprig of green in the spring searching in and out of their little black address books when the leaves were turning, to find who they knew, where they could stay, to watch the colors mellow.

When Mary Catherine walked in the door to Lolly's house the familiar smell of cinnamon candles was encouraging. Going to Lolly and Dave's was like coming home. When she was getting the divorce, Mary Catherine could never accept her and Carlo keeping the same friends. It was out of the question. Lolly and Dave understood. "I don't care who it is," Mary Catherine he said, "but you'll have to choose, me or him. It's an over with life and I don't want any residuals." Some friends couldn't understand at all and thought she was old-fashioned, childish, petulant, churlish. Whatever. Carlo could have his cronies, his drinking buddies, his sailing pals. She kept Lolly and Dave and that's all she really wanted anyway.

"This is Herb and Alice, Mary C. I've told you so much about them, as they say."

"Hello."

They were indeed fat. Alice had short black curly hair, and a pretty pig face. The nostrils turned up and were wide; the eyes, small. She had ham thighs, and Herb's belly was spilling over his belt like a flooding water bed. He was short, had a receding hairline, fleshy inner palms, and untrimmed fingernails.

What is it that they teach, she kept trying to remember.

"I had a student named Mary Catherine," Herb said, leading her to the couch. "She was very Catholic."

"How does one be very Catholic as opposed to just Catholic?" Mary Catherine said, accepting the seat next to the light. John Kenneth Galbraith's book about India was in her direct line of vision.

"Well, you know what I mean. She went to mass every Sunday, still kept fish on Friday, and really wanted to remain a virgin until she got married."

"I remember her," Alice said, sitting in the armchair opposite the coffee table in front of the couch. "She had long, blond hair and about a ten-inch waist."

"That's the one."

"She was in my clinical program."

Psychology, that was it; they both taught psychology.

Dave came in from the kitchen, drying his hands on a towel. "Mary Catherine, love, how are you? You look marvelous." He pulled her up from the couch and gave her a hug. He smelled of curry and Brut. Lolly must have listened to that commercial where Joe Namath's girl purrs into the screen about her man wearing that manly scent and how it must be the sexiest thing since Tarzan's loincloth. She was always doing that and Mary Catherine would call her on it. "Lolly, the man is who he is, he's tweedy and professorial, and why on earth are you sending him off to have his hair styled and his weight trimmed? He is who he is."

"He just doesn't care enough about those things,"

she had said, "and he should." It always amazed Mary
Catherine that he went, always went on those beauty
excursions to please her. Lolly would buy him smoking
jackets and ascots and narrow-cut Italian jackets that
hugged his rounded rear, and he wore them about once
a year, then stuck with his jeans and tweeds and old
windbreakers. But Brut had succeeded in finding its
way to the back of his neck. It didn't suit him at all,
Mary Catherine thought.

"You met the Arnolds, right?"

"Yes, Lolly just introduced us."

"And do you know Myra and Stanley Tenzer?"

The Tenzers were an attractive couple, both very
tall. He had a cleft in his chin and thick hair sprinkled
with stalks of gray. Myra Tenzer was a nervous woman, once very smart and finely chiseled, whose forties
and lack of fortitude had dealt an unkind blow. The
taut bones in her face were in place but the skin over
them had developed hundreds of wrinkles and veins
branching out like the opening of a fan. She com-
plained a lot.

"Mary Catherine, I haven't seen you in ages," Myra
said. "You know, I was thinking about you the other
day. I bumped into Carlo in front of Saks. My, he
looks well. What's he doing these days? He was with
an awfully pretty girl. About twenty-five, I would say."

Of course, this was hardly the first time. Mary
Catherine was, in a way, used to it. People had to
have some frame of reference, some hook to attach
their conversation to, and so if it couldn't be a mutual
interest in Emily Dickinson, and at the moment *Così
Fan Tutte* didn't come into anybody's head, nine times
out of ten it would be Carlo. How someone had seen
him at the ballet, how someone else had encountered
him at a cocktail party in the East Sixties. Or at an
insurance convention, or running for a cab. My, he's

lost weight, or my, he's gained weight, or my, he's getting gray, or my, he's looking young. People never knew exactly what to say, only knowing compulsively that it was incumbent upon them to establish it. That they knew him. They had to mention his name. The ex-husband. Why don't they just talk about the weather like everyone else? Oh well.

"He's with a new company."

"Really, oh, I'm glad. How is Francie? Is she adjusted to it yet? Mary Catherine, I really should see you more often. Can't we have lunch or something? We haven't seen each other in ages. Is she Carlo's latest girl friend?"

She means well. It's not that she wants to be tactless. It's her way. Their way. People do that.

"You know I don't know, Myra. He seems happy and so do I, so I suppose everything is for the best, right? Francie is lovely."

"Is Carlo your ex-husband?"

Herb helped himself to four pieces of shrimp, two toothpicks in each hand, and dunked them all into the cocktail sauce. The red stuff drooled out of both corners of his mouth, as if someone had just shot him in the back.

"Yes."

"Well, that will never happen to us, will it, dear?" Alice was rubbing his shoulder.

Stanley Tenzer's teeth shone. "Never say never."

"It can't to us, we've got a foolproof system."

"Listen, don't get into that so soon," Dave said. "Mary Catherine, what will you drink?"

"Scotch. Scotch, please, and a little water."

That last remark had piqued her curiosity. There was a fire in the fireplace and the coffee table in front of it was laden with hors d'oeuvres. Gypsy, the Bernsteins' dog, was asleep under it, and the curry and cinnamon smells moving in the room made Mary Catherine feel quiet. Comfortable. She didn't quite know what to make of Herb and Alice, however. Stanley Tenzer led her away from the center of the room, his arm in back of her, leaning it on the wall, and began to talk conspiratorially about business. Were houses selling as well as last year, had inflation hit her business like everyone else? He luckily kept rolling along since Campbell Soup and jockey shorts or whatever it was he voiced over were still going strong. She liked Stanley, he flirted and always made one or two suggestive remarks an evening, but there was something good-humored about him. He had had his head bashed in by a Washington policeman years ago when he, his middle-aged self, and hundreds of hippies had stormed the Pentagon. He ended up with a sticky bandage slapped on his head and spent the night in jail. He never talked about it, although Myra did. She was proud of him, but secretly resented his foolhardiness, Mary Catherine always felt.

"Oh, God, I'm so sorry I'm late." Frieda Latner burst in the door. She had two bottles of wine under her arm and some roses from her greenhouse. Frieda never came empty-handed anywhere.

Frieda was big, busty, long-legged, and homely. Her nose was too long, the eyes, like green goldfish, sprung out as though on a spring. She was short-waisted, with a flat behind, and had long slim fingers that toyed continually with a cigarette holder. She was fifty years old, had the energy of a sixteen-year-old, and talked about sex all the time. Frieda was divorced ten years now and had just broken up recently with a man she had been going with for eight years. She got large alimony checks but did very well herself running a chic antiques store. "It's full of expensive knickknacks and if I don't break even in the winter, at least in the summer when the New Yorkers come out in droves I clean up. I up the prices on everything and they still think they're getting a bargain."

"Mary Catherine Romano," she bellowed across the room. "Where have you been. I've been calling you for weeks. We were supposed to have lunch ages ago and what happened, I can't remember." Frieda had a raucous laugh that came from her knees.

"Frieda, you can always get me at the office."

"Listen, Frieda, you're late and the food is going to get cold, go get a fast drink and we're all going to sit down," Lolly shouted from the kitchen.

"O.K., O.K."

A pale little girl came into the room, and without saying anything to anyone went up to Alice and whispered in her ear. "All right, darling, just watch television in the basement. You don't mind, Lolly, do you? Amanda won't eat with us, she's got her shows to watch. She'll just take a plate downstairs, all right?"

"Fine." Lolly was relieved because she didn't want Amanda at the table anyway.

The sideboard was bountiful. Somehow she had managed to cook for three days, at the same time chauffeuring the girls, writing her article, pampering Dave; somehow she had put together a beautiful Indian meal. The coconut, chutney, and raisins sat in the middle of the board next to the meats and curries, rice, and Indian bread she had baked. The centerpiece was a ceramic dish they had bought in India with dried flowers of muted colors inside.

Deborah would fall apart if she saw all the work Lolly put into it, Mary Catherine thought. Deborah was convinced that Lolly could one-upsman every one of them with the variety, beauty, and taste of her meals. But for ten years that's all she ever did, entertain for Dave, make him feel that he had married the chef from the Four Seasons. She did it all herself and Mary Catherine noticed that Dave had sat down and was enjoying himself with the guests while Lolly was still puttering in the kitchen.

Mary Catherine was seated between Herb and Stanley. Alice was on the other side of Frieda, and Mary Catherine was amused as she watched Frieda's bulging eyes bulge farther as Alice bent forward in great intimacy.

"To the hostess," Stanley said, lifting his glass of wine. "As usual, Lolly, you have outdone yourself. The table groans with your excess. My compliments, love."

Lolly shone. It wasn't the Pulitzer Prize, Mary Catherine thought, but it was something. We all need something, for God's sake, something that everyone else loves. Eleanora, whom Mary Catherine adored, was like that a lot. A bottomless well. When she would visit, Eleanora would drag out her new designs, put them all over the floor of the living room, forcing everyone to look at them. Francie said she was a braggart, boasting all the time about this award and that French house coming along and stealing her fall line. We all need something, though, Mary Catherine thought, staring into the candles Lolly had lit all across the table. There was incense in them, and the good crystal caught the light.

"Another toast," Herb said, standing up. He looked a little like he was still sitting down.

"To my wife. To Alice. Long may she wave."

At whom, Mary Catherine thought.

"Who are they?" Stanley mumbled into her ear.

"Old friends of Lolly and Dave's. They're psychologists. Teach somewhere."

"Oh, God, they're the married ones."

"The what? What do you mean?"

"You see, it began with our own excursion in fantasy," Mary Catherine heard on her right. Herb was talking to Frieda on his right.

"Speak up, Herb, so we all can hear." Lolly was playing hostess.

"I really don't know if everyone would be interested, Lolly."

"Oh yes they would. I certainly am. You see everybody. . . ." Lolly was bright-eyed and shining. She had had three glasses of wine in the kitchen as she was putting a little here and there in the food.

"Well, I'm certainly not loath to discuss Alice's and my arrangement. We have what I consider one of the best marriages I know and the reason is," he said and paused to put the meat mixture into the coconut, mix it with the raisins and chutney, pour it all over the rice, and put it into, eventually, his mouth. He chewed slowly. Everyone watched, listening.

"May I have some more wine, Dave?" Mary Catherine said, unable to concentrate on Herb's chewing anymore.

"Sure, anyone else?"

"We have an extended family," Herb continued without skipping a beat. "You see, it began with our own excursion into fantasy. When we would have sex we became brother and sister, famous lovers in history, anything we felt like experimenting with. After all, we'd been married fifteen years, had an eight-year-old child, things were getting stale. Sex became fantastic. We couldn't wait for night to come." He spoke as though he were on *Meet the Press* and Mr. Spivak had just asked his most salient question. He spoke in measured, even tones.

His wife put her hand over his. "It was the beginning of a new life," she said.

Stanley put down his fork. Dave, who had heard it

all before, kept on eating. "Lolly, this is out of this world. You did it again." He blew her a kiss across the table. Lollys eyes were bright. "Go on, Herb."

Herb had taken another mouthful. The salad in his mouth sounded a little like Cracker Jacks since he had taken a double forkful. He washed it down with almost the whole glass of wine. "How about some more, Dave?"

"Fine."

"But then . . ."

"Herb certainly has a sense of the dramatic," Mary Catherine whispered to Stanley. He kicked her under the table. That's what I miss, she thought, someone to kick under the table. I can be without a man, I don't mind going places alone, or doing things by myself or coping, but I do miss kicking someone under the table. She looked quickly across the candle-light. She did not want to offend Myra. She was not in the business of extricating husbands from ladies whom she knew. Other people's husbands were different. Those wives took their chances, but ladies whom she knew could be safe with her, Mary Catherine thought, having developed the divorcée's handbook of her own, chapter 4, paragraph 2. "Never have anything to do with the husband of a lady you know, is a casual acquaintance or a friend. It is not a good practice simply because it makes you out a hypocrite, it is uncomfortable if you attend the same gathering, and it just does not feel very good. There is no sense of power whatsoever."

"But then," Herb continued, "Alice had an affair with Charles, a student who was living with us. He, you see, had had doubts about his virility . . ."

". . . and Alice just took over the situation like Deborah Kerr did with John Kerr in *Tea and Sym-*

pathy," Mary Catherine finished his sentence for him
to herself.

"We discussed it, her affair," he resumed, "and I
participated in her being in love." Maybe that's it,
maybe these people have the answer, Mary Catherine
thought, looking at the whole thing with new respect.
Maybe we old jealous ones, we traditional ones, are
the crazy ones. Every eye at the table was on Herb
now. He finally stopped eating.

"As time went on, Ellen came to live with us."

"Was she a student too?" Mary Catherine just didn't
quite understand the imbalance of it all, the young
students with these middle-aged fatties.

"Yes, of course, we rent out rooms."

And then Bill and Fiona came.

"So then there were four extra people living in the
house with you, your wife and child," said Myra, who
had a need for closure.

"That's right."

"And you all started to sleep with each other?"
Lolly couldn't hide her excitement.

"Well, it emerged that way eventually."

"But how did you manage it? I mean, who slept
with whom, I mean did the men do it too? Herb,
explain how it was. I can't quite visualize the whole
thing, especially since I was a bridesmaid at your
wedding. I mean . . ."

"What's that got to do with anything?" Alice was
annoyed. "It was all very beautiful. Our lives became
very full and lovely. And our child blossomed."

"She knew about all that was going on?" Stanley
asked.

"Of course. She attended the ceremony." Herb
scraped the remaining salad into his dish and handed
it to Lolly, who really wasn't ready to start clearing
up yet. But she got up, as did Mary Catherine to help.

They went around the table picking up dishes as fast as they could.

"What ceremony?"

"The wedding."

"What wedding?"

Herb was beginning to get annoyed with these squares. But with great patience he explained that they had a group marriage. They all did it, together, Alice and Herb, Charles, Ellen, Bill and Fiona. He didn't explain about who got whose names.

As Lolly poured the coffee and put out fresh pineapple and cookies, Alice looked triumphantly at the table.

"You all think it's the sexual variety that was intriguing." Mary Catherine looked at her full lips, her huge flanks spreading on the chair, her little fingers with rings pushing the flesh out. "No, you're wrong, it wasn't. It was the loving several people that was so moving. That meant so much to us. That moved us. If Herb would come home from teaching, exhausted, tense, and I had had four classes that day and came home unable to move, Ellen could give him the comfort and tenderness he needed. It wasn't all on me, or all on him. We could come to each other freshly with joy. Doesn't that make sense to any of you? We were acting out our fantasies and each of us knew what the other was doing. No one was cheating or sneaking around. Our marriage, our love, was intact."

There, it was her words. Intact. It made sense, sure, Mary Catherine thought, but why did these two look so unintact to her? They probably had more sex than they knew what to do with, more variety, more positions, more orifices, more flesh. But why did two middle-aged people need twenty-year-olds to spice up their sex lives, their loving lives?

"You know, it's something a lot of people would

give anything to do but just don't have the courage to. I can understand how you might think that the sexual variety would be the titillating thing. But it was secondary. We all loved each other."

Lolly's hands were folded and her chin rested on them. I can see her creeping in with those two tonight, Mary Catherine thought.

"So where are Ellen, and Charles, and Fiona and Bill now?"

"Well, unfortunately," Herb said, "they're all over."

"What do you mean?' Myra said.

"The administration wasn't happy about the situation."

"Who? What administration?" Dave leaned back and lit his pipe.

"The university authorities. They heard about the marriage. The kids had to leave and I lost my job," Herb said. "They just didn't understand. Ours was not an orgy or lascivious encounter. It was based on love and mutual respect. It's been very hard for us."

"Well, we're working at another college now, and Amanda is getting used to only having two parents again. We write to them all, Ellen wants desperately to come back," Alice said, "and perhaps someday we will find others who would be interested in the same kind of life-style. We're hopeful it will happen."

"You see, we know it's the right thing for us, for our marriage," Herb said to the group which was silent. "It just worked. It was beautiful. And it brought us closer together. Our marriage today is more solid and loving than it had ever been. I'm sure, we wouldn't be together now if we hadn't had that time of the extended family. It saved us."

Alice took Herb's hands in hers and started massaging it again. Amanda came in and put her dishes in the sink, went back downstairs without a word.

"Well," Lolly said. "Let's all go in the other room."

"What did your having been my bridesmaid have to do with anything?" Alice said to Lolly as she pushed her chair in. "What difference does that make?"

"Oh, I don't know, Alice. It's just that traditionalism and alternate life-styles do confuse me a bit, I have to admit it. There is a part of me that's very comfortable in my middle-class mecca here, and another that's just bursting at the seams."

Dave was getting out the brandy and glasses.

"Mary Catherine, come talk to me," Frieda said, holding her arm. "Enough of this stuff. It gives me the willies." They walked into the den, which was book-lined and big enough to house a piano. "Absolutely give me the willies. What's the matter with those people?"

"I don't know if it's so crazy, really."

"Are you kidding? I couldn't share a bathroom with my own kid, no less four other husbands and wives I was alternating my bed with. Cripes, they're sickies."

"I'm not so sure."

"Listen Mary, come off it. You couldn't do it in a million years." She picked up a few records, put on a Locatelli album that was resting on the top of a pile. "It's the only way those two overweight sad sacks can get their kicks, that's all. It's as simple as that, they just don't turn each other on anymore, if they ever did in the first place."

"I don't know. It's all so difficult. We make it all so difficult, this one-man, one-woman business. Not only the sex, but the loving each other. It's so hard, maybe a lot of people just takes the steam out of it."

"Couldn't work if people really loved each other. Couldn't. That's why communes come and go. People are jealous and possessive. It just happens. Whether we want it to or not."

The two settled in front of a fireplace that was blazing, in two low-slung brown cordovan chairs. Dave came in with snifters of brandy.

"It used to be the gentlemen who retired with their brandy," he said. "Well, what do you think?" He came over and sat at Mary Catherine's feet.

"I don't know; Frieda thinks they're a little off."

"They're both brilliant, you know. He was at the top of our class in college. He almost ruined his whole teaching career with this business, though."

"Well, that's not really fair," Mary Catherine said. "People should be able to live the way they want, it seems to me."

Dave kept rubbing his brandy glass against Mary Catherine's knee. Myra and Stanley appeared at the door.

"Dave, I'm really sorry but our sitter called and Bruce isn't feeling well. Stanley's going to go home. We came in two cars, so I'll stay for a while. I haven't been out of the house all week."

"Good-bye, Mary Catherine, Frieda. Two of Eastville's loveliest. Why some South American millionaires haven't snapped you two up in a mystery to me."

"What a coincidence, to me too," Frieda said, stretching out her hand to be kissed. Stanley liked to kiss hands, look into eyes, cup chins. He was harmless. Long ago he had decided that Myra wasn't perfect, but they had both been married before and saw no reason in going through the pain of leaving. Divorces had taken too much out of both of them. So he flirted and made a fool of himself a bit. It was little enough.

"Can I join you?" Myra settled into a couch in the far corner of the room as Dave and Stanley went to the front door.

Turtles. Mary Catherine was thinking of turtles. Slow-moving, heavy, cumbersome, tired turtles.

"O.K., Mary Catherine, now what's new?"

"Oh, Frieda, nothing, nothing at all. What about you?"

Frieda took a long swallow of the brandy.

"Philip and I broke up, you know."

"I'd heard."

"Eight years."

"Oh, Frieda."

"Listen, I've been through it before, probably will go through it again." She crossed and recrossed her long legs. "When I was married I'd had an affair with Ralph for nine years. Did you know that? Nine years. Can you imagine getting away with that for nine years? But I'd rather have that, the cheating and the subterfuge, than the Grand Hotel going right on in my own house like Ted and Alice, Jane and whoever in there. And you know what, Mary Catherine, I probably would have stayed married if Ed himself hadn't been unfaithful. Why are you looking at me as though I had turned purple? It's true. Listen, I've told you that before, I've had a lot of men. That's what I've had in my life, a lot of men. It just turned out that way. Even when I was having the affair I had men. Do you know that once, a week after my divorce, I had sex once, just once, with the vice-president of Metro-Goldwyn-Mayer or the Music Corporation, MGM or MCA or M and MS, I can't remember, something with M, once, mind you, just once, and, you'll never believe this, but he gave me clap and got me pregnant all at the same time. In one blow. Just one blow, like that Russian song. Do you know that marvelous Russian song about a tailor or something that's swatting flies and killing them in just one blow?"

Frieda was getting drunk. She poured herself a large share of the brandy in the decanter. Dave had left on the table. Herb and Alice had set her thinking.

"So I went down to Puerto Rico, this was about ten years ago, of course, and got an abortion for a thousand smackeroos and got such a high fever they had to keep shooting me full of penicillin, if it wasn't so sad, I would think it was funny at this late date. Listen, you know what, I don't know about you, but I hate it."

"What? What do you hate?" Mary Catherine kicked off her shoes. She wondered where the others had gone.

"I can't stand being without a man. I'm different from you. See, I love to do for a man. I like to cook for them, bolster them, be important to them. Listen, I've had them, I've been through every man in this town."

"No kidding." Mary Catherine looked at her. Every man?

"Every single eligible man I've had in this town. I mean it, and they're duds, every one of them. New York too. I've been through that scene too. Forget about it. There's nobody around. Oh, I've got this one and that one. I don't know how you manage, I'm not prying or anything. But since Philip there's been nobody for me. Philip I loved. I think he's probably the only man I ever loved." She leaned her head back against the chair and looked at the ceiling.

"Mary C., he was my best friend, we would gossip and make love forever. And you know what?"

"What."

"He was a cad. An utter cad. Listen, I could have supported him for the rest of his life. I got him out of more scrapes, tax problems, problems with his kids. And you know what, big and substantial and tough as I am, you know what he did. He went off and left me." Her eyes filled with tears and she tossed her hair away from her face.

"He would withhold sex if I didn't pay for things," she continued, "and I started to catch on." Never underestimate the power of the penis, Mary Catherine thought. If Frieda had lived in that extended family thing she could have had several legitimate penises and they would all love each other and live happily ever after, she thought, and she wouldn't be crying now.

"You're well out of it." Mary Catherine twirled the brandy in her glass. She needed some more.

"God, do I know it. Listen, Mary, I was sleeping with others while I was with Philip. Listen, I knew I had to protect myself somehow. Yes, I do not think I could ever love anyone else. Now, listen, I've learned my lesson. I went with a nice Jewish man in Harrison with the house where he lived with his dead wife, right. The whole bit. And I've been thinking these past weeks, maybe that is the thing to do, stop running away from my destiny, forget about the sexy cads who ruin me, and find a nice rich Jewish man who I can hostess for and replace the dead wife for, whose picture is all over the place. Right? Wrong. Well, I presided or whatever you call it over one dinner party for him and that cured me. Talk to those bankers. God. Never again. I gave him his walking papers. You can't go home again. Never."

She sat looking up at the ceiling, tears falling from the corners of her eyes. Mary Catherine put her hands over hers.

"Oh, stop it. I'll be all right. I've had the best. I'm not really complaining. I travel a lot and have fun. My kids are all grown and in beautiful shape. I just need a man, that's all. It's as simple as that. I bluster and act tough, but I like to do for a man. I miss that. What I'm saying is, is it really so terrible to need a man? Listen, I'm fifty years old and I'm not afraid of anybody. I've lived my life and I know what works for me and what doesn't. I've got the career bit and I'm successful, but I don't like coming home to an empty house. I can make as much money as a man and be as shrewd as one. But I'm not embarrassed to say it, there is nothing, but nothing in this world like the interchange between a man and a woman who've got something going. It's the best. And if I make a little less money, and don't exert my executive ability to its ultimate potential because my energies go to a man, then so what. I've got someone to grow old with and who cares if I get appendicitis in the middle of the night.

"Anyway, enough about me, for God's sake, how maudlin can you get, especially after not seeing you for a long time. You always do that to me, all the stuff keeps pouring out of me when I'm near you."

"Frieda, I'm fine. Really."

They had forgotten about Myra, who had settled herself on the couch behind their chairs. She got up and slowly stretched. She came around and stood in front of the two of them.

"You know, I didn't mean to eavesdrop. Really."

"Oh, Myra, I don't care. It's old stuff, yesterday's news."

"But you know what?" Myra asked, feeling her pocket for a cigarette.

"What?"

"You might be lonely, and that's all I kept thinking about that couple in there. Such loneliness, such afraid of being alone together. Such needing others to take away the burden of each other. I feel for that. But you, how would you like it if your kid wanted to die? How would you like that, that's the greatest loneliness of all, the worst, the worst." Mary Catherine lit the cigarette for her.

"Myra, sit down."

"No, I'm going. Stanley's alone with the kids. Gilda's home too. I just had to get away for a while."

"What the matter?"

"All I'm saying is, well, maybe there are no men to love you around and maybe there's pain, but how would you like it if your daughter, age fifteen, sat on the steps of the YMCA and took 300 milligrams of Quaalude that she and two friends had stolen from the pharmary." Dry-eyed, Myra went on. "That's trouble, my dears, that's real trouble, and then this child, this fifteen-year-old who has lived in your house your and her whole life, looks at you after the police have left, after she's almost died, and she tells you that it doesn't matter. 'It doesn't matter, Ma', she said, and this is the third time she's tried it. The third time that fifteen-year-old stomach has been pumped. And she told the police they can lock her up, beat her up, but she's not going to testify against her friend, who they haven't caught yet. 'I will never testify again,' she told me, 'never, never again because you made me testify against Daddy when I was seven and I'll never do it again.'"

"Oh, Myra."

"So, my dears, that's trouble. I fought so hard to keep that child and Ted kidnapped her twice—do you remember that, Frieda? Mary Catherine, you weren't in town then—and I had to keep him away from her. And now she hates me and wants to die. Three hundred milligrams of Quaalude right on the Y steps. They swallowed it there. Just waiting for someone to see them.

"I don't cry anymore. Stanley's wonderful. He helps, and Gilda's been seeing a psychiatrist since she was eight. I thought the drug scene was over. I thought they were going to booze; that would be a comfort, I know what to do about that. But this. Anyway, that's real trouble. You and Herb and Alice, that's nothing. That's kid stuff. O.K. Enough. 'Bye, girls. It really was good to see you, Mary C. If I call, will you come

to dinner? You turned me down about three times and
I stopped calling."

"I don't go out much, Myra. I really don't."

"Well, I'll try. We both like you."

"O.K. O.K., Myra."

"Come on," said Frieda, "let's get out of here. It's
late and it's dark and I forgot to feed the dog. Hell,
I've got to feed somebody."

Chapter Eighteen

"He's driving me crazy."

"Who?"

"Dave."

"Now what?"

The next day Mary Catherine and Lolly were sitting
on the steps of the high school auditorium, waiting to
pick up their girls. Young people in jeans and sweaters
walked by them, books under their arms. It was Thursday afternoon, and the students had begun to unwind
already. The weekend was coming.

"He really is getting paranoid."

"Now what?"

"He really wants me to quit this assignment. Give
it up. Fifteen hundred dollars, and one of the most
interesting things I've ever done. He's crazy and is
driving me to distraction."

"Why Lolly, why? More of the same?"

"If you really want to know, I think he's jealous. I
really do. He just doesn't get the excitement I do out
of his work anymore. He's for women fulfilling them-

selves all right, just so long as his pants still get to the
cleaners and I call the man to come fix the lawn-
mower, and I'm responsive as a geisha girl in bed and
he gets interesting meals, then, then it's fine, just
dandy, then I can be as fulfilled as I want. But who
the hell can be all those people at once? I can shut
myself up in my studio for ten hours at a time, the
hours just fly by, Mary Catherine, I forget all about
him when I do, and the girls, and everything. He yells
because I let the tires on the car go down too low, he
walks around, literally walks around with this little
pocket air-measure thing he bought, measuring how
many pounds of air I've got in the tires. He's got a
profession, he earns a good living, he has stature, and
everybody thinks he's a fine teacher. So what does he
want from me? I do what I have to do, the house is
clean, for God's sake, the kids aren't going barefoot, so
what is his trouble? He's driving me crazy and I'm
telling you, Mary Catherine, I just don't know what to
do about it."

"When did all this happen? Last night things seemed
all right."

"Oh, it's been coming." She bent down to tie a bow
in her sneakers.

"You know what, Mary Catherine. You know what
the worst part of the whole thing is. It's so distracting.
Just damn distracting. I don't get my work done, I'm
so angry at Dave inside for denying me this thing that
gives me such pleasure. 'This is not the girl I married,'
he says to me. 'That was not my expectation,' and
what the hell did he think I was going to do with my
Phi Beta Kappa key, wear it through my nose and
that would be that? He knew he married a bright
woman, that's what attracted him to me in the first
place, so what's the big surprise now that I want to
make use or a little sense out of my brains and my

talent? I'm so disappointed in him I could cry. I
thought he was more secure than that. He swears up
and down he's not threatened, but, Mary Catherine,
he must be. Why would he be putting me through this?"

"Is he afraid you will meet someone else, someone
more interested in your work than he is?"

"No, I don't, I really don't . . . He just doesn't want
his apple cart upset, he doesn't want this housewife
he's had for years to lose her touch."

"So why don't you get a maid?"

"Oh, we have a cleaning woman, you know that,
and she'll cook dinner sometimes. That's not it. He
wants me to do it. Not, for God's sake, that I can do
it better than anyone but only because that's what wives
are supposed to do. You know you've been there when
we have company. If I've been working all day it
doesn't make any difference, he'll serve drinks and
that's it. Just sit there while I make the whole dinner,
move the hors d'oeuvres around, clear the table. I
don't understand him, he is an intelligent man with the
best head in the world, but his mother spoiled him
rotten and I'm paying for it."

A bell rang and tens of doors opened onto the
campus. Students spilled out, chattering singing, holding hands, arms around each other, a great hum filled
the hair.

"Lolly. He's a good man."

Tears were in Lolly's eyes.

"Don't you think I know it, don't you think I know
that I've got one of the best around. I mean, I waver
sometimes in my yearning to know what other men
would be like, I'd give anything to have a few affairs
and not have anything change but I know I can't have it
all ways and that if he screwed around I would die.
Look, maybe he does for all I know, but I don't know,
and I think he doesn't. And I think the reason the sex

has stayed so good all these years is because we have made some kind of commitment, that we want to survive and so we can be free as we want with each other because we know there will be no other partners. I don't know, but that's just it. I don't know how I'm going to be able to get anywhere professionally and keep my husband all the same time."

Francie and Sarah Bernstein walked up to where the two women were sitting.

"And you know what gets me madder?" Lolly's voice became shrill. When she became excited it wailed with the intensity of the banshee.

"What gets me madder is that in company, when we have people over, he is marvelous, just marvelous. You'd never know a goddamned thing was wrong. Would you, when you see him I'm sure you think nothing but what a bright adorable man is sitting over there. And I'm resenting him, I know I am. The last three nights I've just turned over. I can't respond. I'm too boiling, I'm furious inside."

"Lolly, here come the girls."

"It's all I even talk about with Dr. What's his name, fifty dollars an hour to be a broken record. Dave's just got to understand that I'm not who I was, and not only that, I never wanted to be that stay-at-home in the first place."

"Mother, I'm late for my ballet lesson." Sarah Bernstein had hair down to her waist and round black eyes. She wanted to be a ballet dancer, and for the first five years Lolly had dropped everything at two twenty, three times a week, to pick her up and take her to class. In six months she would be sixteen and would be able to drive and Lolly would be free, or freer, since Rebecca still had to be taken to the orthodontist twice a week and driven to her volunteer job at a community center in the next town. Eastville's kids were trapped in a way, relegated to hitchhiking, which their parents frowned on, walking long distances, or encountering the set mouths and tapping feet of mothers longing to be liberated from the tyranny of the car.

"And the magazines are killing me," Lolly continued, not missing a beat. "I read a piece somewhere the other day that just made me sick."

"Let's walk to the car."

"Mother, I've got three minutes to get there."

"O.K., O.K. I'm going. Hello, Francie, how are you? This article, I can't remember where it was, written by this wildly successful feminist with her picture all serene and chic in the left-hand corner. And she's talking about how marvelous it is to be a working mother. Well, sure she concedes that to be affluent is important in the whole picture, since you can always have help to prepare the canapés for the dinner parties or whatever, and of course she lives in the city and is a big-time editor on a ladies' magazine and her husband earns a lot of money, but that still wasn't the point—"

"Mother, I really feel gross when I come in late."

"Sarah darling, here's the key, go warm up the car."

"You do this every time. I could just die.'

"Sarah, I'm coming, for God's sake. All right, I won't drag this out, but anyway, the last line in the article was by the husband, this big successful lawyer who comes home and helps with dinner and gets the kids off to school in the morning since the housekeeper and the lady dynamo sleep late."

"What did he say?"

"He said, 'My wife is the most interesting person I know.' The point being that he allows her to be. A nice secure, affluent man. That, my dear, is of course the key to Women's Liberation, finding the right man, finding a man who is absolutely turned on by a woman's activity. And you know what, Mary Catherine,

Dave is not it. He wants that old insecure Lolly whose major accomplishment of the month was a cherry pie. Can she bake a cherry pie, Davy boy, Davy boy—that's what it comes to, and—"

"Mother, you're mean, you're just being mean. I'm late already."

"Sarah darling, I'm so sorry," Lolly shouted as she stepped into her car. "I'll see you Saturday, Mary C., at Deborah's. God, Dave and the typewriter willing."

"What was all that about?" Francie said, brushing some dust from her mother's shoulder.

"Dave is resentful of Lolly's working."

"I can't understand how a man can be resentful. It's only good for them in the long run."

"How?"

"Because, God, if you're doing something you love, you bring a whole excitement to the house in the evening."

"How have you felt about my working all these years?"

They moved into the car, and Francie buckled the seat belt on her side. Mary Catherine straightened the mirror and buckled herself in.

"I like it."

"That's it? 'I like it'? There must be more."

"I think I'm proud of you and I get a big kick out of you when you get excited after making a big sale. But I hate it when you're not home when I get home from school. I hate it."

Mary Catherine looked at her daughter. There were tears in her eyes.

"Francie, I never knew you felt that strongly."

What's it all about, Mary Catherine thought. What are we here for. To indulge ourselves, to make love on windy Tuesday afternoons, to be as sharp in business as any man could ever be, to be mothers, to cuddle and guide. Who are we, how do we be all these things all at the same time.

"I don't know. When I was little and all the other mothers were always home at three o'clock, I used to pray at night that the next day you would be there with cookies in the oven and hot chocolate waiting for me on the kitchen table. With real whipped cream in it. Is that silly?"

"Of course not. But what do you think you'll do with your kids?"

"I don't know if I'll have them."

Mary Catherine looked at the big eyes, thoughtful.

"Oh, I don't know, Mother, it's dumb to talk about it now. Hilda and I were talking about it the other day. Whether or not we would ever get married, no less have kids. She definitely doesn't want to. I have mixed feelings. . . .

"How can a writer have children and give them the time they need? I wouldn't want to resent them. But I wouldn't want to stick my head in an oven like Sylvia Plath, either, if I got so frustrated."

"Why on earth does it have to be either or?"

"Because it's just what you were talking about with Lolly. If you don't find the right man, forget it. If you don't find a man who understands, forget it. Anyway, what do I know, I'm only sixteen."

Mary Catherine drove on in silence. There were several hitchhikers on the road but she did not want to prick the mood. She passed them by.

"I dreamed you and Dad were together again last night."

"I thought I heard you screaming in your sleep."

"Very funny. It was kind of nice. We were all having dinner together and Dad reached out and smoothed your hair. It was nice."

"Would you like him to come back? Would you like us all to be together again?"

Francie didn't answer right away. It was as though some images had to be conjured in her head first: 3 A.M., screaming slurred words, muffled cries, tears, so many tears.

"No. Drop me at Hilda's, Mom. We're going to tape some songs."

What to say. What to feel. Don't worry. She'll survive. It's not so terrible. So many divorces. Love, your magic spell is everywhere. Not here. Love is a many-splendored thing. Love is where you find it. Love's in bloom. Not here. My child is loving but the unit is torn asunder, no more threesome, no more Mommy, Daddy, and me, no more Daddy shaving in the morning, lather thick, lather he would put on her face when she was little and he would give her an empty razor to shave with. And they would laugh like conspirators. Pals. No more. I will join a commune, I will give my child ten fathers. In a hundred years, the futurists say there won't be any family anyway. No more shaving in the morning.

"What are you thinking about?"

"Why?"

"I could just see the wheels turning. Mom. Are you all right?"

"Oh, I worry about you. About how this all is going to affect you. What boys you will go out with, who your serious relationships will be with. I can't help but be very Freudian and hope the divorce and relationship with Dad won't affect you badly. I worry about it. I would like you to find a loving man. One you could love."

"Mom, I don't want to talk about it. Hilda's is on the next street. You always pass it."

"Sorry. What time will you be home?"

"Dinner, I'll be home for dinner, Mom."

"Yes, dear."

"Don't worry about me. I know. Just don't worry."

Francie flounced out of the car swinging her bag over her shoulder. She leaned down and through the open window thrust her ringed hand at Mary Catherine.

Mary Catherine sat in the car for a long time before starting. She had an appointment to meet Seth at his office in ten minutes.

Chapter Nineteen

There is eating in this world. There is whipped cream melting on your tongue, chocolate mousse disappearing, becoming air, there is butter oozing into bread, covering the hot surface like lava. There is veal and lemon with just a bit of parsley, tart. There is a world of taste and tongues out there and she never knew about it till now.

It was Friday night and Malcolm's wife was in Florida. Mary Catherine was having her last supper. She and Malcolm were ending. She could feel it. She had sensed it this afternoon as they made love in his friend's apartment, a one-room ghost town that smelled of cement caves, where milk soured in the refrigerator, and magazines, from week to week, like cobwebs stuck to stucco, never changed.

They had argued over an Albee play they had seen the night before. "*Seascape* is exactly like a Magritte," he had said, "there is a terrible detachment, yet a painful relevance." Mary Catherine never would have had a discussion with Carlo about Albee, no less Magritte, he being more apt to dissect the innards of his boat than the ideas of a complicated man. But Malcolm sounded like the old *Intellectual Digest*, chewed, swallowed, and regurgitated like the *Reader's Digest*. The commitment was canned, the opinion secondhand. Mary Catherine was sure he had read that about Magritte somewhere.

That first time they had lunch in a fashionable East Side French restaurant in New York, where the maître d' had conspiratorially whispered, "Bonjour, your table is ready, monsieur," he had told her he didn't want to get involved. He had been faithful for thirteen years, and then had fallen in love with a twenty-year-old airline stewardess. It had knocked the hell out of him and he had gone crazy. Sleeping with the stewardess all night, then rushing back to his own bed at five in the morning. He had gotten an ulcer and his hands had begun to shake. And when he broke up with the stewardess, there had been a succession of "lollipops," but for the past several years he had been clean, as he called it.

So they had had lunch four times before they decided to go to bed. "I will go to bed with you," Mary Catherine had said over that lunch, the almonds crunchy on top of the sole, the petals of the single rose in a vase in the center of the table covered with down. After the fencing was over, she had said, "O.K., Malcolm, I will go to bed with you and take the consequences." And she had meant it. At the time.

Tonight, sitting across from him at dinner, she wasn't so sure if the consequences could be taken. When she had gone to the ladies' room and stood looking at herself in the mirror, he was still there inside her from the afternoon lovemaking, and in a rush came pouring out of her, making her warm standing there looking at

herself in the mirror in the ladies' room, the attendant
in the black dress and white apron sitting on a brocade
stool reading a movie magazine.

Looking up, she said, "What's that smell, darling?
Is it Joy? Sure, I knew it. Oh, my God, darling Hazel
Scott gave me a bottle of that ages ago, the cologne.
Fifteen dollars it was. My, that smells good, darling."
She handed Mary Catherine a towel. "Hon, your hem
is turned up, that means you're going to get a new out-
fit." Her brown hands rested on her black uniform.
Mary Catherine heard her two quarters clink into the
dish.

Staring at herself in the mirror, she pursed her lips.
Looked at her mouth. This is the mouth that Malcolm
kissed. This is the mouth that kissed the chest that
touched the thigh that smoothed the hip. This is the
mouth that Malcolm built. She wanted to think of a
word for his thighs, long, hard, white. As she combed
her hair she longed for a vocabulary. Where could she
find the words to equal the pleasure in touching him.
The words are not in *Playgirl,* she thought, with those
flaccid penises lolling lopsidedly between pubic hairs,
pubic hairs red, pubic hairs black.

She loved Malcolm's thighs, and his forearms. What
she liked best was to smooth his face, flat-handed,
cheek by jowl, cheek by ear, cheek by hair. His buttocks were fleshy and appeared womanly, but she liked
them. "I love your body," she had told him this afternoon, rubbing the white flesh with the remains of summer still on it. Men write about the round apples of
women's breasts, what can I call your penis, dormant,
or your steel thighs?

He is cocky, she thought, and self-centered, able
to go on endlessly about his idiotic college pranks and
conquests, and his good mind really is wasted on all
the trivia he talks about. But his charm delights me.

Gathering up her bag, patting more perfume on, she remembered the very first time they had gone to bed. How he had asked her, that very first time, if she had anyone else, because if she didn't it wouldn't be good. Yes, she said, not going into it, answering him after she had asked why he had asked. She let it go until later, when from the bathroom, combing her hair, she had called out, why, do you want to be sure I am protected? He had mumbled something.

In the cab going to the station that first time he had said, "You know, we must be temperate," an odd word she thought at the time, "and not go wild with this thing."

And she remembered lying in bed that night thinking, quite coolly, "On the last day of this affair I will look back on this day and remember." And she recalled thinking that it was impossible, that it would end, and that she wouldn't miss it for anything.

"You're very quiet tonight," Malcolm said, getting up as she sat down.

If I could say what I was thinking, she thought, if I could truly put it into words, I would tell you that we have endured this short time because I decided long ago to take my cue from your casual air. I would say that this is a very civilized affair and for a single woman I am extraordinary in my restraint. I place no demands on you, never mention your wife or that you cannot see me most weekends.

"I always think of our time together like being in a cocoon. It's as though we don't exist except for those moments when we're in bed together."

"True, I suppose that's true. So?"

"So ours is sort of a test tube, isn't it. An experiment, a laboratory love."

"Mary Catherine, what are you driving at? Do you want dessert?"

"No, thank you, just coffee. Truly we have no endearments, no promises, no pain. Right?"

"Right. That's right. But we knew that, didn't we?"

"Are you aware that after we make love you move away? You move away imperceptibly and . . ."

"Go on."

"And do you know where you go, when you move away imperceptibly, you go to somewhere-else land, to office and telephone land, back to wife and children land."

"That's right." He was looking at her, eyes wide.

"You know what we are?" she said, cupping her glass of water with both palms.

"What?"

"We are restrained, affectionate friends. That's what we are. We're like people whose time together doesn't sing a full refrain. Ours is half a chorus, a light opera instead of the full four acts."

"My, you are metaphorical tonight. You are metaphorical and very strange."

"Yes," she said, not listening, "ours is a languid light opera. I can't cry in front of you, and you, you keep your urgency to yourself."

"What are you saying, Mary Catherine?"

"I'm just making an observation. Really, that's really all I'm doing. I understand it. I understand that some songs are like that. Their tune is only suited for humming. Do you know what I mean, Malcolm?"

She looked at him, at his aging pretty-boy face. A middle-aged baby face. That's what you have. Why didn't I notice before? Your eyes are too big and too blue for a fifty-year-old man, and your skin is too smooth, your hair too thick. It is a young face that seems about to crumble at any moment. There is something unreal about it, she thought, the baby face, the youthful pallor held up by an invisible string located somewhere under all that hair, and perhaps if pulled would cause all that pretty-boy Malcolm to fall. Ring around the rosy, pocketful of posy, Malcolm, Malcolm, all fall down, and then it would be all pug nose and pertness and thick lashes and shining teeth down around your shoulders. In repose, she thought, staring straight at him, in repose, when you are not busy being charming or sexy, you look like the fourth stage of Dorian Gray, the young light still shining in your eyes, the creases in your neck just beginning to indent themselves, the tiny lines on either side of your face, next to the ears giving ominous promise of further crumbling.

Malcolm looked relieved. She saw it in his eyes. He was tired, he really was. She was extraordinary and responsive in bed, true, but perhaps too much so because, if he was really honest about it, he wasn't up to it. He, again if he were painfully, scrupulously truthful, would have to admit that her warmth was threatening.

It worried him the day he had cried. He hadn't cried in years and this snip of a woman, smoothing his back, nails lightly skimming the surface of his ribs, had been asking him about his father.

"He died," Malcolm had said.

And when she pursued the question, about how did it feel watching him suffer so terribly those last days, it all came back in a rush, the metallic smell of the hospital, the curved ass of his father's favorite nurse, the endless bottles hanging over his head, the humiliating defeat of his body. How somebody else had taken over his bed, how some wasted thing had moved into his double room behind the green curtains. How he had tried to tell him then in some way that all those college pranks really didn't mean anything, that he would amount to something after all, that he wasn't angry anymore.

That he loved him.

When he said that, that day, lying in the gray afternoon, his legs caught in the twisted sheets, when he
said those words, he cried. From nowhere they came,
the tears. And this woman, this real estate lady, this
affair, this once- or twice-a-week lay had touched his
forehead and kissed his cheek. She held his face in both
her hands and hugged him to her chest. And he couldn't
stop. It all came back, how much he had loved the old
man, and he had felt so relieved when the sobs had
subsided. He hadn't cried like that since he was a little
boy. Certainly not right after the old man died.

He had felt foolish that day, and when it was all
over, feigned an appointment, even though he was free,
and didn't take her to dinner. He put her in a cab and
called his mother to see if she wanted a fast visit from
him.

Worrisome, worrisome someone who can tap your
tears. So that when she starts with the back-to-children
land and office and telephone land and the humming
business instead of the full chorus, or however it is she
mixes her metaphors, the handwriting is on the wall.

Intriguing she is. Different. Very. And if again he
would be confessional about it, he envied the pure
joy she got out of their lovemaking. She loved it.
Sure, well she didn't have to prove anything, just lie
there and take it. But true, he had never known a
woman who could experience sex so fully and so fre-
quently. Hell, he didn't have the stamina. The curiosity,
yes, the energy, no. But what did intrigue him was her
softness. He didn't know who her other lovers were, he
had asked her and was sure she was sleeping with
others, but he didn't want to know, not really. Not
important. But he couldn't understand how she could
be so tender with him, so loving, when he knew they
both knew that theirs was a casual affair. Was she the
same with her other lovers?

Well, it didn't matter really. He just had to do something. He couldn't jeopardize his marriage again, anyway. The good thing about Mary Catherine was that really even though she had backed into this thing, it was with her eyes open. She knew what she was getting into, and seemed wise enough to know how to handle it.

He might miss her, he wasn't sure.

He jotted a note to her on a napkin the next time she went to the ladies' room.

She found it in her coat pocket when she got home.

Dear Mary Catherine.

Some of the things you said tonight have thrown me off stride. Truly, more important, I think, is what you didn't say, since that involves what we do next. Where do we go from here?

Yes, it has been a tune "only suited for humming," but the melody has a haunting quality that surfaces to the consciousness, oddly when it seems to be all but forgotten. I think of French tunes that do not overwhelm, bittersweet and subtle, more like that quiet, deep-hued time after a rain than a brilliant spring day. So much for the metaphor.

There is this continuing feeling that our experiment (bad word but none other comes to mind) has run its course and we cannot go forward in suspended animation. We must now go either up or down. A disaster in either case. It's sad perhaps that we can't get drunk in each other and not worry about the hangover. But that's the fool's courage, essentially selfish and self-deluding, and the debris mocks self-respect. The endless irony. And so forgive me for humming but know that I was tempted to sing.

A big M was the signature.

A bit pretentious, Mary Catherine felt. But not bad.

Well, Dr. Stander, there it was. The risk. The risk-taking you kept talking about, remember? That stuff I was supposed to put myself into. I did it, Mary Catherine thought. Malcolm did move me, just a little bit. And, well, I'm still here, I guess. I'm still in one piece, I guess.

Chapter Twenty

A dry day for Deborah's party.

It was winter, which she hated, great smoky breath and toes that curled inside her fur boots. Still, it was a dry day. No snow, no rain, nothing damp about it. Cold. Too cold; as Joshua Gold would say, the great God Jehovah couldn't make it all of a sudden summer in the middle of February, she knew that. But still she was grateful for small favors. It was dry: no migraines, no sinus, a good day for a party.

"And Saturday shone dry," she wrote in her diary. This is an ostentatious little red book, she thought, writing in red ink. It is pretty stupid for a grown woman to have one of these red-velvet jobs with a tiny keyhole in front with an even tinier key with which to open it. She had kept one since high school, and months would go by sometimes between entries, but she had tens of them all packed away on the top of her closet in a Lord and Taylor hat box.

Today was the day of the party she was giving herself. Next week she would be married. Mrs. Sam Spade. No, of course that won't be her last name. Aronowitz. Oh dear. She preferred Spade. And she would go to Japan and buy one of those dresses with the square bustle over the behind and wear those clogs and mince along the streets with a high black wig with pencils sticking out of it. And Sam would take her to live in his castle in the sky, and if she were unhappy, like Rapunzel she would let down her long golden locks, which unfortunately were neither golden nor long, but she would manage. She would let down her bottle of J & B on a long piece of rope and it would go from the Jersey side across the Hudson river and some great giant Viking like Eric in the cigar commercial would pick up the bottle and read her message, "Help, I am being held prisoner in a penthouse paradise with all the booze I can drink, flowers in every vase, a checkbook in every pot."

Her mind was going too fast today. She had to stop it. Today was Saturday, right? Today was the day of her party for herself. But what was yesterday, where had yesterday gone, what had she done with Friday? She couldn't remember where she had been the night before. Bad sign. Bad sign. They talk about blackouts and I never had them before, but there are beginning to be a lot of days that just disappear.

The buzzer on her bedroom phone belched Essie's arrival.

She rasped into the phone, her first words of the day. "Essie, is that you?"

"Yes, Mrs. Shapiro. It sure is a mess down here."

"Why, what's the matter?"

"The cat got in the garbage, and the neighbor's dogs ripped up *The New York Times* all over the front lawn. What time is the bartender coming tonight?"

"About six, I think. Listen, Essie, do you have

everything you need? I did an enormous shopping yesterday, left a list for you."

"It sure is a mess down here."

"Listen, Essie, I'm going to get dressed and come right down and help you. Thanks for coming early. Could you put a pot of coffee on? Essie, there's a big box of clothes I collected from Mrs. Romano and Mrs. Bernstein's kids for your nieces. It's on the cellar steps."

"Thanks. How are you feeling?"

"Oh, great, just great, dear. How about you?"

"No. I mean really."

"Essie, I'm fine. Coffee would be heaven. Just put it up. I'll be down in a second. I just have to take a shower."

"Did you cut yourself in here last night?"

"What do you mean?"

"There's a trail of dried blood here in the kitchen."

"Not that I can recall. Well, love, I'll be right down."

"O.K. When are they going to deliver the liquor and the flowers?"

"Oh, God, thanks for reminding me. I forgot to order the flowers."

"See you."

She would put perfume in the light bulbs and lampshades like Arlene Dahl says, she would fill paper bags with sand and put candles in them and line the driveway with them, she would have the bartender wear white gloves. She would entertain like Cristina Ford and sweep down the stairs like her mother used to before the guests came to their summer place in Connecticut. Joshua Gold would hold court there, and short as he was, the ladies would succumb, and he would twirl them around the floor of their patio to the tune of "In the Mood." "Dance with me, Debbie, dance with Daddy," he would say, sweeping her in his arms, waltzing across the floor, and she would always stumble, big as she was, and gawky. At thirteen she was already almost taller than he, but he would hold her close and dance "cheek to cheek" with his little girl and she would feel funny and would always trip over her feet or his. "You're not smooth, honey, you've got to be smooth on your feet. That's what boys want when they dance with you, to hold you close and be smooth." But she couldn't be smooth when she danced with Daddy; she could never pull it off. But the ladies loved him. They could be smooth as he held them close and tight around the waist.

You can always tell what kind of lovers people are, she thought, by the way they dance. She smoothed the rumpled sheets on the bed. Tucked them in neatly, hospital-corner prim, like they taught her to do at sleep-away camp.

She and Abe used to fight on the dance floor. He wanted them to astound, to dazzle the ringsiders, she wanted to dance. So she tripped over his feet just as she had tripped over Joshua Gold's feet. But with Abe sometimes she would want to nuzzle up to him in a harmlessly lascivious fashion, and he would push her away, gently enough; he felt the line would be bad. He wanted to be an attractive couple and you couldn't be an attractive couple if your wife was giving you the dry hump on the dance floor in front of the orchestra, the singer with the red boa clutching the microphone, and the elegant folks in the front row.

Dance floors always seemed such mysteriously sexual places to her. Joshua Gold always wanted to dance with her and she was always uncomfortable with him, not knowing what to do with all that feeling attached to his smell, that pungent lemon and rum, the crush of his pinstripes against her cheek, the firmness of his hand around her waist.

In high school it was one of the places you went

to get touched. To get held. Not much opportunity anywhere else, since no one could get a car until they were sixteen and rarely would the parents lend them for dates anyway, so they would take the bus to the movies, arms around the stuffed fake-leather seats, a few fingers drumming nervously on a shoulder. Once in the movies was another thing, and hands could go swiftly to their checkpoint.

But dance floors were something special, especially in darkened roadhouses where she would go and sip her Tom Collins because that's what Joshua Gold told her was a chic, safe drink. To this day she would remember one night. Why could she remember it? How? when she couldn't even remember why there was a trail of blood in yesterday's kitchen. When she was sixteen she was out with Louis LaMotta. In fifth grade Louis used to go to the boys' john with a gang of boys and a ruler, and compare the size of their penises, and somehow get the results back to the girls. In sixth grade he used to pull the bra straps of the girls now that they were wearing them, and in seventh grade tickle the insides of the palm, which meant you know what. Now he was sixteen his yellow fingers smelled of nicotine and he blew air into her ear when they danced. Eddie Blake and Beatrice Sklar were dancing. (How could she remember those names?) They had been going steady since they were fourteen and they were dancing with their mouths pressed against each other, wide open. She could still see them dancing the whole dance that way. And she had envied them. God, she had envied them, as she had always envied them, those couples, all those lovers out there kissing in hallways, mouths open obscenely like blowfish at the beach, eyes closed, tongues touching, sitting on park benches, stopping at red lights, leaning up against store windows.

But Eddie and Bea, dancing in the dark, doing the two-step, their mouths open on each other for the whole time. She would never forget that.

That's the difference between us, Deborah thought, throwing off her robe, running the shower, we ladies of almost fifty who weren't brought up on drugs and dancing by yourself. When we were young there was form, there were steps, one, two, three, back two, three, we would fox-trot and rumba and there were specific things you had to do, not like the people who were young in the sixties who just wiggled around and gyrated on the floor all by themselves. Stepping into the shower, she squeezed her bulbous belly. What excess. That's a lot of belly there. I've got to stop drinking or take up French white wine, I hear it's the least fattening thing of all in the liquor department since they wipe the vats with brine and have less salt or something, not like the Americans or Italians. Anyway, when I am touring Japan in my big black car, handing out yen to the peasants, I will sip my French white wine and my pot will go down.

The hot water ran over her hair, down her face. It's true, she thought, head back, water falling into her mouth. I'm going to be fifty, that's what it is. That's the trouble. We carry with us all kinds of baggage the thirty-year-olds just don't. They were young in the sixties, we weren't. We were full-grown by then. We were brought up with some kind of structure, like steps in a fox-trot, we had some structure to fight against. They just had all the looseness thrust on them whether they wanted it or not. They've got all that sexual freedom and they don't know what to do with it because they're as bad as Mary Catherine, nobody makes them cry either. They never have to worry about getting pregnant like we did all the time, but anyway, that's not the problem, is it, old girl. She poured the shampoo over her hair, rubbing it in. The heat of the water gave her hope.

The problem is, she thought, that some of us are going to turn fifty soon. That's the problem. And the bloom is off some of us already, not to mention any names, and yet we're in our prime. So what do we do about that particular kettle of fish?

Well, she thought, turning off the water, stepping into her terry-cloth robe, which was ripping under both arms, well, I'm not going to think about that just yet so early in the morning on the day of my party.

Rubbing her hair with a towel, she dialed the phone. "Mary Catherine, can I borrow your punch bowl and the cups that go with it and a dozen forks?"

"Of course. I'll bring it over. I'll come over early anyway, Deborah. And Francie said she'll be glad to come over and help."

"Fine, great. I feel like a little girl, like it's my confirmation or something. Do you know that we went through three hundred bottles of champagne at my confirmation? I wore a white dress and smoked my first cigarette and danced with old Josh baby for three dances."

"How do you feel?"

"Oh, God, you sound like Essie."

"Deborah, how do you feel?'"

"I'm fine. As a matter of fact, I'm kind of excited. I love to give parties. I feel like a little girl."

"Have you thought any more about . . ."

"About AA? No, there is no reason for me to think about it, I knew you were going to say it. I am not an alcoholic, and if you continue to press the point I shall hang up."

"Deborah, you are infuriating. You drink too much."

"That, my dear, is rather a frontal assault. If I

remember the literature correctly, you are not supposed to come on so strong."

"Deborah."

"Stop it. Just stop it. No shrinks, no AA. There is nothing the matter with me. Anyway, a nice Jewish rich man like Sam Spade wants his Debdear luscious and straight, and Alcoholics Anonymous with all those drunks—that is not the place for a honeymoon."

"Deborah, you promised."

"When, just when did I promise anything?"

"Last night. Last night in your kitchen."

"Mary C., you sound like you're going to cry. You're certainly getting soft in your old age. Why bother? I'm unresurrectable."

"I am not crying. I am remembering last night at midnight sitting at your kitchen table and cutting my wrist like a blooming idiot and mingling my blood with yours. That's what I'm remembering and I'm as crazy as you are sometimes, it seems to me. Deborah, I'm worried about you."

"Love is a simple thing. There is an old Shaker song that goes, 'Love is a simple thing, is the gift to be simple, is the gift to be free,' or something. Your love is simple and Catholic and pure. But I don't remember mingling blood with you. I would never do that."

"Deborah, you called me up at eleven, made me come over and then wouldn't let me go home until I got the razor and slit my wrist and you did yours and we held them together. Our blood mingled, you said. Don't you remember?"

"That's what Essie said. There's a bunch of blood in the kitchen."

"You cut yourself deeply and it wouldn't stop."

"My God and your God must be smiling up there or down there, as the case may be."

"Promise me you'll go to the church on Monday."

"You know, you sicked that AA guy on me, that guy called me four times and finally I talked to him and he sounded like a blooming evangelist."

"Deborah, all I ask is that you go to one meeting. He said he would pick you up, take you there, and take you home. He's a friend of mine; I sold him a house last year. He's now a group leader. Please. Promise me you'll go. I swear if you don't go on Monday I'm not coming to your party. I mean it."

"Low. Low blow."

"Promise. Promise me, Deborah."

"Why do you bother?"

"Stop it. I don't want to hear any of the self-pity department today. I've got my own problems. I have to go to the tailor, the library, and take Francie for a haircut. I've got a big day. Don't start with me. Just promise me you'll go."

"You're a friend."

"Of course I'm a friend, who else would be having this stuff on the phone early on a Saturday morning? I want to have some coffee, read my *Times,* talk to my child, shave my legs, wash my hair. Put myself in order. Just promise me."

"Deborah, promise me."

"O.K., for Chrissake. I promise. Tell your friend to call me again and I'll go. I'll go to one meeting and if it's all confessional and a whole God bit, I won't stay. I'm Jewish, and I can't go for all that Billy Graham stuff."

"I can't stand this. It has nothing, nothing whatsoever to do with Billy Graham. Why bring Billy Graham into it?"

"There's a whole thing about God in it, and God has nothing to do with me. Do you know that in temple we had to sit upstairs, all the ladies, because

God communed better with the dovening men downstairs? I used to wave to Joshua Gold over the railing. And, Mary Catherine, the women used to wear silver fox jackets to temple on Rosh Hashanah, even if it came out in September, even if it was ninety degrees outside, they would wear those little silver fox jackets and stockings with seams."

"Deborah, God has nothing to do with it. You believe in each other. In yourself. You help each other. Harold Hughes—"

"If you tell me about Harold Hughes one more time, I'll throw up. I don't care if he went and dragged guys out of bars when he was governor of Idaho—"

"Iowa. Get your facts straight if you're going to be abusive."

"Who's abusive? It's just that you're a broken record, you keep saying the same things over and over all the time."

"But regardless of your prejudice. He did. He was AA and he made it. He was on the skids and was driving a cab and picked himself up to become governor, then senator. That's something. And you'll do it too, Deborah."

"I'll never make governor. Listen, don't start, don't start on me. I'll go. I'll go. Tell your friend to pick me up Monday. I'll go to the meeting with him if just to get you off my back. I'll be good. I'll turn over a new leaf. I'll get involved. I'll sign petitions, develop a social conscience, go door to door. Go on peace marches."

"There are no more peace marches. The war's over, so to speak."

"Mary Catherine, why do you bother about me?"

"Forget it. I'm not falling into that trap. I'll bring over the forks, and what else did you say?"

"Punch bowl and cups."

"O.K. I'll come very early with Francie."

"Mary C."

"What?"

"Did I really insist that we mingle bloods?"

"Yes."

"I did that when I was fourteen."

"I know."

"How do you know?"

"You told me."

"It means we're friends."

"We are."

"It's hard to say how I . . ."

"Never mind. . . ."

"How will you ever know?"

"Go to the meeting Monday."

"Yes."

"Love . . . Have a good day. I'll see you tonight. Good-bye."

'Bye, love. 'Bye, love. A friend in need is a friend indeed. Friendship, friendship, just a perfect blendship, when other . . . something be forgot, ours . . . will not da-de-da. Love is a simple thing. No, it isn't.

Chapter Twenty-one

"Francie, dear, please help me wrap these punch glasses in newspaper."

"You think Deborah and Sam will be happy?"

"I doubt it."

"Can't you stop her from marrying him?"

"She's so lonely."

"Roger used to tell me that he'd come home from school last year every afternoon and find her drunk in front of the television. Her eyes closed, the sound blaring. None of the beds were made and dishes would be in the sink from the day before."

"That was before she went to work."

"But when she did, she'd take days off and just sleep. Sleep the whole day long. I used to feel so sorry for him. He practically never comes home on vacations now. He goes to his father's in New York."

"Maybe Sam will give her a good life. Maybe she'll be happy after all, Francie."

"She shouldn't drink so much. Drinking stinks. . . . Who called so early?"

"It was Deborah."

"Mother, do you know Enid Havemeyer?"

"The little thin one who rides her bike over here all the time?"

"Yes. She ran away from home last night. Well, not quite ran away, as a matter of fact, her mother drove her to a friend's house."

"Why? I didn't think kids did that anymore."

"Now don't tell anyone."

"I don't even know the girl, or anyone who knows her."

"Well, her mother has a twenty-four-year-old boy-friend and Enid found out about it. The boyfriend has a wife and child."

"How old is Enid's mother?"

"Thirty-seven."

"You know, I swear this town gets more like Spoon River every day. What is going on with people? What would you do if I came home with a twenty-four-year-old lover?"

"Don't be silly."

"Really, what would you do? Would you run away?"

"No. I don't know. I don't want to talk about it. That isn't why I told you. It was just news."

"Oh."

It was more than just news. Mary Catherine knew that. She knew that Francie had her fears and her phobias, her worries about her mother. About if she ever got married again, she could never get used to another man. And anyway, men leave. Dad left. People leave; no sense in getting attached to them. Her mother, of course, was different. She'd never leave her. But she's really all I've got, Francie reasoned. Just the two of us. She was beginning to get used to it. She missed a man around the house. But it sure was risky.

Mary Catherine did not know how to put Francie's mind at ease, mainly because she was in such a state of turmoil herself. She patted her head.

"O.K., love, what are you going to wear tonight?"

"That dress we bought last week. We bought it for the party. You know, that's so insulting, you never remember anything, Mother."

"Francie, dear, I'm sorry. I forgot."

"You've always got so much on your mind."

"Well, I do. That's what happens when you get older. You get a lot of things on your mind. Enjoy it now, kid. Enjoy this carefree existence."

"Some carefree. I've got two exams on Monday and three papers due next week."

"I think you had better go get dressed. It's getting to be almost five and I told Deborah we'd be over early."

"O.K. I'll go upstairs. Do you think it will be a drunken brawl?"

"Francie."

"Because if it is, I'm just not going to go. I can't help it, Mother, all that drinking makes me sick. Do people your age smoke pot at parties?"

"Some do."

"Do you?"

"No. Not because I have anything against it. I don't like it."

"But you don't want me to."

"No. I think you're too young. Just like I think you're too young to drink. These outside stimulants or depressants or whatever they are do terrible things to the body and mind, and you're just not developed enough in either to take it. That's what I think. I really do. I can't force you to do anything. But all of us, it seems to me, should be able to get along with it in moderation. When I used to drink too much it was because I was unhappy. And it never never made me feel better. Never. Now a glass or two relaxes me, makes me forget about all those things we were talking about that I have on my mind. Does that make any sense to you?" God, don't make me sound like I'm lecturing, Mary Catherine thought.

"Everybody in school smokes pot. You can't go any where without it being offered to you."

"I know" Mary Catherine was waiting. She knew that when she and Carlo were at their worst, Francie was hanging around with kids who were into everything. During these last two years she had returned to her sweet, almost too sensitive self.

"I think I feel the same way you do. I'm not sure. The thing I dislike the most about pot is that people push it on you. As though you aren't a person who can make up your own mind. I don't like people telling me what's good for me. Do you worry about me and pot?"

"Sometimes. For the most part I trust you, I really do, because you know how I feel about it, but sometimes I don't trust the other guys."

"If you're going to worry, you should worry about the drinking. And, Mother, there are still kids in my school who are tripping."

"Why? Why on earth, why? I just can't understand it."

"They're always kids with problems. Most of them drink like crazy."

"There is something about a bunch of kids drinking that makes me furious."

"You sound so condescending about kids. We're people."

"Francie, of course you are. It's just so young."

"You don't have to worry about me, Mom."

Mary Catherine looked at her daughter. Sometimes Francie looked like the mother. As though she were the wise one. The one on whom she could depend. Whither thou goest.

"Read this," Francie said shyly as she ripped a sheet from her French notebook. "I wrote it in French class Friday. Just write me a note about it, don't tell me." And she was away. Mary Catherine heard the shower running.

My breast [the poem began], it yearns to run free
through tunnels made by overlapping
branches weighed down with smooth green leaves
and keep on running until it came to the waterfall;
a battle being fought between the rocks and
    raging waters
but it doesn't want to fall or swim or tumble
helplessly into the waterfall, it wants to
float down; just glide down like a figure
skater on cold ice

and at the bottom of the waterfall is a
person; a stranger but with warmth in his
heart, who is waiting with open arms and
welcoming eyes.
    but not just for my breast;
    for me.

"Francesca Romano, you crack my heart, soothe my
soul, give me such joy. My romantic, my lovely daughter." Signed, Mary Catherine Romano. She wrote it
on the back of a shopping list, and left it in the middle
of the kitchen table. It was one of those moments.

The phone rang. Deborah's voice sounded very high.
Breathless.

"This little girl was at a bar mitzvah, the paper said,
and she went upstairs in the temple to go to the bathroom. And this sixteen-year-old kid from the neighborhood, who wasn't invited, took her in the boys' room.
And raped her. During a bar mitzvah. It's true. It was
in the paper. I saw it in the *Times*." Deborah was crying. "She came running down the stairs almost naked,
with all her clothes ripped, with blood all over her,
crying hysterically. And everyone stopped eating their
chicken liver, and drinking their red wine, and stuffing
the bar mitzvah boy's pockets full of checks or whatever they were doing, and I guess wrapped her in
their coats or prayer shawls and took her to the hospital.
They shouldn't put stories like that in the paper. It
makes me too sad. Mary Catherine, imagine how she
felt, going to a party, having it end that way. The
number thirteen will haunt her forever, every time she
sees a solid gold pen she will shiver."

"Deborah, stop it. . . ."

"It's true. It's the most terrible story I've ever read."

"Deborah, are you all right? I'm just out the door to
bring the stuff over to your house."

"Mary Catherine, I'm never going to read *The New York Times* again."

"Deborah, it is, it is a sad story. Francie and I are leaving now."

"And she probably had to talk to the police, some policewoman I hope, one of that new modern squad of trained people who are trained to talk about rapes, I hope. And all the kids at school would know. And she probably hadn't even had her period yet. I just read it, I hadn't gotten to the *Times* today till just now, till I was dressing, and, Mary C., it's such a sad story. So humiliating."

"Deborah, please don't drink any more." Mary Catherine felt suddenly very tired. The evening was just beginning.

"I haven't had a drop."

"Deborah, dear, please. Is Sam there yet?"

"Soon. He's coming in a hired limousine with a chauffeur."

"My."

"I told him to park it around the back."

"Why?"

"I don't know. I think it'll look funny in front."

"Deborah, I'm coming over now."

Mary Catherine and Francie piled the punch bowl that Carlo's Aunt Sophia had given them for a wedding present, and a dozen cups that her two sisters Angela and Maria had chipped in to give them, in the back seat. Mary Catherine also brought dozens of daisies she had bought from the florist on her way home from town.

Francie was all rosy and sweet-smelling. Perhaps it would be a good evening after all.

A dead raccoon greeted them at the end of the street. The blood spilled out onto the asphalt. Mary Catherine couldn't look at the insides. Francie turned her head away. "I can't stand that, I can't stand that. Why do people do that, Mom? Why do they hit them?"

Whenever she was with Francie she controlled her outrage. Francie's rage dissipated her own. It was necessary to be in command. "I guess they don't want to have an accident, to swerve is to hit something or someone else I guess." She didn't sound very convincing.

"I don't care. It stinks to mash an animal into the pavement."

"It takes a lot of cars . . ."

"Stop it, I don't want to hear about it."

"I know. It kills me every time I see it."

"Well, people should stop it. Do something. Mother, call up the state police and make them get that body off the road. More and more cars will just mash it into nothing. I can't stand it."

Francie's eyes were filled with tears. Of course she's right. People could go around it. Or call up the state police themselves. Or something.

When they reached the corner, she stopped at a phone booth on the street. A gruff voice announcing the number of the Twenty-seventh Barracks answered, and when she gave that voice, which was probably expecting some dire emergency, some monumental accordion pileup on the Belt Parkway, the news about a measly raccoon who was slowly becoming part of Spruce Tree Lane's tar, she was amazed by the solicitousness. "O.K., lady, we'll take care of it. Thanks for calling."

Virtuous. She felt virtuous. A heroine to her child, to herself.

They rode along in silence to Deborah's house. It was almost six o'clock, the stores were just closing. Few people remained in town. It was the weekend. party time, Saturday night, time-to-have-a-good-time.

The streets emptied out suddenly. As though everyone had fled to air-raid shelters. As though some siren somewhere had sounded.

Within minutes it had become a dead town. Dead except, Mary Catherine thought, as she passed through Main Street, for the mannequins in the store windows. The two or three ladies' stores showed lithe ladies in bikinis, their stomachs deliciously concave, with perhaps only a slash of an appendix scar to mar their beauty. The bikinis and flowing terry-cloth robes, the silky slacks and colored blouses seemed frivolous, somehow, in the winter air.

Chapter Twenty-two

There was only one car in Deborah's driveway. They were early. But the kitchen was a whirlwind of activity, where Essie, a round black woman with bifocals, was washing shrimp in the sink, and Essie's daughter, Merrilie, was rolling dough for cheese balls at the breakfast table.

"Hello, Mrs. Romano. She's upstairs dressing. Thanks for the bowl, I need that. And the forks. Hi there, Francie, don't you look lovely."

"Thanks, Essie. Hi, Merrilie." Merrilie was Francie's ago. They lived in Jamaica, which was a long drive, but Essie knew Deborah needed her, especially since the divorce.

Essie was a Democratic committee woman from her district, had brought up four children and put them through college after her husband died. Ever since Abe left, she was sure Deborah was going to come to a bad end. Their relationship over the fifteen years had gone through subtle changes. Deborah had not been the madam for a long time, and yet Essie still called her Mrs. Shapiro. Yet Essie had assumed the maternal role, and while Deborah had relinquished her politically active one, Essie had picked up the banner.

"Yes, go upstairs and see if she's all right. She's been acting peculiar all day. Doesn't stop talking for one minute. She's driving me out of my mind. Just doesn't stop talking. Did you talk to her about AA?"

"Essie, she said she'd go."

"Thank God. When?"

"Monday. She promised me."

"Well, you keep after her. That girl's going to get herself good and sick."

Yet Deborah had ordered the flowers, and arranged them throughout the house. She had done everything she said she was going to do.

She and Abe had built this modern house for years after they were married, when they had moved straight to the suburbs from New York. Mary Catherine, unused to such lavish expenditures of money, always marveled at the extravagant landscaping, designed like delicate Japanese gardens. A renowned architect from Connecticut had designed the house on an unusual piece of property Abe had bought in Eastville, almost on the town line. One had to climb a steep group of steps to get to the front door, but from then on it was glass and brick, a sweep of space, two tones of gray. Joshua Gold had bought the land and given them the down payment for the builder. No one Mary Catherine had ever known had received that kind of generosity from a parent. Her own dowry had been three dresses her mother made, and a few war bonds her father had been saving for her.

Deborah and Abe had used a decorator fifteen years ago when they had moved in and everything had been new and shining. Full of hope.

Deborah had never changed a lampshade in all these years, and now the Oriental rugs were frayed, the authentic Eames chairs weakened by the passage of time, the upholstery ragged. Still, her natural flair gave the place some style, orange and red pillows splashed the white couch in front of the fireplace, and handsomely framed posters and prints enhanced the walls, which badly needed a paint job. Tonight the house worked, Mary Catherine thought, even though it was one of Eleanora's typical dvorcée's neglected palaces. The classic lines saved it, and the flowers and blazing fire and the good crystal shining, the festive air all held a smell of promise. Maybe everything would be all right after all. Maybe.

"Sam's going to be a little late," Deborah said, as Mary Catherine walked into her bedroom.

Deborah was wearing a robe she had bought at a thrift shop, all nineteen-thirties grandeur, with ostrich feathers at the cuffs and hem. Her slippers had puffs of fur on them too, the fuzzy stuff looking the way dandelions get when they're not dandelions anymore but feathery balls. It reminded Mary Catherine of summer when she used to blow them away, the feathers, puff the magic dragon of her breath, one two three puff and then you would know how many children you were going to have.

"Deborah, people are coming very soon."

"Two seconds, that's all it's going to take. I just have to put my face on."

"Deborah, you know that takes ages."

"So what, it's my party."

Mary Catherine looked at her friend. There was something different. She had never, never been mean.

"Sam's going to be late."

"I know."

"How. How do you know?"

"Deborah, you told me."

"When?"

"Just now."

"Oh."

"What are you going to wear?"

"That blue dress. That I got that time in Bloomingdale's."

"The house looks just lovely, Deborah. Essie's busy as a bee."

"I love Essie. I get filled up from Essie."

"What does that mean?"

Tired. I am tired of her innuendos about her terrible life. Please, God, let her stop drinking and become a human being again. Let me stop thinking about her and worrying about her. Let me get back to my own things.

"You want to get a laugh, or a cry, one or the other?"

"What?"

"Look at this. It's a Christmas card from some guy I met at the Parents Without Partners meeting I went to."

The card was large and handmade. It was a crudely drawn picture of a Christmas tree with balls on it. At the top of the page in bold letters it said "New Year's Resolution" and inside each ball was written the New Year fantasy of the sender. He wanted to "play tennis with Deborah, meet Deborah's sons, read poetry with Deborah, make love with Deborah."

"Who is he?"

"A tall skinny guy who had just been divorced. Whose wife ran out on him. He was so lonesome. He called me this morning and asked me how my love life was, which is without a doubt one of the more revolting openers for any conversation. I told him I was getting married and moving to Japan. Is that something."

"Yes."

"Mary Catherine? A terrible thing happened this morning."

"What?"

"I discovered a gray hair in my pubic hair."

She delivered it with such a straight face that Mary Catherine burst out laughing.

"God, you're too much. Just too much."

"It just so happened that it upset me very much. Just one more battle to combat. It's just not like getting them on your head."

"Give in, give in already."

"Do you ever watch David Susskind?"

Deborah had stripped naked in a moment. It was as though the legs belonged on a Barbie doll, so long and thin they were. Her hips were flat. The belly swollen. After forty we get the face we deserve, Mary Catherine thought, but what happens to bodies is that they cease having secrets. The skin, so much thinner now, reveals the veins and capillaries that had been hiding underneath all these years. All those inner workings of the nervous system are displayed like a road map. Deborah's swelling blue veins and skin, coarse and dry, could not be erased despite her lavishing fifty dollars a month of loving attention to it.

"Well, the other night he was interviewing this madam, Mary C., and she was out of this world. Pauline something her name was, and she came from the South or West or something. Anyway, she was very ladylike and pristine about her profession. I liked her so much; she gave it all such class, such dignity."

"Deborah, get dressed."

"I am, I am. I am."

"What time did you invite people for?"

"I don't remember. Anyway, she kept talking about the lovely preachers she had in her whorehouse, politicians, governors, lieutenant governors, judges. She wouldn't allow drinking in her house and all her girls had medical exams. Have you ever wanted to be a whore, Mary C.?"

Deborah had put on the filmy Israeli gown she had bought. It may have suited her in the store mirror, but tonight it hung badly. Yet she still could give the illusion of chic. She had little diamonds in her ears and pointed black-satin shoes. She made up her face with short, swift strokes. She was late. It would just have to do.

"She never allowed her girls to use curse words," she said, "and kept talking about sex being the most beautiful thing in the world but how could people use that terrible four-letter word that they do to describe it, it just doesn't do justice to what intercourse is, she said. She was fat and old and sort of gross, but she had a certain class. People should have class. Don't you think?"

The buzzer sounded. "What is it, Essie?"

"Mr. Aronowitz is here."

"Oh, swell. Tell him I'll be right there. Mary C., do I look all right?"

"Deborah, you look fine. It's going to be a great party." She hugged her.

"I'm nervous. Like a little girl. I haven't had anybody in this house in such a long time."

"I know."

"Thanks, thanks, Mary C."

She turned and flounced out the door, giving herself a final dab of L'Heure Bleue behind the ears.

Mary Catherine followed her down the stairs to the living room.

Sam did indeed look like a penguin, she thought,

viewing him from afar, but he was much more present-able than Deborah had pictured.

"You must be Mary Catherine. Deborah adores you."

"Hello, Sam, I'm so glad to meet you."

"She just thinks you're the cat's meow."

"Would you like a drink, Sam?"

"Love it."

"Deborah's got the bar set up in the dining room."

"Hi there, Charlie, how about a scotch on the rocks?"

Charlie. His name is Ezra. He'll probably never work for Deborah again.

"You're in the real estate business, I hear. How's tricks?"

"Well, not so good, mortgages are hard to get and—"

"Do I ever know it. I closed this deal for downtown Broadway the other day, a quarter-of-a-million job and believe you me, it was almost impossible. But we pulled it off. I have this combine, you see, and we go into deals. Listen, if you ever come across something out here in the sticks that you think I'd be interested in, give us a call." He reached inside to his breast pocket and took out a card. It had maroon writing on it and was embossed.

"Have you caught the Edward Weston show at the Modern?"

Mary Catherine could have kissed him. He was try-ing so hard to be Eastville.

"Well, no as a matter of fact. . . ."

"It's gorgeous. Just fine. Really swell."

Cars started to come into the driveway. Deborah was in the kitchen and Mary Catherine could hear her.

"Francie, Roger called from college today," she heard her say in a high-pitched voice, "he said he was sorry he couldn't make the party. You should see him; he must have grown two inches since he's there and he loves it. Essie, never mind; I'll get the door. Just you continue what you're doing, dear."

From the back of her head Mary Catherine could feel it beginning. The hum. The party hum. Saturday nighthood. And, as if she were holding the shell of the room to her ear, she heard clinking glasses and muted music, voices, the rise and fall of voices. The room was suddenly filled with people.

Every time the door opened, the cold smell mingled with the wood smoke, the cigarette smoke. Saturday night time. Somehow sad.

Sam wandered away. Mary Catherine glimpsed her daughter with a tray full of cold shrimp. She looked older. Contained. Pretty soon, it won't be long now and she'll be gone. An empty bedroom. A quiet house. It won't be long now.

"Mary Catherine, you look sensational. Where have you been keeping yourself?"

"Hello, Keith. How are you? Where's Doris?"

"You haven't heard."

Not another one.

"No. What?"

"Separated. Finished."

Keith was English and worked for an advertising agency. He was younger than Doris and not half as nice. He was wearing an ascot and a double-breasted blue jacket with gold buttons. He looked as though he should go rowing in the park immediately.

"I'm moving to the city. As soon as I can. My experience with the country involves a bunch of divorcées who are frustrated lushes. Present company excluded, of course."

"Of course. Is Doris going to stay here?"

"I suppose so. How about lunch in town sometime?"

"Oh, I'm sorry, Keith. I'm seeing someone seriously."

That's the appropriate term, I think, Mary Catherine

mused, or should it be I'm involved, or should it be go peddle your papers elsewhere?

"Well, that's good news; I hadn't heard that."

"News doesn't get around town as fast as it used to."

"You certainly are looking well, I still think, oh, hi, Jane, where have you been keeping yourself . . . ?" He mumbled a retreat and was gone.

Most of the women had long gowns or flowing skirts, and the men didn't wear ties but sleeveless sweaters over shirts open at the neck or turtlenecks with great knubby stitches. Everyone looked well fed and sleek, toned. The group was very attractive, thought Mary Catherine, looking out at them, hearing the animated sounds coming from corners of the room. Sam seemed to be going over very big with Frieda Latner, who looked down from her height onto his baldness. They seemed to know a lot of people in common. She spotted Frank Snow, who shared an office with Dr. Stander, and kept away from him, since for some reason she felt uncomfortable. As though somehow her secrets had sifted through the walls out into the waiting room and into Snow's four walls.

John Slater was with Miriam Frank. His wife had just run off with a college professor, and Miriam, who had recently terminated a long period of residence with a portrait painter, was free again. Years ago she wouldn't have looked at John. Musical chairs. Changing partners. Incest is next, Mary Catherine thought. The formerly marrieds in a small town just run out of people to see, so they have to start the cycle all over again. Wouldn't it be something, she mused, if we all ended up with the same husband or wife we had in the first place.

It occurred to her that she really didn't want to know all this about everybody. It just came from living here a few years, seeing the same people all the time, absorbing their joys, their miseries, without even realizing it.

There was a great flurry and commotion at the door. Laughter and bubbling. Aunt Eleanora had arrived.

"Wouldn't miss this for the world. Where's the happy couple? Hello, Mary Catherine, love."

"Well, Deborah's around somewhere, that's Sam over there. Hello, Henry."

Henry, the new husband to-be, never did get a word in edgewise, but he absolutely doted on Eleanora and that's what seemed to matter at this stage of the game. Eleanora was wearing a black suit slashed to the belly button with no blouse underneath and an Indian necklace around her neck. Her blue eyes were lined in blue and she had rouged her cheeks.

"Eleanora, you look so well. So beautiful."

"How do you like this suit? Isn't it smashing? I designed it. It's in the new line, coming out at Bonwit's in the spring in shantung. I've decided to bring back shantung. Oh, God, there's Frieda, I haven't seen her since the last time I was here. Let me introduce Henry to her. Take my cape, dear."

And she was off. Mary Catherine went into Deborah's bedroom and laid the cape on the bed. In the mirror on the door of the bathroom she saw a figure, sitting in her chair by the desk holding a glass. A bottle of scotch was on the table.

"Deborah, what are you doing in here? Everyone's here."

"I know, dear, just taking a little rest. What do you think of Sam?"

"He really seems awfully nice. We had a nice talk."

"He's vulgar and he's gross."

"Deborah."

"He's too fat."

"Deborah."

"Oh, I'll be all right. I resent the fact that I need him, I resent the fact that I can't make it on my own."

"You know you can."

"Look, Mary C., just let me sit here a minute. I'll be right out. I see Keith Granger is available again."

"Who wants him?"

"He's attractive. She's so nice. I wonder what happened."

"He's a vain peacock."

"You're so fussy, Mary Catherine, that's what's wrong with you; you'll never fall in love. Me neither, I'll never fall in love either. The trick is not to want to fall in love, to cross it off your list of priorities of things you want out of life."

"Let's go back."

"O.K. Just give me a few minutes. I feel a little shaky."

"You sure?"

"Absolutely. See if Essie's all right. God, Francie is getting gorgeous."

"I know."

"I always wanted a girl. Well, see you in a minute."

The time has come, the walrus said, to talk of many things, let's talk of many things, Deborah thought. Like I don't like this party, that's one thing, stretching out in her easy chair, legs long on the ottoman. If it were at someone else's house, I would have gone home by now. Her bedspread used to be white. There was a whole blue tint to it now. It's dull, the party is, the people are dull, I know what they're all going to say. I don't feel pretty. I used to make such entrances. No more entrances. And Sam. Sam. I can't. I can't do it.

She tried to get up off the chair. This is a bad night. Not a good one. I can feel it. Got to go inside. Got to be a hostess with the mostess, got to eat something, got to get through this night.

The hum had grown louder. A great cacophony now. The food was being served. Everyone applauded as Essie, Francie, and Merrilie brought out the stroganoff and noodles, giant hunks of Italian bread, salad, pitchers of wine, fruit and cheese, and two cakes that Essie had baked, one pie. There was too much food, but Deborah had a theory, if you're going to do something, do it.

She appeared at the door of the dining room. Barefoot, shoes, stockings off. Earrings off.

"Listen, everybody, Essie worked her butt off to make a good feed here, so eat up. The food's fabulous." She was shouting, weight on one foot, her hair in her eyes. Mary Catherine heard her from the other side of the room. Voices seemed to be coming out of the ceiling, off the floor, bouncing off the wall, the music from the hi-fi drowned out the words so that all one heard were the periods and exclamation points. Mary Catherine was determined to keep her eye on Deborah, but one obstacle after another kept putting itself in her way. Deborah was almost percolating, a coffee pot just about ready to boil over, the sound was just right. In a moment. It would all happen. Mary Catherine knew it.

"Lionel, oh, God, you came. Well, I don't know if you came but you certainly arrived at the party." Deborah threw herself into Lionel Forrester's arms. Pressed her body next to his. Lionel was a newscaster for a major network and a coup to have at every party. He tried to extricate himself from Deborah's embrace. Mary Catherine tried to get over to the food table to unglue her. Someone turned the music louder. Someone else must have put perfume into the lamps or something, the place smelled so heavy. It kept getting darker. Sam and Deborah had barely exchanged a few words. Sam couldn't get away from Frieda. Francie, where was Francie, Mary Catherine sipped her scotch, she hadn't eaten all day and the first swallows sang in her head. Sober sober who's got the sober, she thought, got to stay sober. Deborah's daft, Deborah's delirious, got to keep my eye on the sparrow, got to watch Deborah carefully tonight. Mary Catherine moved in and around the skirts and slacks, suede, leather boots. Dave Bernstein came up from behind, putting his arms around her waist.

"Hello, lovely."

Turning, she said, "Oh, Dave, I was wondering where you were. Where's Lolly? I'm missing her."

"Out. Away."

"What does that mean?"

"She did it."

"What, she did what?"

"She took off. Has eleven interviews lined up in seven states on that article. She left this morning. She told me to kiss you good-bye; she didn't have a chance to call you. It came up very fast, or let's say we decided very fast to have her do it."

"Well, I knew she was thinking about it, but it seemed so far off. Is there someone there to do the cooking and take care of the kids in the afternoon?"

She sensed it. Déjà vu. She could predict the next ten sentences.

"Don't worry about it. It's all arranged. Let's give you the kiss she wanted you to have."

"Well."

Dave put his hands on her cheeks and his mouth on hers. His mouth opened. It was wet in there.

Francie was passing by with a platter. "Pickles, Mr. Bernstein?"

Sheepishly Dave released Francie's mother, the head

of her household, the best spaghetti-and-clam-sauce maker on the block, who rubbed her back sometimes and recited Edna St. Vincent Millay to her when she wasn't feeling well.

"Hi, Francie. How are you? God, you're getting big. Just giving your mother regards from Lolly."

She moved on her way as Mary Catherine straightened her blouse, patted her hair.

"Dave, what was that all about?" Her groin hurt. Deborah. Can't lose sight of Deborah. Where did she go?

"Mary Catherine, get a plate, come sit with me in the den."

"Well, I really should see how everyone is doing, and I'm worried about Deborah."

"They're fine, everyone is fine. I want to talk to you."

"Let me get a plate."

The point of the story is, Mary Catherine thought, as she filled up her plate, as her daughter walked by and pinched her on the right buttock, the point of the story is that if it weren't for this and that, she could go for Dave. She liked his calm, his sweetness, she liked the comfort he seemed to have in his sexuality. All these years, she'd suppressed it, forgotten about it, not paid any attention to it, because Lolly was her friend. But all's fair in love and war, Eleanora would be whispering into her ear if she knew about all this, if you can snare him, get him, she would say, knowing that a good man nowadays is hard to find. But Lolly's man, her friend's husband, never. Sister Mary Alice would forgive her for a lot of things but coveting thy neighbor's . . . never.

Fixing a plate for herself and taking a glass of wine, Mary Catherine squeezed herself through people sitting on the floor with plates in their laps, people standing with drinks in their hands.

Somebody turned the radio up even louder, switched from WQXR to a rock station. She smelled pot. Where was Francie? The air was getting close and someone lowered the lights some more. The shadows of the fire on the ceiling had jagged edges as couples got up to dance. It was a party, a real party. She hadn't been anywhere where people were dancing in a long time. She caught a glimpse of Eleanora in the far corner of the long room standing on her head. An Eastville party, Deborah was giving a bona fide Eastville party. Mary Catherine felt exhausted, as though the smile had been drawn on with red grease pencil.

She moved on. She could barely make it to the den. Margaret Apple barred her way.

"Mary Catherine, I've been trying to talk to you all evening."

Her stroganoff was getting cold.

"How are you, Margaret? I heard you were moving to Europe."

"I didn't do it. That's what I wanted to talk to you about. How are you faring? We divorcées should stick together."

We divorcées should stay away from each other.

"Why?"

"Well, we could help each other. You know. There have been so many times I've wanted to call you and have lunch."

Deborah. Where is Deborah? Mary Catherine twisted her head. A kaleidoscope of muted color. No Deborah.

Mary Catherine and Margaret had worked together to raise money for Muscular Dystrophy when she had first moved to town. They were acquaintances; nothing more, but it was like being Catholic together, coming from Boston together, being alone was a club with a large membership.

"I used to travel alone to Europe all the time when I was married, you know. But you can't live there. How on earth can a forty-six-year-old divorcée live in Europe? The few women I've known who have tried it always come back. It's too tough. You need people."

The music was so loud Mary Catherine could barely hear her. Margaret had licked her lipstick off, but the blue eyeshadow still clung to her lids. She had high cheekbones, an almost haughty look. Hers was a classic beauty, much more effective when her makeup wore off, making her more appealing and vulnerable.

"No, I couldn't move. Even though my family's on the Coast. Well, we didn't get along that well with each other to begin with, anyway. Even though my kids are all away at college I still feel I should have a place for them to come home to. Some kind of resting place. So here I stay. Eastville, U.S.A. I really should move but I can't. Where would I go? You get killed in New York no matter where you live, how about you, how are you faring? How's your love life?"

That phrase should be struck from the language. Some day my prince will come, and that ugly witch with the apple will go off in a puff of smoke like the wicked witch of the North.

"I'm fine. Look, why don't we make a date. I promised Dave Bernstein I'd eat with him and have been having the roughest time just getting in the den."

"Have you met any men?" Margaret pursued, relentless. "I don't know what your experience has been, but I've never met such a bunch of neurotics in my life." She was playing with her beads. "I don't know. I'm trapped here and yet it's home to me. I love it. It's beautiful, it's where my friends are. But, I have to admit it, I don't mind saying it to you because I'm sure you understand. It's the loneliness. That's what gets you."

So many. So many like that man who went to the porno with a gun. His date was a .45, he stroked it instead of a soft inner arm.

"I know. It does. Margaret, how about Monday? I'm free and I would love to have a long, lazy lunch with you. Business is so slow I have a lot of time on my hands."

"Fine, I'll call your office Monday morning."

"Margaret, you look lovely. Really, you look so well."

"Do I?" she said, brightening. "Thanks. Do I really?"

Mary Catherine scanned the room, but couldn't find Deborah.

Dave was already on his dessert.

"Well, I knew eventually you would come. I turned away an Egyptian belly dancer, a doctoral candidate in Middle English, and your own daughter. Mary Catherine, I'm sorry about that kiss. I talked to Francie about it."

"Oh, Dave, it's all right. She understands."

No, I don't think she understands.

"I've got to sit down. My legs hurt."

"Sit."

"Cleanliness is next to godliness," was all she could think of saying.

"I know, dear, we all know that. So?"

"And loneliness is next to madness. Somebody told me that recently."

"Probably. They're probably right. Eat, Mary Catherine, that must be ghastly by now, it's so cold. Would you like another plate?" Dave took his pipe out of his pocket, beginning the ritual. The taking-time-to-think ritual of jabbing the old tobacco around before he poured the new in.

"I'm starved," she said, "I haven't eaten all day. I love that feeling, though, don't you, when you're wildly hungry and then you start to eat, warming your stomach, feeling the wine tingle."

"Right. I know what you mean." He had finally lit up.

"I like your sweater."

"Lolly bought it for me as a peace offering."

"What do you mean?"

"Well, before she took off."

"Dave, I don't want to interfere, but really what's so terrible?"

Dave Bernstein was a handsome man. He was slight, although his shoulders were broad for a man not weighing more than 160 pounds. His face was very narrow, with an aquiline nose and pointed chin, and as his forties had come and gone the lines decorated it with a softness worthy of his good nature. Creases at the side of his face when he smiled gave him a gentle air.

Dave had been brought up by an old-fashioned Jewish mother who knew that nothing and nobody were good enough for her Davey. Love and food were synonymous, of course. She had cooked his favorite meals for him through his college days, relieved him of his tension by rubbing his back after having anointed his regal shoulders with olive oil, while Leo Bernstein read his paper. That's about all Dave remembered about the silent kind little man who would come home from work dog tired, who, with the energy beaten out of him by long days squinting through his visor, threading his needle on his machine, sewing endless ladies' garments for the same boss for forty years, had quietly died. As quietly as he had lived. But Becky

Bernstein was a different story and her Dave was her pride and joy.

When he brought home Lolly, whose parents were from the Upper West Side in Manhattan and had their parties catered, Becky was pleased in a way. The girl had a college education, was mousy, but pretty enough, she supposed, but the best thing was that she felt she would take up where Becky left off. Good hot meals. A loving temperament. To always give comfort and succor to her boy.

And this is what Dave had wanted fifteen years ago. And if he had the courage to admit it in these frantic days of women fulfilling themselves till it oozed out of their ears, that's what he wanted now. He was bright, attractive, alert, aware, but a liberated wife was not what he had bargained for. True, Lolly's quickness, her creativity, her good mind that would challenge him deep into the night on issues crucial to them and to the world stimulated him. And true, she was his best friend. And true, he could trust her. And true, he still enjoyed her in bed, her body just beginning to show the signs of middle age, but he wanted it all to stay the old way. Sure she could grow, he didn't want to get bored with her like lots of men did, throwing over the helpmate of fifteen or twenty years for a little piece. He didn't want that. First of all, young girls were terrible in bed. There was never any justice to it. The rewards of that firm body, high ass and breast were only rewards unto themselves, since the girls were usually unresponsive, unknowledgeable in ways of exciting a man. The few times he had found himself in situations where he went to bed with these nubile creatures of excellence it had always been a hollow affair. Aesthetically pleasing, perhaps, as it always was to watch and touch a beautiful body, but bad sex, so who needed that? It had been fun and titillating, nothing else.

But he was trying, he told Lolly, as a man who prided himself on his generosity and openness, to understand her explorations. He had to admit it, he was confused and bewildered. It was as though his world was being blown up, a little *Monitor* and *Merrimack* in his own backyard. Fort Sumter at the Bernsteins. For that was what it was like lately. The busier Lolly got, the more resentful Dave became. The more she would protest, the more stubborn he became. He didn't like it. It confused the hell out of him.

He was beginning to feel unnecessary. The kids were off out in their own little worlds of ballet and horses, Lolly was always holed up in her studio finishing a piece, meeting a deadline. And by the time he came home from the university, by the time he came home after being the breadwinner and earning the money that was feeding, housing, and clothing this female brood living in pretty grand style, no one was paying any attention to him. True, Lolly always left dinner in the refrigerator for him if she had to go out; true, she always arranged for a sitter if they both had to be out; true, the kids really could stay alone now anyway, but where did he fit into all this?

They hadn't had sex in two weeks and it was grating on him. He was frustrated, but worse than that, a connection was becoming frayed. Like a sturdy telephone wire whose fibers were becoming loose, their special continuity was being interrupted. And every time he talked about it he sounded whiny to himself. And he didn't like it. He didn't want to stand in the way of progress. He would be the last man in the world who would hinder a bright woman from developing herself. But not at his expense. That wasn't part of the deal. Dave had been stuffed into the middle class like a letter too big for its envelope. There wasn't much flexibility. He knew he sounded self-righteous at times and hated himself for it. But he felt wronged. He wanted a wife to be a wife. Otherwise why be married, for God's sake. It's not a question of confusion of role, he would tell Lolly, I've always pulled my share. Helped with the kids, the chores. We've been partners, long before the marriage contract business got all that publicity. But, by God, he didn't like her taking off and leaving him alone. He just didn't like it.

"I'm upset, I really am. . . ."

"Dave, you've gone to so many conventions and have traveled without Lolly through the years. Why is this any different?"

"First of all, she doesn't make the kind of money I make."

He was sorry the minute he said it. Even though it really was the way he felt.

"Oh, Dave. Truthfully now, is that it? Is that what it's all about?"

"Goddamn it, yes." He started to shout, banging his pipe on the edge of an ashtray.

"You're going to break that."

"Listen, Mary Catherine, if I'm not the breadwinner, if I'm not the strong one, if I'm not indeed the male in the family, then who am I to them all? Just who am I?"

Mary Catherine looked at him. "Dave, how can I answer that? Only you can. I talk to Lolly and I know how she feels and it's her turn. She feels it's her turn to soar and see what life is like out there. Don't reduce the whole thing to women's movement clichés. That's a real thing going on. You admit that she's bright and she's talented. And the extra income she brings in always helps."

"The money she makes costs me money. It actually does. Unless she makes some kind of real money I might as well take it out of my pocket and give it to her."

He didn't mean it to sound that way. He couldn't be honest, that was all. Mary Catherine was all right, but it was like talking to Lolly and it was getting so he couldn't be honest with her either.

He hurt. He felt terrified, in a way, that no one would be there to take care of him. Odd as it might sound, which was why he would never say it out loud, because it almost didn't make sense. He didn't want to relinquish the big-man, I'll-take-care-of-everything pose, and yet he desperately wanted a place to cry in. That was it. That's what he felt was beginning to go. A soft place. A place for him to be the little boy in. Where could he do it? With his students he was wise and fatherly, giving out advice, being supportive. He could listen for hours as a tearful coed would sit in his office and confide in him. He was responsible, he was sturdy. He was superb in emergencies; when Sarah went head first through the plate-glass window and had to have eight stitches in her forehead, he had scooped her up and taken her to the hospital with all the coolness and expertise of a person to be counted on.

But he couldn't have his soft place, his sweet place, if his wife wasn't there when he needed her. I never have a place to cry, he thought. I never have a place where I can shed all those poses like yesterday's skin. Where do I go with my panic, my fear? Lolly's my best friend, sure, so where is she, in Minneapolis or some damn place writing some piece that she'll get a couple of hundred dollars for and I have to pay the air fare and hotel room, so that means she'll clear about a hundred bucks. I want a woman when I want her.

"Look, I'm not going to get into this kind of discussion because obviously you've had it often with Lolly. Still, for you to reduce the whole thing to money makes me sick, and you know I'm not a big-deal feminist. That's not the point."

Dave's blue eyes had turned soft. He was looking at her hair and it made her nervous. He wasn't listening to what she was saying.

"O.K., babe, forget it. At least I know where you stand, and stand pat. Look, don't worry about it. We'll be all right, we'll work this out just the same way we've worked a lot of other things out. How about some coffee?"

"Oh, fine, Dave. Friends?"

"Honey, we'll always be friends. You know that. Are you wearing your hair in a different way?"

"No. Why?"

"It looks different, fuller or something."

"No. Not at all."

"You're still a good-looking woman, Mary Catherine. When are you going to get married?" His hand was on her knee.

"Ha. You sound like my mother. Who knows. Maybe sometime, maybe never."

He took her hand. "You're a good kid. You really made these last years work for you."

"I guess so."

He closed his large palm over her small one. Took it to his mouth and kissed it.

"Friends?"

"Friends."

A great crash from inside. Glass shattering. Splinters.

"Oh, God." For a moment Mary Catherine had forgotten Deborah, she had enjoyed Dave's hand on her knee, the titillation of the conversation. No wife should trust her with her husband, regardless of the Romano Rules of Order. If he puts his hand on her knee, all kinds of involuntary actions act. The sound made her jump. She ran into the other room.

"I've got to go to see Deborah. I know something's wrong. Something's wrong."

Deborah was standing in the middle of what had been a glass coffee table a moment ago. She had obviously been dancing on it, Ginger Rogers, the gay divorcée, was not so gay tonight and had given a guarded rendition of "Putting on the Ritz" or something and had fallen through the shatterproof glass which was not able to withstand her 142 pounds. Mary Catherine saw Sam brushing the dandruff off Frieda's shoulder. Essie stood at the kitchen door with a towel in her hand, Merrilie had her hand on her breast. If Deborah moved backward she would be cut by the pointed ends of the broken glass.

"So you see," Deborah was saying, waving her drink, "this insurance guy calls me up and says, what, you don't have any major medical. So I said, no sir, I don't. What shall I do, sir? So he says, well, Mrs. Shapiro, how old are you? So, demurely, blushing, with a confidential tone, I told him I was in my middle forties, which I thought was fair enough, so you know what happened . . . ?" She laughed a hoarse, raucous laugh. Mary Catherine moved closer to the circle. No one was helping her out of the snake pit. "He must have computed on his little computer or something and he said, well, Mrs. Shapiro, that will cost you about four hundred dollars a year. What, I bellowed, that's a lot of bread, and he said, as they do with tact, with charm, well, women of your age are prone to things happening to them, you know the body and all, and well, the insurance rates get higher. So you see, ladies and gentlemen, that is why I plan never to get a protracted illness because I'm sure as hell not going to spend four hundred dollars for medical insurance just because my mother had me the year that she did. After all, what's so terrible about being forty? Nothing except that your insurance rates soar."

People drifted nervously back to the food table, over to the bar. They laughed uncomfortably, patted her on the shoulder, offered hands to get her out of her jagged island.

"Dave, do something for God's sake, get her out of there."

"Deborah, come step out, hon, time for dessert." Dave's tone was soft, winning.

"Oh, sure. How about a hand?" Docilely she put all her weight on Dave's shoulders and was hoisted out of the glass prison. "Some mess. Lotsa glass. Some mess. Abe's gonna have a fit. And Joshua Gold will undoubtedly puke. Sam darling, there you are."

Sam, who had been standing at the door to the dining room for the past few minutes, came over to Deborah. He was appalled. She could see the disgust in his eyes. What was he getting himself into? Who was this raving maniac, whose hair was stringy, whose owl eyes were ringed with soot? She looked older than he did, for God's sakes, and the wrinkles were deep around her eyes. Too damn much, sun, why hadn't he seen them before?

Tanked up, she's just tanked up, and although he'd seen her drink a lot before, he had never seen her so out of control, so crazy. Who needs that, for God's sake? She'd lose more deals for him, that's for sure. She's a raving maniac, that's what she is.

He put his hands on her shoulder. Deborah whirled around and stumbled down onto the couch.

"You're all right, Sam, you really are, but why, oh

why, do you use all those creams on your face? Do
you know, Mary C., he's got these rows upon rows
of dermotol . . . dermatologi . . . whatever, skin
creams lined up on his bathroom shelves? Like grave-
stones. A regular Arlington National Cemetery right
in his bathroom in his castle high in the sky. And
you know what else? He's got this suit of armor in
the hallway, holding a scepter or whatever that long
thing is with a ball on the end of it and . . ."

"Debdear, I'm leaving."

"Oh, Sam, don't be silly, stay, stay, the party hasn't
even started yet." She couldn't get up off the couch.

She spread both arms out like an eagle preparing
for flight and knocked Mary Catherine's glass out of
her hand. Her other hand hit a giant glass ashtray,
sending it spinning to the floor.

"Listen, Deb, don't bother, don't bother to get up.
I can see myself to the door. Really, dear, don't worry
about a thing. I'll call in the morning. Sleep it off,
hon."

He waddled to the door, took his coat and hat from
the hall closet and, without turning around, opened
the front door and slammed it. The sleigh bells hanging
on the other side bounced against the wood.

"Whatsa matter with him? All I said was that he
was too fat and used face creams prescribed by the
dermatologists. Listen, could someone help me for
God sake, I've got to pee."

Mary Catherine offered both hands. Deborah stood
up unsteadily and put her arms around her neck.
"Listen, kid, I'm so glad you never dyed that streak
in your hair, it's smashing. You're all right, Mary C.,
you'll go far. You're a winner. No matter what, you're
all right, kid, so glad to have bumped into you."

"Deborah, I'm going with you."

"Listen, I'm just going for a minute to pee. I have

to pee so bad and I've got this thing about bathrooms, the only place I like to go is my bedroom bathroom. Be down soon. Been down so long it almost seems like up or something. See you anon." She stumbled away.

Mary Catherine followed her upstairs. Her uneasiness made her itch. Her breasts itched. She knew her symptoms. Deborah had locked her door.

"Deb, come on, open up."

"Scram, love, be right out. Go enjoy yourself."

"Deborah, open the door immediately." Like to Francie when she was ten.

"Let me pee in peace."

"Open up."

"Come back, love, come back in two seconds."

"No. Now. I want to come in. Now, Deborah, or I'll get Dave and break the door down. I'm telling you, now open up."

"Two minutes, give me two minutes. Mary. Please." Plaintive, like a little girl.

"All right. All right. Pee, and I'll be back in two seconds, I swear, then you come out and tell everyone to go home and you go the hell to sleep. Deborah, do you hear me?"

"Yes. I'm peeing in my pants. Go away. Come back."

"My uncle's a detective and he only handles cases involving runaway wives," she heard someone say, back in the living room. "He's doing a thriving business and sometimes he finds them for the husbands and sometimes he doesn't. He told me that when he finds them they're bitter and say they've been faking orgasms for years and they say they don't want men, they don't need them. They leave the big houses and the Puccis in the closet and strip their lives down to nothing. He told me. It's wild."

"I wouldn't have the nerve."

"Listen, everybody, I think Deborah's not feeling

too well and perhaps you all ought to go. I'm sorry, but she's gone to bed."

"It's all very fine to be so marvelously liberated, so Amazonian, but where are the men to share everything, if of course you believe in sharing, and I do." Frieda was holding forth. "No point to living without sharing. So where are they, pray tell, where are they? I tell my boys in college to cherish these girls they're meeting now. You're not going to meet them later in life, I tell them, not those girls with the kinds of intelligence and sensitiveness that you're looking for."

"Go home. Please, everybody. Go home."

Mary Catherine's voice was shrill.

Dave, without a word, played a giant chord on the piano.

"Party's over. Deb's a bit under the weather. Sorry, everybody."

"So how come so many young men are becoming impotent?"

"Everybody's so worried about protecting their identities, but what about good old-fashioned responsibility?"

"They're scared, the men are scared as the women. That's why they're running off with the twenty-year-olds."

People kept sipping their drinks as they wandered to the door. No one skipped a beat in the conversation.

"When I was a kid, my father would come in and turn on the light and there I'd be fumbling for my hairpins and straightening my clothes and this lovely boy would be telling me my body was like a Stradivarius. Me, I go down when my kid's in the family room with her boyfriend and play 'The Star-Spangled Banner' on the piano and he knows it's time to go home."

The party broke up.

An air of uncertainty, uncomfortable embarrassment, had hovered after Deborah's outburst. No one wanted to stay anyway. Essie had already left, the bartender had gone home.

"Do something about your friend," Eleanora whispered to Mary Catherine as she slid into her Chinese brocade cape. "I'm telling you, she's gone off the deep end. She's just about lost her looks, that's for sure. Call us tomorrow, love. I have a fabulous suggestion, by the way, get out of town. There's nothing, but nothing here for you, I'm convinced of it. I've decided. Let's talk about it tomorrow. Not till noon, now. 'Bye, love."

Henry dutifully kissed Mary Catherine's cheek. He had spent the whole evening playing chess in the den with Stanley Tenzer.

Mary Catherine was deathly worried about Deborah, but was left in a maze of farewell amenities at the door. She had to put order back into these rooms. Somehow.

The Tenzers said they would take Francie home, kissed Mary Catherine good-bye, Margaret and Frieda made a date to play indoor tennis tomorrow. The rest of the guests made their exit quickly.

A roar of engines, puffs of steam and headlights flooded the driveway. Suddenly it was still. They were all gone.

Mary Catherine turned and ran down the hall. Dave, who was sitting alone in the living room puffing on his pipe, followed.

Deborah had tripped over her long blue gown. My sweet little Deborah blue gown, she hummed. In the bathroom, she squatted on the toilet but missed. The urine came out in a stream on the floor. Down on her hands and knees, she tried to clean it up, but the toilet paper kept getting too wet. Her head was swirling. The sky is falling, she thought, struggling up to put some cold water on her face.

In the bedroom she tripped over the ottoman next to her easy chair, and made her way to the desk. Piles of clippings were stacked in a corner. She picked up the little one on top, cut out of *The Village Voice*. The edges were jagged. The Singles Social Success Institute of New York was advertising. Squinting, she read, "Learn the secrets of social and business success. Develop personal charisma, persuasive charm, conversation control. Learn the art of manipulating people for personal and business purposes. Develop individual magnetism and positive reaction techniques. Learn the art of developing and handling intimate relationships." I always meant to call them, she thought.

Feeling the top of her table for her red diary, she knocked half the stack of clippings to the floor. "Damn," she said, trying to pick them up. She found it hard to focus. Shuffling them together, she saw a page she had cut out of a fashion magazine. The bold type read: "Learn How the Liberated Woman Always Gets Her Man." What did I ever do about that one, she thought, peering more closely. I could have learned how to pick up a man, the "three secrets the stewardesses know, how and where to meet rich men, how to meet the marrying kind, seven ways to be sexy, why a woman doesn't have to be beautiful, how to make the first move." Why didn't I even order that book, she wondered. Struggling to stand up, she took the whole pile and threw it in the wastepaper basket.

"Deborah, open up."

"O.K. O.K." She unlocked the door. "Mary Catherine, I'm thinking about strength. Do you think you're a strong person? How about it, Mary Catherine?"

"How about some coffee?"

"Are you kidding, this is the shank of the evening. Answer my question. Strength. What is it? Some people say women are stronger than men."

"Many women are," Mary Catherine said. "Deborah, get into bed."

"No, you know, that Helen Reddy song, about being invincible. Well, me, I'm the most vincible person I know." She was having trouble talking. "No. I can't imagine men worrying because they're alone and not strong. It's too hard. Too hard to be strong."

She started talking softly, sitting there at the edge of her bed, no stockings, no shoes. She looked straight at Mary Catherine. "I've been thinking. We're all expected to be so goddamn strong. Well, I can't. I just can't. I've been doing a lot of thinking. And I've got all kinds of spunk and spirit and God knows what, but I'm tired. I read where Shirley MacLaine is tired of making movies about those poor little victims like that round-faced thing she was in *The Apartment,* prey, victim to all the Fred MacMurrays of the world. No more she said, in the article, I'm going off to make a film about Amelia Earhart.

"Fine. Great. More power to her. But how many are there like that who can go off into the wild blue yonder like Amelia Earhart, for God sakes? There are some of us who just need a man first, who are somehow beaten down by being alone, who somehow need a man and his comfort and bigness and his sex more than anything. And we'll do anything to get it, sell our kids, go into white slavery maybe. I don't know. We exist. I exist.

"I'm scared. The bloom is off, Mary Catherine. No more bloom. No more shiny face. When I was young my face used to shine. The skin was so taut across my forehead that after I had scrubbed it clean with soap and water I could almost see my own reflection in it. I used to shine.

"There was an odor about my skin that I remember; lying in bed at night, my mouth would fall on my shoulder and I smelled sweet. I don't smell sweet anymore. I smell of all kinds of artificial things and booze and cigarettes and my own failure. Success smells sweet, right? That's what everyone says. I smell bad. I smell old. I smell getting old. No more bloom. And then, and then, just one more month and I'm fifty. Fifty. And all the Women's Liberation in the world isn't going to give it back to me. That shine. That lovely odor of my own skin.

"Bleating. I'm bleating. I know it. The magazines are telling me ten times a day that I'm a cop-out, a loser, a giver in, a baby. Maybe so. Maybe so."

Deborah was swaying back and forth, her drink in her hand. She took a long gulp.

"This is my party, right? My wedding, my funeral, right? So let's have another drink. Get one for yourself and let's liven things up a bit here.

"Do you remember, Mary Catherine, when we were in high school we would always compete with the girls in our class? Whether we realized we were doing it or not. We girls were just natural enemies. We outdressed each other, little dickies sticking out of pink cashmere sweaters. Remember? Bad to compete, the Women's Lib ladies are saying. Love thy neighbor. Love thy sister. I say bullshit. I think the competition is there as much as now, even more. So we don't compete for prettiest or most popular or biggest tits or whatever it was in those school popularity polls. But today it's who can be a psychiatric neurosurgeon with a minor in medieval madrigals and bake the tastiest banana bread, mix your own martini, and bring up the best-adjusted kids on the block, all at the same time.

"Well, you know what, you know what, I quit. I abdicate. I give up the throne for the woman I love. Me. I am out of the running. The fulfillment race. I will be unfulfilled. I will not be reschooled and go into special education like everyone else, I will not be the president of the first women's airline because I can't. I don't measure up. My potential, ladies and gentlemen, will remain untapped."

"Deborah, please sit down." Deborah was struggling to stand. Mary Catherine put her arms around her shoulders.

"I'm fine, love, just fine.

"And another thing," she continued, crumpling suddenly into a cross-legged position on the bed. "I am not Shirley MacLaine and I do not have her energy, her looks, her drive, or her ability to attract brilliant men."

"For God's sake, Deborah, who said you have to? Leave Shirley MacLaine alone, for God's sakes. I'm getting a little sick of all this, really. Deborah, what is the matter with you?"

"Mary Catherine, I'm just me. Just me. I can't be Shirley MacLaine. I try to be bigger and better all the time but it's obviously not enough because I always end up being me. The panic overtakes me. The panic," she started to whisper, pulling on Mary Catherine's long skirt, "those long dark halls inside my stomach are endless like that scene in *Caligari* where what's-his-name Conrad something stumbles across that hall, those endless halls, and he was sleepwalking, a sona-mul . . . amonbulist or something, and he stumbled and held on to the walls for dear life and that's what I am doing except that I don't hold on to the walls, I drink. Did you know that I drink? I drink instead, because there is nothing else at this point. I shall go nuts from the loneliness, from the absence of things.

"You know what, Mary Catherine." She spoke in a mock whisper. It came out loud. "Did you know that Robert Ryan went and died on me? That's what he did. When he did that, getting cancer the way he did, wasting away the way he did, I cried. He made me cry. The big Irish health of him, all cocky and cruel in those early movies, had turned into softness. I saw him once as Antony on the stage and his legs were beautiful and he was so fair. His eyes twinkled and his *A*'s were flat, both bad for Antony, but for me he was everything. He could take care of anything, I figured. There was a man who would never walk out on you. So what did he do. He went and died on me. Just like Abe, he went and left me. And he lost all his flesh tone, you know. Did you see him in *Iceman?* He looked green. His skin was green. He was dying then. Robert Ryan went and died on me."

Mary Catherine began to cry.

"Please, Deborah, please take some coffee, dear."

"Mary C., you don't understand what I'm talking about. This is very serious. I've got to get it all out. I've got to talk about it because you see I'm scared. You see, Sam isn't really so bad and I do understand him but"—and she whispered confidentially into Mary Catherine's ear—"his body on top of me suffocates me. I will die under there someday, my friend, I am afraid of smothering. I am so deadly afraid of having no air, of not having enough air, and when he is on top of me his belly pushes the life out of me. There is no life.

"Old Joshua Gold, the patriarch of this illustrious family, the paterfamilias, used to put his feet in my face, I was a little girl, and he would roll around with me on the lawn and I would squeal, we would be having fun, but when he would get me in such a position that his bare feet, pudgy they were, would be in my face and I couldn't breathe, you see, and that wasn't very nice of him. I used to be scared.

"Mary Catherine."

"Yes, dear."

"Do me a big favor."

"Anything."

"Go get Dave, see if he can fix my TV. I can't get Channel 13. I like to fall asleep with Channel 13. I've never had anyone here who could get me Channel 13. I want Channel 13 so badly. It's just a little adjustment he has to do and I can't do it. Mary C. Just go get him, all right, love? Please."

"Now?"

"Yes. Please, Mary C. Please."

"O.K. Of course, Deborah, look, put your nightgown on. I'll put up some fresh coffee. Get into bed. I'll rub your back."

"Lovely. Just go get Dave."

"O.K."

"Mary Catherine?"

"Yes."

"See you."

"I'll be right back."

After Mary Catherine had shut the door, Deborah struggled up, and locked it.

Lurching into the bathroom, she opened the medicine chest, and pulled out her bottle of Seconal. Sleep, she had to sleep. Tomorrow was Sunday. Sitting on her bed, she poured out about twenty capsules. A lot, she thought, I need a lot to make me sleep. Opening the tablets, she poured their insides into her glass of scotch, which was half full. Stirring it with her finger, she thought, it's enough already. I've had enough Sundays for a while. She went to her chest of drawers and took out her beige cashmere sweater stuffed inside a transparent plastic bag. She kept sipping the scotch.

The party's over.

I'm sleepy. I feel the fear oozing out of me. I'm not afraid anymore. No more Sundays. Joshua Gold, son of none, you never had a son of your own, it was just me, just Deborah Ruth Gold and I couldn't go to temple with you and I couldn't play golf with you, but we would wrestle on the lawn and you bought me a husband and put your feet in my face when I was a little girl. I was so afraid because I couldn't breathe, but I'm not afraid now. I'm not afraid anymore.

She took her beige cashmere sweater out of the plastic bag, threw it on the floor, and put the bag over her head. It was a cellophane world out there, an amusement-park hall-of-mirrors world out there, a world from the bottom of the glass world out there. To tie it tight around her neck, she broke off a piece of waxed dental floss that was resting next to the phone on her night table.

Chapter Twenty-three

Dave had to smash the door in with his shoulder.

Deborah was lying on the floor. She had toppled off the bed into a heap. Her mouth was open, her head to one side. Her face had a purple tint.

Oh, God. Mary Catherine stood in the doorway, Dave behind her.

Oh, God. Oh, God.

Dave rushed in the room, took a small pocketknife off his key chain, and slit open the bag. Deborah was big and very heavy. He couldn't get her up on the bed.

"Oh, God. She was so afraid of no air. Of not having any air. I should have come back faster. I should have. I shouldn't have left."

"She didn't mean it, I know she didn't mean it. I know it," Dave said. "She didn't know what she was doing, the liquor just got to her. There's a bottle of sleeping pills. She did that first."

"But she's always taken them. Oh, God, what difference does it make?" Deborah, wake up, you're just sleeping, aren't you, just resting, just waiting. Aren't you, waiting till someone would come and keep you company. She hated to be alone. I should have been there. I should have stayed. "We've got to call her father, the police."

"It's a sin." Mary Catherine's fists were clenched.

"Stop it. I know she didn't mean it."

"I can't believe it. I can't believe it." Deborah, Mary Catherine thought, wake up. Please, Deborah, have a drink. I know you didn't mean to bump into me with your car. Deborah, wake up, Deborah, get married. Read a book. Be happy. Deborah, wake up.

Then the tears started to come. Mary Catherine couldn't stop them. Dave put his arms around her. They stood there holding each other like Hansel and Gretel in the middle of the Black Forest. Her face was in his chest.

"Don't, don't."

He stroked her back.

And she felt him get hard.

Stop, she said soundlessly to someone in the room, stop, she said as he moved his hands down around her waist, stop, she said to the Mary Catherine in her head as she pressed harder against him.

Suddenly their mouths, their faces were moving in Mary Catherine's tears. His hands felt her body. He pushed up under her skirt, feeling beyond her tears.

No.

No. She pushed against him with both hands so that he almost landed next to Deborah's outstretched leg. He looked at Deborah sleeping. No telling tales.

"Call the police," Mary Catherine finally found her voice, "the fire department, do something. Call a priest, call a rabbi, call Sam, call God, just don't touch me. Don't touch me, Dave. No fair. No fair."

She walked out of the room. Go play in your own backyard, she thought. It's enough. Enough. Just enough.

Chapter Twenty-four

The next day was Sunday.

Mary Catherine was lying in bed, her hands behind her head. Crying.

The phone rang early. It was Seth.

"Listen, Mary. I heard about a motel in town that's got water beds, porno films, and mirrors on the ceiling. What do you say? I'm free tonight."

"No."

"Why no? What's the matter. Oh, God. I did hear about it downtown when I went to get the Sunday papers. Your friend Deborah. I heard about it. What a blow. Jesus, I'm sorry. I really am. I know how you cared about her. I'm sorry, Mary."

"O.K., Seth."

"So?"

"So what."

"Well, can you see me? I'd really like to see you, babe."

"No. No more, Seth."

"Oh, honey, you'll get over it. It takes time, you get over it. You get over everything. You will. Maybe you should go away for a while."

"No. No more, Seth."

"What do you mean?"

"No more."

"You're the horniest girl I've ever known."

"So what."

"Can I call you?"

"No, Seth. Don't call."

"I hate to lose . . ."

Such an apt pupil. Thanks, but it's enough. Thanks, but no thanks.

"Mary Catherine. Thanks."

"I know."

"I really like you, you know."

"I know."

"I've known my wife for twenty years and she's a good egg but we never——"

"I know, Seth."

"I'm flip and cool, crazy and experimental, you know that about me, Mary C. She doesn't. I can't talk to her about things. Mary C., I like you."

"I know, Seth."

"You're sure you won't reconsider?"

"No."

"O.K., kid. O.K. But you're something. Something else. So long."

"I'm something more, not something else," she shouted into the dead phone.

I tried, Deborah, she thought. I tried I really cared about you. You were so funny and so self-pitying and I wanted you to be happy. And I thought I really did it. I thought I was something. I thought I finally got you to go for help. I feel so bad.

She rolled over on her side and held her stomach. She had a bellyache. She heard herself crying. Putting her hand over her mouth, she remembered how early it was, that she didn't want to wake Francie. Such a feeling of emptiness. Sorrow. I feel sorrow. I loved her.

She got up and sat in the rocking chair.

It was hard to love you, Deborah. Hard to love anyone. Hard to care. Maybe because you needed me so much, maybe that's what made it easier for me. Hard to give to a woman. Hard to love a woman, no less a man. With it all, with all your sickness, and your vulnerability, there was something about the force, the ferocity of your determination to have it the way you wanted it or not at all. So you decided on not at all. Could I have stopped you? Could I have mingled my blood better with yours, earlier with yours? Could I have somehow made you feel that my love insisted that you stay alive? Could I have done that? Deborah, dear Deborah, you made me laugh and you made me feel stronger about myself. But you wanted so badly to be loved, you wanted so badly to be able to give that big body of yours to somebody. I feel so bad, so bad.

Mary Catherine rocked back and forth, barely hearing the squeak of the chair. Love is hard. It's so easy to mistake it for something else. You needed me so I loved you, she thought. Was that it, or was it more? You weren't as pretty as I am or as accomplished, I could always feel more important, stronger than you, was that it, was the love based on that? Why didn't I stop you? I sensed it, by God, I sensed it, all day long I sensed it. Didn't I love you enough? Can you love a woman enough? Yes I can. Yes I can. I did and I do, she heard herself shouting.

Deborah, I did want you to be happy. I didn't do

enough. We don't do enough because we can't identify
it when we see it. That love. I hope you knew, Deborah.
I hope you knew somewhere, somehow, that I loved
you. You'd be pleased, Deborah, she thought, her
elbow on her knee, rocking, rocking up and down,
I'm dovening, dovening for you, Deborah.

O.K., kid, so what's next? What's next on the
agenda, she thought, breathing deeply. Can't possibly
go back to the same old thing. Who can I call up?
437-8920 won't be there. Deborah, do you realize that
if I call your number you won't be there anymore?
Robert Ryan went and died on you but, Deborah
Shapiro, you died on me. How dare you? There is
no one to call up anymore. No one to trust anymore.
And now there is no one left to trust. No one but me.

Sitting there, rocking back and forth, Mary Catherine invoked every saint's name she could remember.
It didn't matter why.

O.K. What's next? Where do we go from here, from
the song of the same name. I know where I'm going,
from the song of the same name. So you've had one
man for a long time, Mary Catherine Romano, and
then a lot of men all at the same time, Mary Catherine Romano, and neither plan seems to fit the bill.
What's next? What's the future shock plan for you?

No one to trust anyone. No one but me. But, by
God, I do trust me. That may be what I've got now,
and if there's no more Deborah, at least there is a
Mary Catherine. And if I was unsure about that ever
before, I'm positive about it now. I trust me. Yes I do.
I'll get by as long as I have me. From the song of the
same name. She was getting giddy. Sartre said it his
way and I'll sing it my way. I'll get by as long as I
have me. I'd like more, sure I'd like more, one man,
maybe two, who knows, maybe even three, who knows,
the shadows knows and he's about all at this point.

But what difference does it make. She leaned her head back and closed her eyes. The tears were sticky on her cheeks.

She heard church bells. Maybe she would go to mass. Maybe she wouldn't. Maybe she'd take Francie out to brunch and have bloody Marys and shirred eggs. Maybe she wouldn't. Maybe she'd settle down with the Encyclopaedia Britannica, starting with All Saint's Day. Maybe she would just sit and think.

It just so happens, she thought, wishing she could tell Deborah, it just so happens, she said out loud, that I am tired of fleshing out men's fantasies. That's one thing that's for sure. I am finally tired of filling in red those white spaces in colorless marriages. Color me tired. I'm tired of being a visitor in so many lives. I'm tired of men who get up and go. I want one who stays.

Being single presupposes that I am available for married men's dreams, she thought. Why didn't I think of it that way before? Why don't they talk to their wives, those husbands? Why don't wives talk to their husbands? Why don't they listen to each other? I don't want anyone else's husband. I want a man of my own. I had a man of my own and I didn't want him anymore. There's got to be some resting place somewhere for me that includes the outrageous, the sense of adventure. There's just got to be.

So I've learned about this gift. This body. This pleasure factory that I walk around in. O.K. Late bloomers bloom late. Now what to do with it, where to put it? But one thing I know, she thought, fists clenched. Teeth tight, one thing I know.

No more married men.

No more married men for me, she chanted. Cleaning house I am. Cleaning out closets, no more suits. Cleaning out garages, no more cars. No more, no more married men. I extricate myself from the proceedings. Onward and upward. Love, your magic spell is everywhere. Not her.

Call up Eleanora. Look at the *New York Times* classified, apartments, take your child and leave. Go while the getting is good. No more married men. Love is where you find it, in the shade of the old apple tree, in the arms of Morpheus, down by the old mill stream, anywhere. Love, your magic spell is everywhere. Not here. But whatever, no more, no married men for me. That much I know, "that much," she said out loud, "that much I know." And now, and now, she thought, putting her feet on the cold floor, pulling off her nightgown, damp with tears and perspiration, and now I think I'll try happiness. I've tried everything else.

And the tears? she thought, blowing her nose, these warm wet loving tears on my face are for you, my dear Deborah. Rest, my friend. Be safe. My dear friend.

Francie walked in the room. Her hair was tangled. there was a rip in the hem of her nightgown. She was carrying a cup of coffee and the Sunday papers. She had an apple in her mouth. "Have I got the guy for you," she said, putting the papers on the bed. "Mother, put some clothes on for goodness' sake, you'll catch pneumonia. This Frenchman is quoted on the front page of the *Times* today. Let me read it to you."

"Francie . . ."

"Mere, Mother, put your robe on. 'From 35 to 45 women are old,' he says, 'at 45'—this is the good part. Listen to this, Mom—'at 45 the devil takes over and they're beautiful, splendid, maternal, proud. The acidities are gone. When I see them my mouth waters.' How do you like that? That's what I call smart. Of course, he's seventy-seven years old, but what's that got to do with anything?"

Mary Catherine started to laugh. Tying her robe around her, she laughed so hard her belly was sore, her chest hurt. She pulled her daughter to her, stroked her hair, kissed her loudly, roundly on the cheek.

"Francesca Romano, my pride, my joy. Sit down. Sit down, love. I have to tell you something."

Keep Up With The BESTSELLERS!